"You don't know what a fine woman you are.

"Last Friday night you nearly apologized for *not* having slept around, as if experience was some sort of substitute for passion. It isn't. Technique without true feeling leaves both partners more lonely than ever."

Kelly felt her face growing warm at Justin's compliment and at the memory of those few moments on Friday when she'd been in his arms. "Maybe I'm more modern than you think," she said quietly.

"Modern?" he repeated. "Labels like that don't mean anything. What's important is that you be true to yourself. Do what you feel is right for you."

Could she? Kelly knew she was trembling. "Right now," she whispered, "I feel like kissing you." And to her amazement, she did....

ABOUT THE AUTHOR

"I spent about ten years working in television," says Natalie Grant. "And like the heroine of *In the Know,* my favorite television job was working on a talk show. But one day, when I was producing yet another show on a self-help book, I took the author's advice about pursuing my dream and left television for writing romance." Natalie currently lives in Boston, but still considers Louisville, Kentucky, home.

In the Know

NATALIE GRANT

Harlequin Books

TORONTO • NEW YORK • LONDON
AMSTERDAM • PARIS • SYDNEY • HAMBURG
STOCKHOLM • ATHENS • TOKYO • MILAN

Published June 1991

ISBN 0-373-70454-2

IN THE KNOW

For my family,
with affection that can't be measured.

CHAPTER ONE

"MEN TODAY ARE so afraid to commit," the talk show panelist sighed. "Why, I had a guy string me along for two years before he broke down and confessed—tearfully—that he wasn't good enough for me." She shook her head in anger, her red curls bobbing. "The jerk was right!"

Television producer Kelly Ferris increased the sound on her home VCR. The show she was watching had been executive-produced by her new boss, the much-talked about Justin Benedict. In one hour they would meet, and Kelly wanted to scrutinize again the work of the man who was being brought in to "jazz up" her beloved talk show, Boston's *In the Know*. The executive producer's position had been vacant for some time, allowing Kelly the freedom to produce in her own way. Now she gazed at the videotape of her new boss's style. His confrontational format was eliciting some lively conversation on the subject of relationships, but it was at the cost of real understanding and real answers.

"Hey, it's not just men who are afraid to commit," the talk show's host shot back. He was a good-looking man with a knack for stirring up his panelists. "My network offered me a great opportunity, but it meant moving to another city. My fiancée, or I should say my *ex*-fiancée, refused to move because of her job.'' He turned to the studio audience. ''Was that fair?''

The mostly male audience exploded with a collective ''Noooo!''

Kelly grimaced at these antics. She'd bet her eye-teeth that the host was goading his female guest simply to generate the sparks that would increase his ratings. Kelly also bet that he'd been encouraged to do this by his executive producer, who was now *her* new executive producer, Justin Benedict.

The spunky redheaded panelist did seem nettled, but she managed to retort, ''That's such a typical reaction. *Your* job, *your* big opportunity, *your* needs. Men say they're all for equality, but at home they still expect the woman to do ninety percent of the housework and child rearing. If they should, every now and then, make a bed, they act as if they deserve a medal.''

''I make my bed every day!'' a rather quiet man interjected from an opposite couch.

Bully for you, Kelly thought.

''Bully for you,'' the woman said, smoothing back her auburn hair. ''But when was the last time you stayed home from work because your child was sick?''

''Aha!'' Kelly exclaimed out loud, waking Cecil Ferris, her cat, who stretched out on Kelly's unmade bed.

''Well,'' the man confessed, ''if one of us has to stay home, my wife and I usually agree it will be her. I mean, it's not that my wife's job isn't important, but men are the primary breadwinners and women are the primary care-givers.''

"What if you have to be both?" Kelly snapped, furious at the man who still lived in the 1950s world of Ozzie and Harriet.

"What are you yelling about?" Kelly's sixteen-year-old sister Sylvie asked from the bedroom doorway. In one hand she had her schoolbooks, and in the other a can of diet soda.

"What is that?" Kelly inquired, ignoring the question and pointing to the soft drink.

"Breakfast."

"Sylvie! We've been over this a million times."

"Hey, I'll eat oatmeal if you will. Besides, you didn't answer my question. Why were you ready to punch out the screen?"

Kelly turned off the program. She had been yelling, she realized. To her surprise she'd become involved in the sensationalistic program. But that didn't make it worthwhile television. "I was watching an example of my new executive producer's work."

"You mean that cute guy I saw in the newspaper?"

Kelly chuckled. "Sylvie, looks may be important to you, but I'm more concerned with his approach. It's fast-food television no matter how good it looks."

The young girl walked to the unmade bed where Kelly sat and plopped down beside her. "If his awesome good looks have absolutely no effect on you, then taking care of me since Mom and Dad died has exhausted you more than I thought."

Kelly turned to her kid sister and noticed the mischievous look in her eyes. They didn't look much like sisters, Kelly thought. Sylvie's curly brown hair, cut in a French pageboy style, framed her round hazel eyes and olive skin. Kelly's eyes were almond-shaped, dove-gray in color and surrounded by a fringe of black lashes. Her skin was so pale as to be nearly alabaster, and her long black hair hung straight. Today it was tied in a businesslike chignon. Both sisters shared one thing—they were petite, barely reaching five feet two inches. People who spoke to Kelly on the phone were always surprised when they met her. "You sounded taller," they invariably said.

"I'm not immune to blue eyes and dimples," Kelly replied, bending down to punch the rewind button. "I'm just more concerned that he'll make a mess of *In the Know*."

"He was brought in to help the show," Sylvie pointed out.

Kelly hit the eject button a little harder than necessary. "Yes, I know the ratings are a little low," she said. "But we're putting on a serious issues-oriented talk show and we've got a bubble-brain for a host!"

"Oh, Gilda," Sylvie said with sympathy.

"Yes, Gilda Simone, that 'controversial, irrepressible stick of blond Boston dynamite,'" Kelly said, quoting the station's publicity. "They got the blond part right."

"He's blond, too, isn't he?"

"Who?"

"Justin Benedict. Mr. Right, who you'll meet as soon as you bother to get dressed. Why don't you wear your black knit? It makes you look sexy. He isn't married, is he?"

Kelly groaned. "Aren't you rushing things? Rumor has it that he's divorced." She eyed her sister tolerantly. "It just so happens, Sylvie, that I dress appropriately for my position."

"Are you producing board meetings now?" Sylvie asked in mock innocence.

Kelly ignored this remark. Her clothes had another purpose besides just keeping her warm. She intended them to convey confidence and a sense of being in control. Still, the criticism nettled. "I just hope I can work with him," she said.

Sylvie slipped one arm around her sister's shoulders and offered her a sip of soda. "Kelly," she began, "I worry about you. You're twenty-nine, and all you ever do is work. Where else will you meet a guy?"

"Right now I'm just too busy," Kelly said. "Too busy with the show, and," she paused, "with the oatmeal I'm about to make."

"Oh, gross!"

KELLY EASED HER ANCIENT, rattling Ford onto Massachusetts Avenue. Her hands left damp smears on the steering wheel, despite the coolness of the early October day. Just who was this Justin Benedict? And how dedicated was he to the kind of thought-provoking television she strove for? Kelly had been producing the show for two years. Since then there had been two new program managers. The latest, Larry Bishop, had hired Benedict straight from Chicago as executive producer to spruce up all local programming, not just *In the Know*. Although he would report to Larry, Benedict would be the real force in the programming department. Every producer would be answerable to him. *In the Know* was the biggest money-maker, despite the fact that its rating had dropped three crucial points, and the show still led in its time period, 1:00 to 2:00 p.m. each weekday, even beating the soap opera,

Phoenix City Hospital. As such, it would fall under Benedict's closer scrutiny.

And so will I, Kelly thought, her pulse involuntarily accelerating. She *had* been affected by his picture in the paper, but there was no sense admitting that to Sylvie. She was already too boy crazy.

Since their parents had died in a car accident two years ago, Kelly had been Sylvie's only real parental figure. They had a brother, Paul, but he was in the army.

Being thrust into the role of single parent hadn't been an easy adjustment for Kelly to make. Learning that she couldn't be just a pal to Sylvie, now that she had to be a parent, had been difficult. The responsibility weighed heavily, as did producing *In the Know.* But the show was her pride and joy, her baby. It reflected her commitment to the community and her love of intelligent conversation.

Kelly had decided that if she worked very hard, slept very little and kissed her private life goodbye, neither Sylvie nor the show would get shortchanged. She simply had to stay in charge of her priorities.

She turned the radio on but found that Sylvie had programmed all the buttons to popular teen stations. Hard rock couldn't ease Kelly's tense mood. Staying in control of her life was getting harder. Producing a live talk show five times a week wasn't a nine-to-five job. Raising a hormone-charged teenager was a full-time job, too. It was a tough juggling act, and after two years of it, Kelly worried about losing her grip. And now Justin Benedict, Mr. Fast-Food Television, was going to complicate her life further. She gritted her teeth as she pulled into the parking lot of WMAS-TV.

When Kelly passed the office of Larry Bishop, she heard laughter filtering through the closed door. The high-pitched guffaws belonged to Larry, but the low, rumbling laughter of another man sounded unfamiliar. How nice, she figured, Justin Benedict was already ingratiating himself with management.

By the time she reached the *In the Know* office area, she needed a cup of tea, or something stronger.

"What'll it be this bright Monday morning?" Peg Lanihan, her associate producer, inquired. "Herbal tea or that deeply satisfying jolt of caffeine?"

"Caffeine, definitely caffeine," Kelly said, hanging her jacket in a small coat closet. The *In the Know* office area wasn't big, but it boasted more magazines, newspapers, books, phones and typewriters per square inch than even the newsroom. A huge bulletin board adorned one wall, with yellow cardboard squares for each upcoming show stating the date and topic. Usually topics were booked a couple of weeks in advance, but some squares reflected dates as far away as December or January, due to the necessity of committing to an author or celebrity in advance.

A large bookcase stuck in the middle of the room sectioned off the space between Kelly's desk and Peg's and Gilda's. The bookcase overflowed, as did all available counter space, with current magazines, phone books, newspapers, reference guides and files. Occasionally a work-study student organized them. One cabinet housed videocassettes of *In the Know*'s "greatest hits." A sign thumbtacked to the wall read Bless This Mess.

Kelly's desk was a rectangular oasis of neatness. In response to the chaos around her, she kept it religiously tidy. She made her way to her corner now, seeking sanctuary, and in the middle of her clean desk, where she had most definitely not left it, found a piece of paper.

Kelly picked it up. "What's this?" she asked.

"Tea first!" Peg sang out. She thrust a mug under Kelly's nose, but Kelly's eyes were glued to the memo on her desk.

"What...is...this?" Kelly said again.

"Now, Kelly, it was on your desk when I came in. I'm not sure whose idea it is."

Kelly held up the typed sheet of paper and read it out loud. "'Kelly, here's a great idea for a show. I read in a local paper that there's a stripper in town who contributes the money she makes from her profession to the Boy Scouts. How about having the stripper on, plus a representative of the Boy Scouts to explain why they appreciate her efforts—or if they're even aware of what she does. Finally, why not have someone on who thinks the whole thing is in bad taste.'"

"Bad taste!" Kelly exploded. "*Bad taste!* The whole idea is in bad taste." She dropped the memo on her desk. "I can see why it's unsigned. Normally this sounds like Larry, but after viewing the sample tape of our new executive producer's work, I'm not so sure." She accepted a mug of tea from Peg, but the liquid failed to soothe her. "Peg, I'm worried, really worried about what they're going to do to the show."

"Who?"

"Larry and our new Mr. Fix-it, Justin Benedict."

Peg shook her head. "Kelly, you don't know he wrote this memo. I haven't even seen him yet."

"Oh, he's here," she replied, dropping wearily into a chair. "Yakking it up with Larry in Larry's office. It's only 9:03, but already he's flattering his boss and infuriating his staff."

"Who's furious?" a deep voice inquired.

Kelly wheeled around to face Justin Benedict.

For a moment she was too stunned to speak. And as she took stock of Justin Benedict, she became even more flustered. His picture didn't do him justice. A black-and-white photo couldn't portray the startling blue of his eyes, hooded and seemingly drowsy but, Kelly suspected, very alert. Nor could a one-dimensional picture capture the lithe, sinewy frame decked out in a navy pinstriped suit. The conservative cut of his suit and thick blond hair contrasted with a face that always seemed on the verge of a smile. Even though she had insulted him, he looked that way now, his lips curling up at the ends, deepening his dimples. And why his face exuded a boyish zest was a puzzle, since his square jaw, high cheekbones and forthright nose cast a more stalwart image. It was those eyes, changing even as she gazed at them, from sapphire to the color of a still lagoon, that gave him away. Wicked, drowsy eyes.

Kelly struggled to convey only mild surprise at his unexpected appearance, but she knew she was staring. Where were those dimples in the photo? And his hair startled her with its burnished richness, practically demanding that someone's fingers muss it a little. He was striking all right, but her heart did a swan dive when she realized that the maddeningly attractive man before her was not only her boss, but in all probability a professional adversary. Now he had the final word on her show, a shift in power that threatened everything she'd worked for in the past two years. Although she had to tilt her head up, she made herself meet his gaze with calm assurance. She decided that those blue eyes could handle the direct approach.

"I'm upset, Mr. Benedict," she said, holding up the memo, "because while I know you're here to change *In the Know,* I hope this isn't the direction you want to move it in."

He walked over to where she was sitting and took the memo from her. Kelly was shocked—no after-shave. Every hotshot she'd ever worked for simply slathered on cologne. He was lean but hard, she suspected, underneath his suit.

"Larry's just trying to be helpful," he said, dropping the memo into the trash can, "but this isn't precisely my style."

His reply snapped her out of her pleasurable but ridiculous speculation. It also made her slightly hopeful. "What is your style?" she asked.

"Why don't I leave you two to discuss it," Peg offered, making a beeline for the door.

A dimple deepened ever so slightly on Justin's left cheek as he pulled up a chair and sat down next to Kelly. "Just this," he said. "I'll do anything I can to get a rating point, no matter how crass, commercial, exploitative or silly."

Kelly realized immediately that it had been a mistake to sip her tea as he spoke. She began to cough and choke.

"Go down the wrong way?" Justin inquired, dramatically rising to his feet and moving behind Kelly where he gently tapped her on the back. He also gallantly offered her his handkerchief.

Between coughs and an attempt to wipe the tea off her black knit, she managed to utter "You can't be serious!"

He sat down again opposite her. His drowsy eyes seemed amused. "No, I'm not serious," he said as he put his slightly damp handkerchief back into his pocket, "but that's what you think of me, isn't it?" He smiled ever so slightly. The boyish sweetness of his smile seemed to defy anyone not to trust him. Kelly caught herself.

"Not," she said, still breathing hard, "entirely."

"Oh, come on," he insisted.

"If you're asking me if I'm a little concerned over your arrival, the answer is yes. You want to change something I helped create."

"Modify, I think would be a better term," Justin said. "There are a lot of good things about *In the Know.*"

Kelly already knew that, but she bit back this reply. Perhaps his comment meant that he didn't want to change the show radically. "Why don't you tell me what you think is wrong with the show."

He shifted in his chair and rubbed his lower lip with his index finger. "It's not entertaining," he finally said.

Kelly silently counted to ten. "What do you mean?"

"It's not fun."

Ah, Gilda's favorite word, Kelly thought. "It wasn't created to be *fun,*" she said dryly. "It was created to make people think, not just be a pause between going to the refrigerator and the bathroom."

He examined the crease in his slacks and then stared at her. Kelly knew her bluntness could be her undoing, but certain things had to be said.

"Can't it be both?" he said. "Can't a television show inform and entertain? Most news magazine programs have at least one lighthearted segment per show. Why shouldn't we vary the tone of *In the Know?*"

"Because our format is basically serious and we don't do segments. We take on one topic per hour. I might add," she said, "that since we created the show, no one has seriously tampered with the format." She hoped that this would lend weight to her argument.

Justin nodded as if the fact did impress him. "That was two years ago, right? From what I've heard there's been so much change in upper management that the show has been left alone by default. But now I'm here."

The statement had the ring of permanence to it. Even as a chill swept over her, Kelly also felt an inexplicable rush of excitement. She'd never backed away from a challenge in her life, and Justin Benedict promised to be a challenge.

"We still beat our competition," she shot back.

"But your lead is dropping," Justin said, leaning closer to her. The wry smile vanished. Kelly felt his intensity. It matched her own, and even though she dreaded his next words, she recognized a kindred spirit.

"More of your audience is switching to *Phoenix City Hospital.*"

Kelly exhaled an exasperated sigh. "Sex and surgery."

Justin threw her a shrewd, unsettling look. It was impossible, Kelly thought, for him to know about the drought in her love life, but she didn't like his ironic glance, anyway.

"Listen," he said. "Most adults think about sex. They think about why they're having sex, if they're doing it right, and if they're not, why not. Why person A makes them want to do it more than person B, if they're having sex too often or," he paused, "not often enough."

Kelly colored slightly.

"It's a topic on everyone's mind," he continued, "but I noticed from the monthly reports I've read that you don't feature it very often."

"Oh, come on, strippers and Boy Scouts!"

Justin laughed. "You'd be surprised how often it crosses the minds of Boy Scouts."

"Is this a personal recollection?" Kelly asked.

The tenseness went out of his body, and the wicked gleam reappeared. "I was a lousy Boy Scout."

"Why doesn't that surprise me," Kelly replied with a smile. Despite her fears for the show she had to admit that Justin Benedict possessed a clever wit and a quick mind. "But every show can't focus on sex. How exactly do you plan to inject fun into a serious program?"

"I don't suggest doing away with all serious shows, just interspersing them with more unconventional topics."

"Such as?"

"Oh, there are dozens of topics," he said, rubbing his hands. "Diets, for instance."

"I do shows on health," Kelly said.

"I'm talking about the new 'in' diets on the market now."

"Some of them are dangerous fads."

"Then we say so," he countered, "but a woman who's being bombarded by television, newspaper and radio ads promising some diet will change her life wants to know if it will, not hear a nutritionist talk about the four major food groups."

Kelly got the point, but she didn't like it. "What else?"

"Human interest stories. I saw an article in the paper about high school sweethearts who were reunited years later and married. Handled properly, a show like that could be sweet but not saccharine. Another possibility is a show on beauty contests. People love them, and we could have former winners tell how they prepared for a contest."

"Does today's woman care about beauty contests?" Kelly asked.

"If she didn't, there wouldn't be any."

He had her there. And the high school sweethearts idea could work. Justin Benedict promised to be a fountain of suggestions. His vitality pushed her into a higher level of competition and, to her surprise, her body reacted like a cat that had just been stroked. Perhaps Justin's lean body, so inadequately camouflaged by his conservative suit, produced this purring. Kelly mentally shook herself. After all, this was the man who wanted former beauty queens on to share their hairspray secrets.

"What else?" she asked.

"Show business. People love a glimpse at glamour, and stars are always on tour, pushing their tell-all books."

"You mean where they tell how often they make love, with whom and why it was fabulous?"

"Relax," he said, touching her arm. "I'm just adding some spice to an already great stew."

"Then why am I getting indigestion?"

Justin's lips curled into a neat smile. Despite herself Kelly warmed to him. Suddenly she realized he was touching her. She moved her arm, and he quickly removed his hand. His grip had been firm, but not tight. Kelly wondered if it was to reassure or warn her. *I'm the boss,* his strong fingers seemed to be saying. *Get used to it!*

He looked slightly embarrassed at having touched her. His gaze lowered to her black knit dress and, for a fraction of a second, Kelly saw appreciation in them for every curve the dress revealed. Kelly felt a confusing flash of pure pleasure. How could she react this way to a man who threatened the integrity of her show? Miserably she checked her options. She couldn't quit; she had to support Sylvie. But her pride rebelled against handing over her show without a fight.

Her resolve must have shown on her face. "Kelly," Justin said matter-of-factly, "this change is going to happen. It has to. If the show doesn't loosen up, it may have to be canceled."

Kelly was stunned. Was the situation as bad as he said? "At least it would go with some dignity," she said, immediately regretting this impetuous remark.

He inhaled sharply. "I don't talk down to the audience."

"No, we'll leave that to Gilda," Peg put in.

Kelly hadn't noticed her reentering. She gave Peg a look that Peg ignored.

"So you think Gilda's the problem," Justin said.

Kelly hesitated, then nodded. "Yes, I do. I have from the beginning, but I didn't pick her. Management overruled me."

Justin leaned back in his chair. "Larry told me confidentially that you've been lobbying to get Gilda a cohost. Tell me why you think she's bad for the show."

Kelly sighed. "Well, for one thing, she has no journalism experience at all."

Justin's wide shoulders rose briefly, then fell. "Most talk show hosts aren't journalists these days. Sure it's regrettable, but that's the way it is."

"There's also the fact," Peg said, pulling up a chair, "that when she's overwhelmed by a topic, she freezes."

Justin's astute glance moved from Peg to Kelly, waiting for her to refute it. She didn't.

"Then these lighthearted shows I was talking about should relax her," Justin said. "She's an excellent interviewer. I've seen several shows that Larry sent me."

"Gilda can be competent," Kelly admitted, "when she's not talking about herself. Most of the time she acts as if she's more interesting than the topic."

"She *is* the star of the show," Justin replied. "Just like Oprah Winfrey and Phil Donahue are definitely stars."

Kelly shook her head slightly. "But they can handle complex subjects as well as the glitzy and offbeat. It would bother me less that Gilda's taste leans toward gold lamé jumpsuits if she could competently field a serious show."

Justin gave up his casual pose and leaned close to Kelly. "You don't like Gilda because she's not your idea of a talk show host. She is, however, appealing to most of our audience, or the show would never have lasted this long. Do you think Donahue would be running for so many years if people didn't like Phil—no matter what he was talking about?"

"And I thought it was all those shows on sex," Kelly said, trying to lighten the tone of the conversation. She had definitely been too frank, too fast.

"Donahue's a personality," he continued. "Oprah's a personality and so is Gilda. Her personality has been buried under too much seriousness. We need to let it out."

Kelly's lips thinned into a closed line. Now she knew why Larry had thwarted her attempts to find a cohost! Justin planned to reshape Gilda. Or, as Kelly feared, let Gilda loose to be herself.

Justin paused, watching her carefully for a moment before continuing. When he did, his voice had a flat, case-closed tone. "You're mad because the topics aren't the star of the show, and Gilda is. Whether or not that's the way it should be, that's the way it is, and it hurts your professional pride."

Kelly barely suppressed an angry protest. What rankled her the most was that there was a grain of truth in what he'd said. But just a grain. "Content should always be more important than glitter," she insisted. "However, Gilda *will* be able to talk to diet quacks, strippers and other assorted celebrities on their own level."

Justin shook his head. "You'd better get used to this. I'm not the enemy."

Kelly wondered why he bothered to say that. She was so preoccupied with her thoughts that she didn't immediately notice the heavy gardenia fragrance that had wafted into the room. It was the favorite scent of Gilda Simone.

"You must be Justin Benedict," Gilda exclaimed. "I can't tell you how excited I am that you're here." She draped her mink coat on a chair. The full-length fur was a tad heavy for early October, Kelly thought, but then Gilda had definite ideas about her clothes.

Gilda Simone was a woman at war with her image, or rather the image Kelly had encouraged. Kelly wanted seriousness; Gilda wanted glamour. Years before, Gilda had gone to Hollywood to be a star and failed, save for a brief stint as a host on a cooking show. *In the Know* was her last shot at being a celebrity, and she tried to look the part.

A star, according to Gilda, dressed in the latest fashion. So she adopted every fad that came along, whether it flattered her or not. Kelly inwardly groaned when she saw the maroon business suit that she had picked out for Gilda. Gilda had raised the hem to dizzying heights. Nobody at WMAS had the nerve to tell Gilda that the resurgence of the miniskirt was not for everyone—especially not someone who was *pre*-baby boom.

The outfits she picked out herself rarely looked as good on her as they did on the models in the magazines. Her weight wasn't the problem. In fact, Kelly thought Gilda's constant dieting had made her too thin. The problem was Gilda's taste, and she disliked Kelly's.

In pursuing a glitzy image Gilda had ironically camouflaged her best features. Heavy, inappropriate makeup hid her pretty face, and an unflattering hair color and style concealed how luxurious her hair really was.

Kelly sighed. Gilda would never believe that her rapport with the average person was more important than designer clothes. She'd been so malleable two years ago when she was plucked from obscurity by one of WMAS's less creative program managers. Now her ego had expanded to the size of Harvard Stadium, and only *she* knew what was best for *In the Know*. Recently Gilda had recommended to Larry that he transfer Kelly to the promotion department, where she could produce public service spots that would air at three in the morning. Gilda's rationale was that Kelly only wanted to work on serious issues.

Kelly glanced at Justin for his first "in person" reaction. He'd already seen Gilda on the tapes Larry had sent him, but never this close. His expression showed no surprise. Gilda, however, left no doubt as to her reaction to Justin. She looked as if she'd just received an early Christmas present.

"Welcome to Boston," Gilda said, extending her hand. "I came in early to meet you."

"Thank you," Justin replied as he rose to greet her.

Gilda's regal pose took a painful tumble when she stepped forward to receive him. One of her spiked heels got caught in the rug, and she fell—with an awkward, obviously unplanned screech—into Justin's arms.

"Does this mean you're happy to see me?" Justin quipped.

Even Gilda joined in the laughter, and Kelly admired the way he'd saved an embarrassing situation.

"Happy?" Gilda repeated. "You're what I've been praying for!" As she straightened, she added, "If I have to do another show on the changing tax laws, I'll just die!''

At that moment Kelly considered homicide. "You know, Gilda," she said, "you haven't done too badly by me. We're still number one in our time period."

Gilda shrugged away this fact. "Kelly, no one can match you with the serious stuff, but I don't believe it showcases the range of my talent." She sat down in a chair, causing her mini to hike up even farther on her thighs. Then she crossed her legs.

This produced a momentary silence. Gilda took the silence as further encouragement to expound. "I've noticed the direction that talk shows have been taking and, frankly, I couldn't be more delighted," she said, gazing at Justin.

Her overstated features softened when she looked at him, and Kelly was annoyed that her own reaction had been similar to Gilda's. She'd thought they had nothing in common.

"There's a widening gap between talk and hard news," Gilda continued, "and I say good. Let reporters do what they're trained for, and I'll do what I'm trained for."

Which is? Kelly wondered.

"Entertainment, human interest," Gilda explained, even though no one asked. "Offbeat, *provocative* topics that will showcase the spontaneous side of my personality. That's my real strength! People are tired of serious topics day after day. They want to feel good about themselves when they watch us."

"We can't promise easy answers to complex problems in sixty minutes," Kelly interjected.

"We can offer hope," Justin said.

"Of course," Kelly and Gilda answered in unison, but Kelly wondered to what extent "hope" meant pat assurances. Just how far would Justin go to make people happy?

"Larry showed me the stripper idea," Gilda enthused, "and I said yes! That's the direction we should go in. Sure, it's wacky, but I can have *fun* with it. Let's rev up this show till—"

"Till it sparkles like yourself," Justin finished.

"Exactly!" Gilda said. She smiled such a happy, genuine smile that Kelly was momentarily disarmed. All Gilda had ever wanted was to be a star and here, looking at her with enthusiasm and kindness, was the man who was going to make it happen for her. Kelly thought back to Sylvie's comment that morning about Justin. Her young sister had miscalculated. Justin Benedict definitely fitted the category of Mr. Right—but not for Kelly.

"Perhaps we could discuss this further over a cup of coffee," he suggested.

Gilda picked up her purse. "I have an idea. Why don't you and I have a drink after work?"

Kelly and Peg exchanged glances at their exclusion from this event. Justin said, "I thought we all could meet. Thursday's my best day."

Gilda spread her arms expansively. "I meant all of us."

Smiling, Peg got up. "Nights are bad for me because I'm in a master's program at Lesley College. But perhaps the three of you could meet." She winked at Kelly and then left the room.

Justin turned to Kelly. "Could you make it?"

"Sylvie has ice-skating every Thursday night," Kelly said quietly.

Justin looked at her keenly. "Is Sylvie your daughter?"

"No, my sister. I'm raising her," Kelly explained.

"Could she reschedule—just this one time?" he asked.

Kelly shifted in her chair. "She could, she has, but there's only so much rearranging you can ask your family to do because of your job."

The remark curiously silenced him. He glanced away from her.

Gilda draped her mink over her shoulders. "I think it's remarkable the way Kelly juggles work and parenting, but I'm afraid I don't have any children, Justin. *My* priority is the show. So I'd be very interested in hearing your new ideas on Thursday. Let's say six o'clock at the Channels Bar and Grill across the street? I'm sure you're just what we need to fix things around here."

The way Gilda emphasized *new* and *fix* was a slap at everything Kelly had done for the show, and all those present knew it. Kelly remained cool, despite the acidic churning of her stomach. Was this humiliation going to be a daily occurrence now? Gilda's ego was stupendous, but she wasn't a stupid woman. She had shrewdly assessed the impact of having Justin on the team and knew it would put Kelly on the defensive.

"Gilda," Justin said in a steely voice Kelly hadn't heard before, "we're *all* going to work together. Each of us must respect the other person, be supportive. That's how I've found people work best."

Gilda flicked a piece of lint off her skirt. "Of course. Naturally," she said, as if being a team player excited her. "Whatever is best for the show. I know our demographics are off. We need topics that rile up our audience either to laugh or cry or get mad as hell—like that show you're putting together, Kelly, on guns in the classroom."

"What about it?" Kelly said.

"Do we have teens on who've been caught carrying guns in school?"

"Of course, several," Kelly replied, "plus I booked parents, school administrators, policemen—"

"Fine, fine," Gilda interrupted, "but how *angry* are our guests? Will the parents stand up and yell, 'How can this be happening in our schools?' Will the administrators accuse the parents of irresponsibility? Will the students refuse to give up their guns? Will confiscated guns be on the set?"

"In other words," Kelly said, "will this turn into a free-for-all?"

"What's wrong with honest emotions?" Gilda countered.

"Nothing," Kelly said. "All my guests feel strongly about the topic, but I can't guarantee a shoot-out, Gilda. I booked these people for their ability to express themselves—in words," she hastily added. "The boy who accidentally shot his best friend—"

"Is he a guest?" Gilda interjected. "*Great.* I definitely want close-ups of his face, and—"

"I promised that we would shoot his face in shadow," Kelly stated, "to protect his privacy, and the other boy's family."

[handwritten in left margin: IB Gilda The wicked other woman]

Gilda threw up her hands. "But we need to see his face, to feel his grief, his guilt."

Kelly winced at Gilda's insensitivity. "His story is powerful enough without seeing his face," she snapped.

Justin had been quiet throughout the exchange, but Kelly felt certain he'd been sizing it up. Just what kind of boss would he be?

He barely shook his head. "No," he said. "The boy should stay in shadow. Kelly's right."

Kelly sighed in relief.

"Oh," Gilda said, slightly surprised. "Well, I suppose we couldn't change things at this point." She picked up a file from her desk. "You'll have to excuse me, Justin. I have to go over the research again for today's show. If anyone needs me, I'll be in the downstairs dressing room." She walked out, carrying notes that Kelly had worked hard on, but that Gilda probably hadn't read yet.

Kelly's head ached. She felt as if Gilda's high heels were tap dancing on her forehead. She rubbed her temples, but the pounding wouldn't stop. "I appreciate your support."

"There was no other answer possible," Justin replied firmly. "We can't exploit a vulnerable child."

Kelly stopped rubbing her temples. She gazed at his casual expression, but felt the conviction behind his words. Perhaps she'd been hasty in judging him.

"Normally, though, I'm against putting people in shadow," he added.

A vague weariness settled in again. "Of course."

He seemed to sense her disappointment. "Look," he said, "I'll be honest. I need you. I need your talent.

Larry knows, I know, you know, and Peg knows that Gilda would never be where she is without you. It would certainly be nice if Gilda recognized it, but Gilda isn't your boss. I am, and I like your style."

His face had lost its detachment. Kelly was drawn as much by its intensity as by the words he was saying.

"Working with people like Gilda can be...delicate," he went on, "and I see you do it with humor and tenacity. I was brought in to complement your strengths, not replace them. I'm well aware that this collaboration of ours will be difficult for you, and you might even be wondering, why bother? You could get another job. Your reputation is solid. But I'm asking you to stay, to give it a chance. I promise, if you'll try, I'll keep the work environment supportive and professional."

It wasn't an outright declaration that he would keep Gilda in line, but he obviously wasn't blind to the situation, either.

"You tell Gilda what she wants to hear," Kelly said, "and you tell me what I want to hear. I think I could learn diplomacy from you."

Justin smiled. "I mean what I say. Give it a chance."

His face looked so concerned that, skeptical as she was, Kelly began to believe him. "We'll see," she conceded. *But it's unfair,* she added silently, *that Justin Benedict should have such physical appeal and I should be so susceptible to it!*

"SO WHAT HAPPENED NEXT?" Sylvie asked. "Did he like your black knit?"

"Oh, Sylvie," Kelly laughed. "You've got a one-track mind."

Sylvie took a gulp of her after-dinner diet soda. The two of them were sitting around the kitchen table. "What's wrong with thinking about boys?" she asked. "I think about Kevin all the time. I told him so. He loves it."

The mention of Sylvie's current boyfriend always put Kelly on her guard. She didn't like Kevin Lucas. The son of a wealthy and powerful father, Kevin thought that normal rules didn't apply to him. Sylvie thrilled to his preppie exterior and rebel interior. Kelly didn't.

"Hmm," she said, trying to play it cool. "What does that mean?"

Sylvie gave her a knowing look. "Ease up on him, will you? He just likes it that I'm honest about my feelings and don't play games."

"What does *that* mean?"

Sylvie emitted a long, dramatic sigh. "Kelly, you're not my mother."

"I'm the closest thing you've got!"

"That doesn't mean you can tell me who to date! Kevin's my first real boyfriend."

Kelly reached out and took Sylvie's free hand. "I know. I'm just worried about you, that's all. And, like it or not, I'll always be nosy about who you see and what you're doing. With Paul in the army, it's you and me, kid."

Sylvie returned the squeeze. "I know, but don't worry. I can take care of myself."

Now there was a phrase to strike terror in the heart of any parent, Kelly thought. She knew that Sylvie's fragile ego had gotten a real boost from Kevin's attention. Beneath all her confident talk was a less-than-confident girl. "If you should ever feel you're being pushed into anything," Kelly said, "you know you can always talk to me—about anything."

Sylvie blushed. "Yeah, thanks, but don't worry about me. Kevin loves me."

"Sylvie, love isn't—"

"Please! No lectures! Besides you changed the subject."

"I did not."

"Did so. You were about to tell me what Justin Benedict did next."

Kelly tossed her napkin onto the table. "He went into a series of meetings, and I barely spoke to him the rest of the day."

Sylvie was disappointed. "Aw, too bad," she said as she got up to scrape the dishes. "But you'll see him every day. Won't that be fun?"

Fun. Kelly blanched at the word. Still, Justin Benedict's arrival signaled a change in her life. That much was certain. Today she'd given as good as she'd got, and he'd shown he could take it. Justin Benedict was going to keep her on her toes, and the prospect excited her. *He* excited her with his easy grace and sexy grin. "I don't know if it'll be fun," she said to Sylvie, "but it won't be boring."

JUSTIN BENEDICT FLICKED off the television in his hotel room. He couldn't concentrate on the local news. Kelly Ferris hadn't completely bought his plea this morning. But she hadn't threatened to quit, either. He'd meant everything he'd said, yet those big gray eyes had been disbelieving. Well, reality was reality. The show would have to change, adjust to the demands of the competition if it wanted to stay on. That was the painful truth, "dignity" notwithstanding.

Just who was she to throw words like that at him! Why did it bother him so? He'd worked hard for his reputation as a man who could turn shows around. Take good shows and make them more watchable. That didn't mean he'd lost his standards.

He admired her fierce devotion to the show. Such passion and commitment. It reminded him of his early idealism, and Justin wondered if perhaps he was too cynical at thirty-five. No, he quickly decided, not cynical. Pragmatic. Kelly wanted all the topics to be serious, and all the hosts to be journalists. That wasn't the real world. And Kelly would have to learn that. In the meantime her stubbornness impressed him. Behind her beguiling gray eyes was a fighter. She was like him, and in more ways than one. It was only a hunch, but he suspected she was a bit lonely, too. Or was he just projecting his own loneliness? If her lushly petite figure distracted him, that was *his* problem. He knew she wouldn't willingly alter the show, and any victory would be hard won.

But he needed her. From the shows he'd seen she had excellent judgment in booking guests, her research for the shows was impeccable and her questions penetrating. Together he and Kelly could make *In the Know* a winner, possibly even syndicate it. To do that required compromising on her part, and Justin was surprised at how ambivalent he was about it. Although it would make his job easier, he didn't want Kelly to lose the fire he'd seen today. It made her so interesting. He didn't want her to leave, because she was crucial to the increased success of the show, and he'd abandoned everything in Chicago for this opportunity.

Justin kicked his shoes off and angrily pulled the covers back on his bed. Without her help he'd fail, making his decision to come to Boston a professional mistake—if indeed it wasn't already a personal mistake. Closing his eyes, he saw the tear-stained face of his five-year-old son. Leaving Tommy in Chicago had torn Justin apart, but he'd felt he had no choice. Tommy had finally made friends at the expensive kindergarten he went to. The security of his world was so fragile, especially after the pain of Mommy and Daddy divorcing. Justin couldn't shatter his son's security, and the job in Boston offered him the ability to support two households. There were planes to Chicago, right?

Someone had once said that money was the root of all evil. Justin knew that the *lack* of money caused even more misery. Still, the decision to leave his boy anguished him. If Kelly wouldn't help him, coming to Boston would cost him too much for too little.

CHAPTER TWO

JUST THIS ONCE Sylvie would have to be late for her skating lesson, Kelly decided as she took a sip of her wine spritzer. She looked around the bar from her corner table. Neither Justin nor Gilda had shown up yet. Channels Bar and Grill was relatively empty at 5:45 p.m. When the local news ended at seven, the place would fill up immediately with the station's dinner crowd, hungry for a Channels burger and brew. Kelly wasn't hungry. At the last minute she'd decided that she *had* to join Justin and Gilda for their planned drink, even if she couldn't stay very long.

Strategically she needed to be there. After only four days on the job, Justin had meddled with this afternoon's *In the Know*. Kelly felt the change hadn't been an improvement. She was determined to get her views across tonight.

A gravelly voice rang out. "Great show today, Kelly!"

Kelly looked up to see Ernie Banks, the portly owner of Channels standing by her table. Since a good percentage of his business came from WMAS staffers, Ernie kept his bar television permanently on that channel, making him an unofficial critic of the station. Kelly usually enjoyed his critiques, but praise for today's show only increased her bad mood.

"You *liked* today's show?" she asked incredulously.

Ernie's moon-shaped face broke into a raspy chuckle. "Yeah, I liked it," he said. "It ain't often, Kelly, that I laugh at your show."

"Usually you're not supposed to."

"But *today,* well, when that seventy-year-old woman talked about why she married the twenty-year-old boy, I had to crack up!" To reiterate his point, Ernie let out a loud belly laugh.

Kelly groaned. The original title of the show had been "May-December Marriages—Do They Work?" She had hoped to make a point that love could withstand the problems of age difference. She'd carefully booked the panel with articulate couples whose age differences spanned between ten and twenty years. At the last minute, however, Justin had unearthed the septuagenarian and the schoolboy and insisted that they be included.

This odd couple completely unbalanced the show. Gilda immediately focused on them and the titillating facts about their sex life. The program's original intent went out the window as the couple cheerfully described the most intimate details of their lives.

"Yeah," Ernie said, wiping his eyes, "it was hard to keep a straight face when that kid called the old lady a foxy chick! You planning to do more shows like that?"

"That remains to be seen," Kelly replied, wondering the same thing.

"I hope so," Ernie said, moving on. "I give this show a thumbs-up!"

"I'm *so* glad," Kelly murmured. She took a deep draw on her spritzer. Justin's "contribution" to her show today still rankled. And here she was, sitting alone in a bar, waiting for him to show up.

A man in a business suit, sipping a large martini, glanced her way. His expression turned appreciative, with a suggestion that he was willing to be more so. Determinedly Kelly focused on the television set positioned on one side of the bar. WMAS's news rang out to the basically uninterested patrons, but one story caught her eye. Budget cutbacks statewide were having a disastrous effect on education, especially colleges. A show on this crisis would be timely and, if booked correctly, incisive. She was assembling her dream panel when she heard that unmistakably deep voice.

"So you could make it."

She turned in her chair to see Justin's handsome face looking down at her. The overhead lights glinted in his thick blond hair, making it the color of wheat on a sunny day. His glen plaid suit brought out the tan in his skin, and he was smiling a smile that, despite her irritation with him, was all but irresistible. It was those damn dimples. Out of the corner of her eyes she saw the interested patron look him over, then glance away in apparent retreat.

Justin sat down opposite her and motioned to the waiter. Then he turned his attention back to Kelly.

"I'm glad you came," he said. "But what about your sister? Did she have to miss her lesson?"

"No, I'm just taking her a little later," Kelly said, surprised that he had remembered. "I can't stay too long." She took a long pull on her wine spritzer, bracing herself.

Justin peered at her drink. "Is that water or lemonade?" he asked, amused.

"It's a spritzer," she said stiffly.

Justin grinned. Dimples and all.

Kelly straightened in her chair. "I have a long night ahead of me. I have to keep my wits about me."

Justin eyed her thoughtfully. "Is that a priority?"

"What?"

"Keeping your wits about you. Always being in control."

Kelly set her drink down. "I'd prefer to call it always being responsible," she parried, "and, yes, I do like it. But I noticed that being in control seems to suit *you*. That couple you forced on me today—"

"Hey, I showed you their marriage certificate. They were legitimate."

"They ruined the show," she protested. "Who could take them seriously?"

"Why must every guest be serious? They were lighthearted and charming. They *made* the show!"

Kelly bridled at this remark. "It doesn't surprise me that you think so," she said, stirring her drink with her straw. "For all my efforts the show was basically about sex. Could the twenty-year-old make whoopie with the seventy-year-old. And if so, how, and how often."

Justin accepted a menu from a waiter. "I'd like to be making whoopie at seventy."

Kelly snorted. "I'm sure you will be! If I'm still producing, I'll book you on a 'Sex after Seventy' show, and you can give pointers!"

She hadn't meant it as a compliment, but Justin burst out laughing. In spite of herself Kelly felt drawn to his infectious chuckle. Then she remembered that a laugh could be just as superficial as the show she'd produced today.

"I'll have a Scotch on the rocks," Justin said to the waiter. "Would you like another spritzer Kelly, or would two send you out of control?"

She met his sardonic gaze unruffled. "No, two makes me insufferably lighthearted and charming."

A dimple deepened ever so slightly on his cheek. When the waiter left, Justin mused, "I wonder what you'd be like with your hair down, figuratively I mean."

In an almost unconscious gesture, Kelly touched her French braid. It was still immaculately coiled, although for one mad, impulsive second she wanted to tear out all the pins and let her hair tumble free. Why did Justin affect her this way?

To cover up her confusion she retorted, "And I wonder if you take anything seriously."

To her surprise Justin's face became closed, guarded. "Yes, I take some things seriously."

"Such as?"

"Such as...dinner. I'm starved. Will you have something to eat?"

Kelly wondered at the evasion. "No, I really can't stay that long."

Justin scrutinized the menu. "What's good here?"

"Burgers."

"What about chicken à la Channels?"

"Occasionally they miss a few feathers. I suggest the burgers."

"Fish and chips?"

"Possibly. It's early enough in the week. But their specialty really is—"

"Burgers," Justin finished. "I'm beginning to understand. A small voice tells me to take your advice."

Kelly leaned back in her chair. "A wise move. You won't regret it."

Justin put down his menu. His smile, so sassy yet sweet, reached out to Kelly like a soft kiss. *Be careful,* she warned herself. *He probably smiles at everyone this way.*

"I have every intention of taking your advice," he said, loosening his tie. "So tell me, with all your years of experience . . . ?"

"Yes?"

"Should I have a baked potato or fries?"

In spite of herself she smiled. "Fries, and get the Indian pudding for dessert." She pushed a piece of paper across the table toward him. He glanced at it—an outline of her ideas for the education piece—then glanced up at her, questioning.

Kelly cleared her throat and plunged in. "Now that I've advised you on the matter of food, I have another suggestion. The state legislature is making massive cutbacks in education to balance the budget. It means layoffs for teachers, fewer students admitted to state universities, the elimination of many special education programs—well, you get the idea. Education is a major industry in Massachusetts, and this is a crisis. I see at least two shows, maybe a whole week. Here are some guests I'd book."

Justin picked up the paper. He read it over, nodding at some of the names. But when he placed the note back on the table, Kelly knew he hadn't been dazzled by her idea. Before he even opened his mouth she felt herself starting to tense up.

Justin's Scotch arrived. He gave his burger and fries order while Kelly waited for him to answer her.

"It's an interesting idea," he said finally, "but what's the hook? Where's the drama?"

"The drama," Kelly said in exasperation, "is in what every parent has to lose. I'll have on mothers who can't get their kids into college or—" she paused "—you want drama? How about a mother who'll protest that the budget cuts will deny her handicapped child the special education classes he needs? That's pretty dramatic."

Justin held up one hand in a peace gesture. "I'm not saying this won't make for one interesting show."

"One?" Her voice rose. "I thought perhaps we could do a week."

"But," he continued, "I disagree with you on your sense of urgency. State legislatures are always in a bind concerning education. You might say that education today is in a perpetual state of crisis. Everyone's tired of hearing it. Don't get me wrong. I'm all for enlightening our viewers as long as they're entertained, as well. *In the Know* is so...so *earnest*. That has to change."

Kelly grabbed her note back. "I'm sure I can find the lighter side of some of the new diseases out today," she snapped.

He eyed her coolly. "A show on medicine doesn't have to be about a disease," he said. "It could be about the newest advances in plastic surgery."

"That's not a bad idea," Kelly said, surprised. "Surgeons are doing some wonderful reconstruction on birth defects these days."

"Well, there's that, but I was thinking more along the lines of cosmetic surgery."

"Ah, fantasies of youth forever."

"Yes, fantasy," he said. "I think the housewife at home would like a glimpse at what *doesn't* plague her day after day. Like plastic surgery for cosmetic reasons."

"Like escape from the real world," Kelly countered.

Justin swirled his drink around in the glass, then glanced toward her again. "You talk about the real world as if it's some grim place. I think our viewers want to see the possibilities, not the probabilities in life. They want fantasy, adventure, the offbeat. Look—" he pulled a newspaper clipping from his pocket "—a strange cult that worships snakes moved next door to this woman. She discovered it when she spotted a cobra behind her rosebushes." He handed her the clipping. "Extraordinary things happening to ordinary people. I'd like to do a whole show on weird cults, have some of the members on."

"Cults can be dangerous! Things could get out of control."

"So much the better. We won't shy away from controversy. In fact, I want more emotion injected into our shows, not less."

Kelly started to object, but Justin cut her off, intent on making his point. "Have you ever been abducted by aliens," he asked, "or suspected that you had a past life? Don't shrug it off. Some people truly believe in reincarnation, and the rest are fascinated by the possibility."

"So you feel that our average viewer would rather ponder the mysteries of UFOs than the immediate dilemma of why Johnny can't go to college?"

He met her gaze evenly. "Yes, although we will do the education idea. I told you yesterday that I wanted a mix of topics. I'm sure you can meet the challenge."

Kelly watched him sip his Scotch, too angry to thank him for this "compliment." Did he think she'd be satisfied with a few crumbs? If he suspected just how upset she was, he didn't show it. In fact, he leaned a little closer to her.

"Suppose we get back to our average viewer, Kelly. The woman twenty-five to forty-nine. *Your* age, more or less."

Kelly gave him a startled, wary look.

"What does she think about, dream about?"

The question caught Kelly off balance, a condition Justin seemed adept at creating. She struggled to switch gears.

"Um, let's see," she said. "What do women think about? Well, there's the problem of affordable daycare, the demand for equal pay for equal work, the high cost of..." Justin stopped her with a shake of his head. "What?" she said somewhat defensively. "I'm answering your question."

Justin took a short sip of his Scotch. "I know, but let me rephrase. I want to do shows on women's deepest hopes and dreams. Tell me, what one dream do you think most women have?"

"World peace."

One corner of his mouth turned up in a slow smile. "I'm sure that's one, but guess again."

Kelly didn't spend much time on dreams. Life had been so full of responsibilities lately that her dreams had taken a back seat to reality. But reality now was Justin, staring at her with interest, challenge and more than a hint of personal speculation.

Insidiously an old aching dream invaded her thoughts. Buried deep within her, almost denied, this dream contained no vision of Emmy acceptance speeches. It involved herself and a man, a vibrant, passionate man who—Justin's eyes interrupted her reverie. Their sapphire gaze seemed to penetrate through her body, right to the spreading warmth of her dream. For a horrible moment Kelly felt embarrassed color flood her cheeks. But then she pinched herself. Justin didn't know her. He couldn't guess her dream. He was merely waiting for an answer.

"Relationships," she got out. "Most women dream about relationships that last."

Justin nodded, his handsome face thoughtful. "I would have said true love," he said, smiling briefly, "but relationships is probably a more accurate term."

"What do most men dream about?" she asked.

"The same thing," he said softly.

"Is that your dream?"

He met her eyes, and for a fraction of a second Kelly thought she saw acknowledgment of that shared dream, that shared fantasy. He glanced away as if embarrassed. "Me?" He laughed. "No. My dream is a twenty-five percent increase in the show's ratings." He looked up. "So I want to really explore relationships on the show. If we can find happy endings for our topics, wonderful. But if there's a controversial aspect to them, then we go with that."

Kelly thought *she* must have been dreaming to think that his priorities could be anything but increased ratings. "Make 'em laugh or make 'em cry," she muttered, "just don't make 'em think."

"Make 'em do *both*," Justin said emphatically. "Entertainment isn't a dirty word. Feelings matter more to people than facts."

An awkward silence fell, during which a juicy, greasy Channels' burger was placed before Justin. "You'd better have some french fries, Kelly," he said, breaking the silence. "I ordered them because you told me to." He pushed the platter over to her.

"It seems like the last piece of advice you took from me," she said dryly. She picked up the catsup bottle and shook it, but the catsup refused to appear. Frustrated, she tapped the back of the bottle with the palm of her hand. Still no catsup. Furious now, not only with the damn bottle but also with Justin, the world of television and her own loss of control, she slapped the bottle so hard that most of its contents spilled over the french fries, drowning them and splashing red dots on herself and Justin.

"Oh, no!" she gasped, horrified. "Oh, I'm sorry!"

Justin looked at Kelly, then down at his crimson plate. Finally he asked, "How did you know I liked my fries that way?"

Despite her mortification Kelly burst out laughing.

Spearing a soggy fry with a fork, he raised it to his mouth and took a bite. "Umm," he said, "perfect, with just that hint of potato."

Kelly pulled napkins from the dispenser and handed some to Justin. "Of course I'll pay for the cleaning," she stated, furiously wiping her blouse and hands.

"Just let me know how much it is. Or I'll bring the suit in myself or replace—"

"Hey, no problem," Justin said, cutting off her babble. "This suit has been through worse than catsup—spaghetti sauce, peanut butter, ground-up animal crackers."

Instantly Kelly saw Justin blink in mild dismay. She paused in her cleanup. "Animal crackers?"

Justin sighed softly and, for a moment, concentrated on wiping his hands. When he looked at Kelly again, his face contained a curious mixture of pride and reluctance.

"My son, Tommy, likes animal crackers. He lives in Chicago with his mother. He's very young, very bright and very messy."

A son! Kelly racked her brains, trying to remember if she'd seen a picture or a plastic cube full of snapshots on his desk. Odd that he should seem reluctant to talk about his own child.

"A son," she said conversationally. "How nice. Does he take after you?"

"Too much," Justin said with a hint of a smile. Then, as if he feared he'd just divulged something important, he added, "We're both messy. Chances are, Kelly, that I'd have dumped something on you if you hadn't gotten to me first."

Kelly thought ruefully that he'd been dumping on her for the past four days. She glanced at his now impassive face and wondered what it would take to shake up that handsome facade. Not even the accidental mention of his son gave him more than a moment's discomfort—but why should it have given him any?

"How old is—?"

"Aghh," Justin let out, touching his head, "I've got catsup in my hair. By the way, so do you." He pulled out a napkin, and before Kelly realized what he was doing, he dabbed some spots on her inky hair and gently touched a spot on her face that she'd missed.

His touch set off a tremor of sensuality within her. The unexpected sensation confused Kelly, though she made no move to disengage. How could Justin's slender fingers produce this pleasant, languid feeling when his professional beliefs produced such aggravation? She had no rational answer. He wasn't an easy man to categorize, pin down or penetrate. When they touched on anything personal, like his son, he deftly changed the subject. Kelly begrudgingly admired how he manipulated situations and conversations to suit his purposes, but that slick side of him also put her on her guard. His touch, however, produced the opposite reaction.

His thumb briefly grazed the soft skin under her cheekbone. Could he feel her skin warm to it? Kelly couldn't meet his gaze for fear he would see how his touch affected her.

Her vulnerability angered her, made her feel defenseless. Oh, why had that crazy romantic dream been unleashed from her subconscious? Justin hadn't mentioned a woman or even a child in *his* dream. *My dream is a twenty-five percent increase in the show's ratings,* he'd said. Maybe he really was that mercenary. Maybe he needed no one but himself.

Justin knew he should remove his hand from her cheek, but he didn't. One more second. He wanted one more second with Kelly's face looking so...ethereal. The change in expression surprised him. He hadn't expected this hint of vulnerability, and it intrigued him. He also suspected that it was fleeting. Letting her emotions loose seemed to alarm Kelly.

"Well, this is a cozy little meeting, I must say," rang out the robust tones of Boston's favorite talk show hostess.

Kelly and Justin both looked up in surprise to see Gilda. Decked out today in her silver fox jacket, she cordially greeted Justin, but although her smile remained fixed, Kelly felt that Gilda wasn't as thrilled to see her. "Why, Kelly," she said with honey-dripping friendliness, "I thought you weren't coming tonight. You didn't mention it."

"I changed my mind at the last minute," Kelly explained. Gilda obviously wasn't pleased. Somehow Gilda's intimate tête-à-tête with Justin had become an uncomfortable threesome.

"Yes, I see, and—what happened?"

Kelly finished wiping her blouse. "I had a small mishap with a catsup bottle," she said.

"Yes, a small mishap," Justin concurred with a deadpan expression as he stared at his catsup-drenched plate.

They laughed. Gilda didn't, although her mouth stretched into a semblance of a smile. Kelly feared that her already delicate relationship with Gilda had just taken a turn for the worse.

Suddenly a round of applause exploded from the bar. Led by Ernie, the patrons clapped and whistled, with Ernie yelling, "Great show today, Gilda! You're really on a roll!"

Startled, Gilda froze in amazement. Then she let out a whoop of delight and took a bow. "Thank you, thank you. Oh, I *love* you," she said, accepting a complimentary glass of champagne from Ernie. She took a sip, held the glass up and said to more applause, "You ain't seen nothing yet!"

Kelly watched this homage with a sinking heart. When Gilda turned and made a bow to Justin, he dipped his head in a cozy show of mutual admiration. Ernie's tribute was just the kind of proof he needed to make his case for changing the show.

Gilda pulled a chair up near Justin and sat down. In a whisper she said, "Ernie could scour the sinks with this champagne." She scooted her chair closer to Justin's. "My, you two got here early."

Justin picked up his hamburger. "It's six-forty, Gilda."

She laughed. "Is it? I must be late."

Kelly glanced at her watch. "So am I." She rose.

"You're leaving?" Gilda asked with a bit too much enthusiasm.

Kelly put on her suit jacket. "Yes, I have to take Sylvie to her skating lesson." She faced Justin. "I'm glad we had this chance to talk away from the station," she said formally. "I think I have a *clearer picture* of the kind of shows you want in the future."

"I have some suggestions for the future," Gilda announced.

"And I look forward to hearing them," Justin said, not missing a beat. "Speaking of the future, let's see if we can't book a show on psychics soon. Get a crystal ball reader, a tarot card reader, an astrologer—"

"We can book *my* astrologer!" Gilda said.

Kelly pulled her chair away. "Perfect," she said. "Just perfect."

CHAPTER THREE

"I SEE...I see a man in your future."

Kelly tried very hard to suppress a grin. Madame Myra was one of several psychics who had just appeared on *In the Know*'s "psychic predictions" show that day. Two weeks had passed since Justin had suggested the topic during the meeting at Channels. At Kelly's insistence they'd had a skeptic on the panel, but Justin claimed it wasn't necessary. No one *really* believed psychics—they were just fun.

"Tell me you don't read your horoscope every day," he'd said to Kelly earlier.

She'd resisted a snappy retort because, again, Justin was right. She did read her horoscope. Didn't everybody? He'd put his finger on a common ritual and made a successful show out of it. Even though the show was over, the studio audience had remained, asking the psychic "experts" more questions.

In one corner the Amazing Tony was trying to help a woman find her lost dog. In another Juliana gazed into a crystal ball and told a suddenly depressed mother that her son was coming down with chicken pox. Madame Myra, who saw the future in your vocal "auras," warned Kelly about this new man in her life.

"It won't be an easy romance," Myra cautioned. "There's turbulence in your aura." The Madame, whose real name was Betty, looked so earnest that Kelly assured her she would be on the lookout for a turbulent man.

Kelly sighed. Zoltan the Astrologer had commandeered the set's coffee table to lay out some charts. "Be prepared for big changes in your life!" she heard him exclaim to Gilda. In five minutes all these people would have to leave to make way for another production. It seemed a shame. Everyone was having so much fun!

"Enjoying yourself?"

Kelly turned to see Justin's smiling face. He always seemed to be around at just the moment when she was admitting to herself that an idea of his had worked. How he anticipated these moments, she didn't know. She suspected, however, that of all the shows he oversaw, *In the Know* affected him the most personally.

At the sight of his drowsy blue eyes a small electric charge ran up her spine. Nearly three weeks of working with him hadn't diminished his physical appeal. It was crazy. They argued every day, and each show was a fiercely bargained-for compromise of their differing tastes. But he had a way about him that made even arguing with him interesting.

His wizardry with words, his endless supply of ideas and his wily, unpredictable defense of those ideas daily tested Kelly's more cautious, analytic mind. Exasperating, yes, but also refreshing and exciting. Not only that, but he particularly seemed to enjoy their sparring matches.

"Who was it," she asked him, "who said, 'There's a sucker born every minute'?"

"Kelly, Kelly," he said, shaking his head. "I thought *I* was supposed to be the cynic."

"Madame Myra told me there was turbulence in my future."

Justin bent down his head to whisper. "That's not your future. That's your present."

Kelly tried not to blush. Was there real feeling behind his teasing? It was absurd to care. Yet she did, more than she wanted to admit. But there was too much at stake on the show to risk finding out that it was only her ego—or her hormones—working overtime.

She tried to lean casually against a television monitor mounted on a cart. "Madame Myra also told me that if I persevere, I'll get what I want," she replied, "so I guess I can handle this turbulence."

Justin walked a few steps to the first row of audience seats and sat down. "Excellent," he said, "then you can handle this guest I want you to book."

Kelly knew she was being charmed! "Who?" she asked warily, moving to the second row of seats. They were raised slightly higher than the first. Being short, Kelly always tried to look down on Justin when they were talking.

He reached into his pocket for a piece of paper. "Her name is Mildred Cokely and, if I understand correctly, she can read the minds of animals."

"Justin!"

"Now it's not as crazy as it sounds! Along with Mildred, we'll have veterinarians on to talk about pet problems. It will be informative as well as amusing."

Kelly felt like a fool. "Wait a minute," she said, "whose mind is Mildred going to read?"

"I figure a dog or two, a cat, a bird and maybe a hamster."

"A hamster? We'll be laughed off the air!"

Justin's face became impassive, but Kelly had learned in the past weeks that there was nothing passive about him. "No one's laughing at us," he said quietly. "The recent ratings have been cause for envy. In fact, the competition is beginning to copy *us*."

"A dubious achievement," Kelly said, throwing program notes into a folder.

"I'll accept it as a compliment," Justin replied. "And you can't deny that half our shows remain serious and hard-hitting."

"No," Kelly conceded. But for how long? she wondered. Justin's penchant for wacky topics had only grown over the past few weeks. Even more unnerving was his conspirator in craziness—Gilda.

An awkward silence fell. Kelly glanced around the studio. A few people remained on the set, listening to Zoltan. They sat on the cobalt-blue couches and looked at the charts strewn on the black slate coffee table. She sighed and took the scrap of paper from Justin's hand. Looking down at him, Kelly mused over his lazy grace. Although he sat languidly on the audience chair, Kelly could feel the latent power in his lean body. She wondered if his sinewy strength could turn to gentleness on the right occasion.

"I better call Mildred," she said, snapping out of her crazy speculation. "I've always wanted to know what my cat Cecil really thinks of me."

Justin watched her walk away. As always, he was unsettled by his attraction to Kelly. It wasn't just physical, although he wondered if her skin was as creamy between her breasts as it was on her face and neck. No, the attraction was far more dangerous—she challenged him. She saw beneath his style, straight through to the substance of what he was saying and squared off with him there. She caused him to think about every decision, to stretch his talent to counter her demands, and yes, he admitted to himself, to want to impress her.

Just once he'd love to dig beneath her professional cool, but that desire spelled trouble. Mixing business with pleasure usually ended with little pleasure and much heartache. Justin rubbed his brow. Wasn't he getting ahead of himself? Kelly hadn't exactly indicated interest, certainly not in an obvious way. And their professional relationship wasn't the most tranquil. Winning a point with him gave her more than ordinary pleasure. And, though Kelly acknowledged his clout, she wasn't cowed by it. Nor was she jealous, as some were, of his swift rise to management.

So far he'd had an enviable career. Breaks had come his way. But he'd worked hard, damn hard. In the beginning it hadn't seemed like work. He'd always loved television. As a boy, it had been a magical escape from the constant bickering of his parents over money. Drawn to the screen, he could imagine that he was a cowboy, a detective, a starship commander—anything other than what he was—a poor boy from an unhappy family.

As he grew older, girls and sports grabbed more of his attention, but television remained an enduring passion. Thanks to a track scholarship, he made it to college where he majored in television. The business fascinated him. Why did people watch one show and ignore another? What was it about the show, or the personalities in it that connected with the viewers? How did this change over time?

Years of viewing had given him a sixth sense for just these questions. He never complained about the hours or the demands. Success had bred success.

Justin made his way back to his office. In the past year, however, he hadn't felt like a success.

When he'd seen his own son make a beeline for the television set to avoid the emotional fallout from yet another fight between Mommy and Daddy, Justin knew that history was repeating itself. The divorce had shattered his dreams for a happy family. Perhaps families like that existed only on television.

Justin accepted responsibility for the fact that the demands and constant pressures of working in television contributed to the breakup of his marriage. But wasn't a man's first obligation to provide for his family? This Boston job allowed him to support two households comfortably. No hand-me-downs for his kid.

But it wasn't just a matter of old jeans versus new. He wanted Tommy's childhood to be different from his. Whereas Justin remembered a boyhood of struggle and strain, he wanted Tommy's to be carefree and fun, with no worries about whether Dad could pay the rent or buy him a new pair of sneakers so that he could join the track team. Being a good provider, Justin thought, was a major part of being a good father.

And yet…he had doubts. As he picked up his phone, he worried about Tommy's reaction to the news that Justin wouldn't be able to fly in for the boy's Halloween pageant that weekend. An unexpected change in the date of a WMAS board meeting put it squarely on the day of Tommy's kindergarten pageant. Several members of the board had expressed an interest in meeting Justin. He couldn't turn down this special invitation, even if he'd rather be many miles away.

He heard the phone ring and then a click.

"Benedict residence."

"Tommy?"

"Dad!"

"Tommy, you sounded so grown-up just now! I never heard you answer the phone that way."

Tommy's sweet giggle made Justin horribly lonely. "Billy Noonan told me at school that he answers the phone that way," the boy chattered. "He said it sorta snotty, so I told him I could do it, too."

"That's right! Can't let those Noonans think they're better than us."

Tommy squealed in delight. "Yeah! And...Daddy? My Halloween costume is ten times better than Billy's. I can't wait for you to see it."

Justin felt his throat tighten. "Um, son, I have some bad news. I'm really sorry, but I can't come to your Halloween pageant."

Justin heard a small gasp, then silence.

"Tommy? Tommy, are you there? I'm sorry, truly I am, but something's come up at work and I can't get—"

"But you promised!"

"I know, I know. God, I hate it, too, but you're coming to see me a week after the pageant. Can't I see your cowboy costume then?"

"No! It'll be too late!" The angry tone had a quiver in it that broke Justin's heart. "You...you were gonna draw a mustache on me with Mommy's makeup pencil.''

"Mommy can do that."

"I want *you* to do it. I want you to come. Everybody else's Dad will be there."

"Tommy I can't."

Tommy started to cry. "You're mean," he said between sobs, "you broke your promise."

His little sobs were like blows. "Oh, Tommy, don't cry," Justin pleaded. "Please don't cry."

He heard the phone hit either a wall or a counter, and then the cool voice of his ex-wife came on the line. He explained to her what had happened. She said Tommy had run into his room. She promised to talk to him and call Justin back. Justin hung up the phone. He'd come to Boston thinking it was for the boy's ultimate good, but he had the nagging feeling that he was letting Tommy down. This melancholy notion clung to Justin for the rest of the afternoon. Even his four o'clock meeting with Kelly to discuss a show failed to brighten his depression.

She entered his office with a twinkle in her eye. Justin noticed that the tailored lines of Kelly's dress couldn't hide her curves. How lovely she looked. Justin enjoyed her occasional change from suits, but refrained from complimenting her on this. The subject of clothes, or more specifically image, was a sensitive one at *In the Know.* He also suspected that the brainstorm he'd just had concerning Gilda's image would wipe the smile off her face.

He didn't want to do that. She looked so happy. Besides, his idea was just in the planning stage. Perhaps Kelly's high spirits would rub off on him.

"What's the matter?" she asked, sitting down.

"Nothing," Justin replied, surprised that she'd picked up on his mood so quickly. But those gray eyes noticed everything. "Nothing's the matter," he repeated.

Kelly didn't buy this for a second. It wasn't just his expression that confirmed her hunch. Justin radiated a palpable sadness, which completely contradicted his normal self-assurance. The paradox was poignant, and she felt the need to cheer him up. "We haven't slipped in the ratings, have we?" she asked.

He laughed, rather artificially she thought. "No, the ratings haven't gone down. Believe it or not, there *are* other things that can upset me."

Kelly hadn't meant it as a criticism. She started to explain, but his face had already rearranged itself into its slightly bemused mask.

"What's your show idea?" he asked.

"I think you'll love it," she replied, handing him an outline. "My idea is to have on child stars from old television series to talk about what it's like to be famous so young."

"That's been done."

"And their parents."

"Oh." Justin rubbed his jaw with his index finger. His silence encouraged Kelly to go on.

"We're in a ratings period right now, so we can justify the expense of flying them in. The angle I'm looking for is, do you give up your childhood when you become a child actor? Did you resent your parents then, do you resent them now? Do the parents feel they pushed too hard? Did family life get neglected?"

Justin fidgeted with his shirt cuff. "Too much smothering, too much attention...it's bad for a child."

"The only thing worse is too little," Kelly said. To her surprise Justin looked slightly rattled. What had she said? "If you don't like this..." she began.

"No, it's fine," Justin quickly replied. "Do you have any guests lined up?"

Kelly pointed at the outline. "Yes. I've got the girl who played Sandy Powers on the old *Across the Galaxy* show, and her mother. You might remember the program. It was about a family whose ship got blown off course while they were trying to get to their home planet of—"

"Terra," Justin said. Kelly looked up from her notes. "And they were pursued by the evil—"

"Drago," she replied, giving him a slight nod. He couldn't possibly know as much trivia on this show as she did. It had been one of her childhood favorites. She asked, "Their spaceship's name was...?"

"The Flyright," Justin answered. "And it was kept in shape by their engineer—"

"Barney," Kelly trumpeted, leaning forward in her chair. "Sandy had a special pet. What was his name?"

"Dog, which was actually a robot built to look like a dog!" A faint smile was returned to Justin's face. "Remember how his fur kept falling off?"

"And they had to solder it on. Remember how the beds in the spaceship made themselves?"

"And Sandy and Scott Junior never seemed to go to school," Justin said wistfully. He handed back her outline. "Okay, Ms. Expert, so you think you know *everything* about *Across the Galaxy?*"

Kelly slipped the sheet into a folder. "In all modesty, yes."

"So you wouldn't mind answering one *minor* question about Dr. Scott Powers, patriarch of the Powers family, its defender against nasty aliens and all-round swell guy."

"Lay it on me," Kelly said. His mysterious depression seemed to be lifting. He smiled in a way that made her eager for his next question. There was no way she'd miss it.

"What was Dr. Powers's doctorate in?"

"His doctorate?"

"Yes, you know, his Ph.D."

"Wasn't he a medical doctor? No wait! They never got sick!"

Justin lightly tapped his fingers against each other. "Out of the goodness of my heart I won't count that as an answer."

Kelly fixed him with a sour look. What *was* Dr. Powers's specialty? She racked her brain, but the answer eluded her. Justin's smug expression forced her to hazard a guess. "Doctor of Spaceology!"

Justin burst out laughing, his dimples deepening in his pale olive skin. Ah, those dimples. Kelly began to chuckle.

"Okay, okay," she said, "what was his doctorate in?"

Justin stopped laughing, but his sly expression remained. "In the six years that *Across the Galaxy* was on the air they never said what his doctorate was in."

"Why you—that was a trick question!"

"It was not," Justin protested. "If you'd really been an expert, you'd have known it."

"I am an expert. I have a Ph.D. in trivia." This ridiculous declaration started her giggling. "It's as authentic as Dr. Powers's," she said before dissolving into laughter. Justin joined her, and for a few minutes Kelly forgot he was her boss. She wiped her eyes. "My father used to say he was just like Dr. Powers—an expert on everything. He was joking, of course."

"My father rarely cracked jokes. Life was too deadly serious for him."

This glimpse into the private Justin startled Kelly. His smooth public image so dazzled the WMAS staffers that they never seemed curious about what was behind the flawless exterior. Kelly was curious. "What about your mother?"

His face became closed. "She didn't have much to laugh at, either. Money was scarce around our house. That caused a lot of tension. She was quite lovely, though, when she was young." Then, as if he realized he'd stumbled onto a sensitive area, he asked, "Was your family, um, like the Powers?" He attempted a weak smile.

"Not exactly, but we were close, very close."

"You miss them?" he asked quietly.

"Every day. They were my friends as well as my parents." Kelly rarely talked about her parents' death, but it seemed easy with Justin. "Are your parents living?"

"No, which is sad, because now I could help them financially. They could have had some happiness."

"Money would have made them happy?"

"Money makes everyone happy," Justin stated, as if any other notion was naive.

Kelly smoothed the skirt of her dress. "I doubt that," she said, meeting his blue eyes evenly. "It can't tell you how to raise a teenager."

A glint of humor returned to his blue eyes. "I expect you have your own ideas on that subject."

"They don't always sit too well with a sixteen-year-old," Kelly said ruefully.

"I imagine you can handle anything."

The compliment caught Kelly off guard. She gazed deeply into his blue eyes and realized he'd meant what he'd said. Oddly enough that pleased her enormously.

"Yes, well, I would be the perfect parent," she said, "if I wasn't such a coward."

"A coward, you?"

"Uh-huh," Kelly agreed morosely. "I'm supposed to be teaching Sylvie to drive, but after one lesson in a mall parking lot, I'm scared to try it again."

"What seems to be the problem?"

"Other drivers."

Justin smiled, but when he saw she was serious, he stopped.

"We nearly hit *three* cars, and that was in a parking lot!" Kelly exclaimed. "I know Sylvie's confidence is a little shaky right now, but the problem is my nervousness. I thought about buying her lessons, but, well, my father taught my mother to drive, my mother taught me, I taught my brother, and if Paul were here, he'd teach Sylvie. But he's not, and there's no reason why I can't teach her, except for mortal terror. You know what a driver's license means to a teenager. I'm afraid I'm letting her down."

I'm afraid I'm letting her down—the very thought Justin had had about his relationship with his son. A wave of sympathy, no *empathy*, for Kelly sprang up in him. He loved her acerbic retorts and her take-charge enthusiasm, but this endearingly human side touched him in a deeper way.

A solution to her problem was clear. "I'll give Sylvie a lesson," he suggested.

"What?" Kelly exclaimed. Then she sputtered. "Oh, no, I couldn't ask you to do that!"

"You didn't. I offered," he pointed out. "And don't think I don't have experience. I taught one sister and three cousins to drive without a single fender bender."

"No, no, it isn't that," Kelly protested. "I just couldn't take up your time."

"I'm new to the city. I have free time. In fact, I'm free tonight."

"Friday night?" Kelly couldn't believe he didn't have plans.

"Unless you have plans."

Kelly shifted in her seat. "Um, no," she admitted, "although I think Sylvie has a date."

"We'll go right after work," Justin said, unaccountably happy at this news. "It's still light then. You can sit in the back seat and give directions. If things get hairy, close your eyes. Look," he said, flashing his driver's license in front of her with the only unflattering picture she'd ever seen of him.

"You look like you're wanted for armed robbery."

"So what do you say?" he asked softly.

What could she say? His offer was the answer to her dilemma. And he looked as if he really wanted to help, *needed* to help, although she couldn't say why.

Justin watched Kelly make up her mind. He knew his offer surprised her. Hell, it surprised him. Jumping into someone else's family wouldn't solve his family problems, but it made him feel as if he was helping someone. Besides, seeing Kelly after work appealed to him. What would she be like, he wondered, in an entirely personal situation away from the pressures of the station?

"I'll call Sylvie," she finally said. "She'll be thrilled. But this . . . is very generous of you, Justin."

"That's what friends are for," he said. And he meant it.

"THIS IS THE CAR she'll be driving?"

Justin's incredulous tone of voice accurately reflected the condition of her car, but it annoyed Kelly, anyway. "Looks aren't everything," she said.

"Obviously."

"But he's sound under the hood."

"He?"

"Yes, er, President Ford. That's what Sylvie and I call the car."

"President Ford?" Justin let out a whoop.

Kelly enjoyed watching him laugh. His face always seemed on the verge of a smile, so a hearty laugh only looked more natural. His dimples deepened and his eyes turned the color of sapphires. Justin's laugh drew you in, making it seem like a private joke between just the two of you. He was at his most unguarded when he laughed, and she knew that his unguarded moments were rare.

"Think you can follow me home in your jalopy?" Kelly asked.

His grin remained. "I'll try." He crossed the WMAS parking lot to his Mercedes convertible, got in and revved the engine, as if bragging.

"Gee, your left valve sounds bad," Kelly called over.

Justin gunned the engine again in reply.

"Aren't guys who drive these cars real insecure?" she shouted. "Like, the longer the car, the shorter…?"

His car suddenly lurched in reverse, missing Kelly by a whisker.

"Hey, you nearly hit me!" she yelled.

"I think *nearly* is the operative word here," he said through his open side window. "We manly men never hit women."

Kelly laughed and climbed into her car. Ten minutes later she pulled up in front of her apartment. Sylvie was standing on the curb and started to wave when she saw the car. Her eyes widened when she spotted Justin's.

Kelly rolled down her window. "Forget it," she said. "You're learning in the President."

Sylvie groaned. "I can dream, can't I?"

Justin pulled in behind Kelly and got out of his car.

"Nice car, Mr. Benedict," Sylvie said.

"Call me Justin. Yes, I like it, but your sister seems to think it's too macho."

"A station wagon," Kelly said. "Give me a man who drives a station wagon, with two kids and four bags of groceries in the back."

"You like children?" Justin asked.

"Yes," Kelly replied, "I even like teenagers." Then, turning to her sister, she said, "Sylvie, daylight's going fast. Let's get started."

Kelly got into the back and watched Justin settle himself in the passenger seat of President Ford. His pained look amused her.

"Kelly, the interior is just as unique as the exterior," he commented.

"We like it," she said.

"It's a dump," Sylvie said.

"How old *is* this car?" he asked.

"The joke in our family," Sylvie explained, "is that Kelly got the President *when* President Ford was in the White House."

Kelly laughed. "A gross exaggeration. He had just left office, but the car still runs, so let's get going."

Kelly watched Justin patiently explain the basic components of the car. She relaxed a little. He obviously knew what he was doing, and Sylvie was giving him the rapt attention that Kelly was sure wouldn't have been given to an older sister.

Sylvie turned on the engine. She nervously looked behind to see if any cars were coming up their one-way street. Kelly caught her eye and winked in support. The young girl smiled.

Sylvie eased the car onto Lancaster. Since it was in first gear, they sputtered along at fifteen miles per hour till Justin said, "Now shift into second." Sylvie grappled with the stick and clutch, but didn't have an easy touch yet. The car stalled.

"That's okay," Justin said. "Just start the car again."

Sylvie did, and again they rode up the street at a snail's pace. Cars filed behind the Ford on the narrow one-way street.

Sylvie's second attempt at shifting stalled the car again. She sighed and glanced behind.

"Pay no attention to them," Justin said. "They'll wait. Just start the car again and I'll shift with you."

Sylvie did, and Kelly watched Justin put his hand on Sylvie's and guide her into second gear.

The car lurched into the new gear, but Sylvie increased her speed only slightly. A yellow Mustang behind them honked.

Boston drivers, Kelly fumed. She noticed Sylvie biting her lip.

Still, the President went no faster. Another car honked. Justin said gently, "Let's move it into third. Why don't you try it alone, first."

Kelly grimaced when Sylvie took her foot off the clutch too soon. The car stalled.

Now they were surrounded by a cacophony of impatient honks. Kelly saw Sylvie's lower lip tremble as Justin quietly talked her through the start-up procedure. He was unflappable, soothing. But Kelly was livid. The Mustang's driver leaned out of his side window and yelled, "What's the matter? Can't you drive!"

Kelly leaned out of her window and shouted, "She's learning. What's your excuse, you jerk!"

Suddenly Sylvie found first gear, and the car jerked forward, leaving the Mustang's driver behind, open-mouthed.

Sylvie and Justin burst out laughing.

"What's so funny?" Kelly asked.

"You are," Justin said. "A tigress and her cub."

Kelly colored but laughed. "I just can't stand rudeness."

"You're the one who called him a jerk," Sylvie pointed out. Then she successfully shifted into second.

Both Justin and Kelly congratulated her, but it was Justin whom Sylvie smiled at with shy pride.

He smiled back, and it was such an encouraging smile that gratitude and warmth toward him flooded Kelly's heart. How different he'd been with Sylvie from the slick executive Kelly knew at the office. This Justin was kind, patient. It must have shown on her face, because when he glanced at her, his expression changed. His face became graver, but the smile no less sweet.

What a lovely face, Justin thought. Those gray eyes missed nothing, but her full lips, parted now in a hesitant smile, betrayed a vulnerability that Justin found irresistible. Suddenly another, more vulnerable face flashed into his mind, and a wave of guilt and loneliness hit him so hard that he didn't know if he could stand it. He closed his eyes in pain. What was he doing barging in on *this* family?

He felt a hand lightly shake his shoulder. Reluctantly he opened his eyes and turned around. He half expected Kelly's face to reflect the inner harshness he was feeling about himself. But it didn't. He saw a face that was confused, but also worried and compassionate. At that moment he wanted very much to kiss her.

"Hey," she said softly, "I'm the one who's supposed to close my eyes."

He smiled, grateful that she hadn't asked him what was wrong.

"What now Justin?" Sylvie asked.

"Harvard Square is coming up," he told her. "It looks jammed. Take your next right."

"Okay, but I want you to know I feel fine now. I can handle traffic," Sylvie boasted.

"It's coming up," Justin said.

"Sure, sure, but as I was saying—"

"Sylvie, pay attention," Kelly said.

"I am!" the young girl snapped.

"You missed it," Justin said.

Kelly groaned.

"No, I didn't!" Sylvie said, making a hard right, which caused Kelly and Justin to grab their seats to keep from toppling to the left. The car behind them honked at the surprise turn, and the President careened violently and shuddered while Sylvie attempted to shift down.

"Hold on," Justin commanded as he slid over and took the wheel just in time to swerve the car from colliding with a fire hydrant. Sylvie's foot hit the brakes, and when the car stopped, Kelly found it was half on the sidewalk.

"That's not how you make a turn!" Kelly gasped. "You slow down, put on your turn signal and *then* turn the car!"

Sylvie stared straight ahead. "All right! I made a mistake. I'm learning."

Kelly was on the verge of a lecture, but she paused. Justin's calm way had proved more effective. "Sylvie," she said mildly, "we're alive and the car's in one piece—I think. Just be more careful." She turned to Justin. "You saved our lives."

He smoothed back his thick blond hair. "In another culture you'd now owe me yours."

Kelly grinned. "Well, Sylvie can repay you by not asking you to drive with her again."

"Very funny," Sylvie said, starting the car.

"And you?" Justin asked softly.

Kelly gazed into his suddenly serious face. "I don't know," she said shyly. "Perhaps we can talk about that."

"Let's do," he agreed.

The atmosphere inside the ancient car was calm again. Justin had a knack for telling Sylvie what to do without getting her dander up, a talent Kelly wished she had. She watched him take Sylvie through the charming side streets of Cambridge. They looped through Harvard University and Lesley College.

"I'm very impressed, honey," Kelly said.

"Thanks, sweetie," Justin replied with a grin.

Sylvie giggled, then asked Kelly the quickest way back. The sun was setting, and she did have a date.

As Sylvie pulled into their apartment parking lot, Kelly noticed a red sports car parked illegally in someone's space. Kevin Lucas was here.

"Oh, great!" Sylvie said, spotting the car. Then turning to Justin, she said, "Thank you so much for my lesson. You were wonderful, and I really appreciate it."

"No problem, Sylvie," Justin said as he got out of the car. He held the seat back for Kelly and helped her out. He smiled at her, but Kelly's face was tense. She was looking at Kevin.

On the surface Kevin Lucas was a parent's dream, Kelly thought. He was polite, personable, with an engaging grin in a smooth baby face. His family lived in a mansion on Brattle Street, one of Cambridge's better addresses.

But underneath the handsome facade Kelly suspected he was willful and spoiled. His parents put few restrictions on him, even enjoying some of his high jinks, like half filling their gin and vodka bottles with water to see if anyone noticed the difference. Where the missing gin and vodka went obviously didn't concern them, and Sylvie had thought it a hilarious joke.

That concerned Kelly. From the few facts she could squeeze out of Sylvie, she surmised that Kevin was quite popular with all the girls. Sylvie had been thrilled by his attentions. Kevin always got what he wanted, and Kelly suspected he wanted Sylvie.

She walked to his car with Justin. Kevin got out and greeted Sylvie with a kiss. As Sylvie made introductions, Kelly glanced into the tiny back seat. There on the floor almost concealed by a sweater was a six-pack of beer.

CHAPTER FOUR

"THIS MAY BE the shortest date on record," Kelly said, more to herself than to the three people making small talk around her. She hated to make a scene, but the situation demanded action—and fast.

"Um, Kevin," she said louder. "There's beer in the back seat of your car."

Polite smiles froze on the faces of Justin, Sylvie and Kevin. For a moment no one spoke.

"Really?" Kevin said, widening his soft brown eyes. "I'd better look." With Sylvie right behind him he went and looked in his car. Justin remained where he was, Kelly noticed, as if he didn't want to interfere. His eyes, however, seemed to be studying Kevin.

"I know how that got there!" Kevin exclaimed, opening the car door and reaching in. Sylvie's anxious face strained to see what he was pulling out. It wasn't a sweater, as Kelly had originally thought, but a sweatshirt with Harvard and the school crest on it.

"My older brother borrowed my car yesterday and must have left this and the beer in here by mistake," he explained. His face took on an expression of earnest sincerity that Kelly didn't buy for a second. He reached into the car and pulled out the six-pack. "Here, take the beer. No, take it. I really didn't know it was there."

Kelly accepted the six-pack but didn't return his tentative smile. He knew she didn't allow Sylvie to drink. She had made her rule clear to both teenagers.

"Doesn't your older brother have a car of his own?" she asked.

Kevin's eyes flickered with surprise, but he answered smoothly. "Yes, he does, but it's in the shop. You know how foreign cars are always breaking down."

"No, I don't," Kelly replied. "I own a Ford myself."

Kevin shifted uneasily on his feet, but his face remained bland. Sylvie slipped one hand into his. When her eyes met Kelly's, they seemed to implore her to believe him, to let them go without a fuss.

But Kelly couldn't. She trusted Sylvie, but she did not trust Kevin Lucas. Sylvie often accused her of being overprotective, but Kelly felt strong parental concern.

"Tell me," she said, walking closer to Sylvie, "what are you two planning to do tonight?"

Kevin shrugged. "We thought we'd hang out."

"Oh? Where?"

"Well, there's a good movie on cable," Kevin said. "We might watch it at my house."

Kelly said as casually as she could, "Will your parents be home?"

Sylvie fumed at this question. "You really don't trust us."

"It's a reasonable question," Kelly replied.

"Yeah, if I was twelve or thirteen," Sylvie protested, "but I'm not a kid anymore. When will you understand that I've grown up!"

"I was sixteen once," Kelly said. "I remember."

"Were you as perfect then as you are now?" Sylvie shot back.

The accusation caught Kelly off balance. Sylvie always grumbled about the rules. But she was wrong if she thought Kelly believed herself perfect. Kelly was doing the best she could as a single parent. Right now, with Sylvie glaring at her mutinously, Kelly recalled her own feelings at sixteen. Parental rules had bugged her a lot, too. During the past two years, however, she'd come to appreciate the necessity for them.

Justin stepped forward. "I've got an idea. Why sit home tonight? Why not go out?"

"What?" Kevin asked suspiciously. He'd been examining a grease spot on the blacktop.

Kelly, too, was surprised. She looked into Justin's cool blue eyes. "Go out where?" she asked.

He smiled casually. "I think I saw in the paper that a place called O'Callahan's is having a no-alcohol night tonight for anyone who's interested in some great music and serious dancing. I didn't catch where it was, though."

"O'Callahan's is in Teele Square," Sylvie said, "near Tufts. That's not too far from here." She tugged at Kevin's arm. "I think the Wild Cards are playing there. I heard they were great."

Kevin nodded but asked, "Are you sure about O'Callahan's?"

Justin shrugged. "I could be wrong. I wasn't paying the closest attention. We could check the paper or call them."

Sylvie squeezed Kevin's hand. "I might like to go, Kevin."

"But we had other plans," he half whispered. Kevin's pursed lips and sudden slouch showed that he didn't appreciate Justin's great idea. But Kelly did. She smiled in gratitude. Justin's eyes softened and he barely nodded.

"I think it sounds like fun," Kelly said to Sylvie.

The young girl smiled. "Believe it or not, I think so, too."

Justin turned to Kelly. "If it sounds like such fun to you, why don't we go, as well?"

"What?" Kelly and Kevin exclaimed in unison.

"Sure," Sylvie said. "You like to dance, or at least you used to. Why don't we all go? It's been ages since you did anything except sit home and wait up for me."

The tactless, teenage remark made her sound like a wallflower. In spite of herself Kelly glanced at Justin. His reaction was to step closer to her.

"I...I haven't gone dancing in years." She couldn't remember when such a casual invitation had jangled her so.

"Come on," he urged, "take a chance."

Kelly gazed into those hooded blue eyes. They seemed to promise that *this* Friday night would be different from so many previous ones. "I'd love to," she replied, amazed at how quickly the words came out. "I'll just need to change."

As the four of them walked to the Ferris apartment, Kelly wondered how a driving lesson had turned into a date.

Kelly and Sylvie described their apartment as "rent control chic." It consisted of two bedrooms, a kitchen, a bath, a living room and a cat so large that they claimed he deserved a third bedroom.

The living room, where Justin and Kevin now waited, was a hodgepodge of styles that collectively exuded a charming warmth. The comfy chintz couch complemented the more subdued art deco rug, both pieces inherited from Kelly and Sylvie's parents. A sleek bleached wood coffee table, an inexpensive wall unit containing books and a stereo, and a less than sleek desk were Kelly's contributions.

In the fall and winter visitors sitting on the couch were treated to the melodious clanging of the ancient pipes. As an added bonus, the pipes occasionally spurted hot water. The couch afforded a lovely view of the restored Victorian across the street. The entire neighborhood boasted authentic New England charm which, thanks to Cambridge's inflated real-estate market, Kelly couldn't afford to buy into.

She was slipping into a pale mauve silk dress when there was a knock on her bedroom door.

"It's me," Sylvie said.

"Come in," Kelly replied. She wondered if the dress was too fancy for O'Callahan's, but its frankly feminine style matched her mood.

Sylvie walked in wearing a red minidress. "I…I want to apologize," she said haltingly. "For the crack I made earlier. You know, about your being perfect."

Surprised and touched, Kelly put her arm around her sister's shoulders. "You mean I'm not perfect?"

Both sisters laughed. Kelly knew she would have to have a serious talk with Sylvie about Kevin, but not tonight. Sylvie threw one arm around Kelly's shoulders and whispered, "Kelly! This is a real live date with a non-dork!"

"Well, it's not exactly a date." She released Sylvie, walked to her vanity table and unwound her French braid to let her thick black hair tumble in waves over her shoulders.

Sylvie came up behind Kelly and cast a withering look into the vanity mirror. "If it's not a date, why are you wearing that dress?"

O'CALLAHAN'S WAS an old ballroom that had changed with the times. Gone was the bandstand where Tommy Dorsey and Benny Goodman had played sentimental ballads and upbeat swing backed by a twenty-piece orchestra. Today the best rock bands in New England performed there. Its original art deco interior had nearly vanished, but a few fixtures remained. They created a streamlined counterpoint to the more colorful posters and lights added in later years.

By the time Kelly, Justin, Sylvie and Kevin arrived the place was already packed. Sylvie and Kevin mingled with the young crowd. Since the teenage couple had come in Kevin's car, Kelly didn't count on seeing much of them until Sylvie came home at her curfew. The defection suited Kelly. She hadn't expected the double date to last all evening. And, in all honesty, she would have been disappointed if it had.

Kelly looked around. She and Justin were the oldest couple there. Justin had discarded his suit jacket and tie, but his gray slacks and blue oxford cloth shirt still contrasted with the outlandish inventions of the rest of the crowd. It amused Kelly when two girls with earrings in their noses glanced at Justin with frank appreciation. *A handsome man is a handsome man,* Kelly thought, *whatever the age.*

Justin whispered in her ear, "If I'd known everybody's hair would be purple, I'd have dyed mine."

Kelly chuckled. "That's all right. I like you, even if you are different."

"Do you really?" he asked. His tone suggested he wasn't posing an idle question. Something had changed between them during the hair-raising ride with Sylvie and the confrontation afterward. She'd discovered a caring man behind the witty, ambitious facade.

"Yes, I like you," she said softly.

Justin smiled. It wasn't the cavalier, slightly mocking smile he used in their arguments at the station. This smile showed an eagerness, a hint of shyness. Kelly felt its warmth steal over her body like an unexpected caress.

Suddenly a deafening noise ripped through the room. Justin and Kelly jumped in surprise. The awful screech turned out to be the Wild Cards beginning a tune. Kelly covered her ears with her hands.

"Would you like to sit down?" she shouted.

"No, let's dance," Justin said. "This song's got a great beat, even if I can't understand the lyrics."

Kelly laughed. "It's probably better that way."

He grasped her hand and led her out onto the dance floor. They were surrounded by gyrating bodies in outrageous attire. The lights dimmed suddenly as the band's light show clicked on. Colored strobe lights flashed in counterrhythm to the beat of the music, the colors changing in rapid progression from blue to yellow to green to magenta.

Glancing around her, Kelly made a sound of wry surprise that was lost in the deafening music. She glanced back at Justin

He had already started to dance. Kelly knew immediately that here was a man at ease with his body. The music blared so loudly that they couldn't talk. But words were unnecessary. His every step relayed a physical joy in movement, in the pounding beat that made the body itchy to get up and, as Sylvie would say, "get down." Justin's hips seemed synchronized with the beat of the drums. Gone was the guarded executive. In his place danced a man as uninhibited as the kids around him.

At first Kelly couldn't let go. It had been so long since she'd danced that she felt rusty, clumsy.

The unbridled delight in Justin's face, however, was as impossible to miss as it was infectious. Her legs soon found their pace and her hips got into the rhythm. Suddenly her upper body and arms seemed charged with energy. She felt she could dance the night away to nonstop rock and roll.

When the song ended, Kelly asked, "How about another?"

Slightly out of breath, Justin managed a nod. Then they were off again. Kelly couldn't remember ever having had so much...

"I can say it!" she yelled to him. "I can say the 'F' word."

"What?" Justin asked.

"Fun!" she shouted. "I'm having fun!"

Justin roared with laughter. In the middle of one song Kelly noticed a particularly interesting step done by a boy with a studded leather jacket. She tried the step out for Justin. To her amusement he copied another dancer, then she copied another dancer, until the two of them were competing as much on the dance floor as they did in the studio.

During the next number, Justin grabbed Kelly and began to jitterbug. Unsure of the steps, but liking his arms around her, Kelly tried to follow. The teenagers stared at them as if they'd commenced the minuet.

Kelly loved the jitterbug! She loved Justin's sure grip when he twirled her around, then reeled her back into his arms again. The fact that she couldn't get the steps down immediately didn't bother him. He didn't even care when she stepped on his toes. As long as she was enjoying herself, he seemed happy.

He swung her into his arms again and then dramatically dipped her whole body close to the floor. Kelly gasped in surprise at the sheer romance of the gesture. Suspended in the air that way, she felt weightless and protected. The other dancers ceased to exist. The universe had narrowed to just her and Justin.

"Would you like to see a few more moves?" he asked, gently bringing her back up.

She didn't have time to answer. As if reading her mind, the Wild Cards launched into a slow, crooning ballad. The strobe lights blinked out, and the room was illuminated with the revolving, multicolored lights of a 1940s ballroom.

She smiled in assent. Justin drew her into his arms. He held her tight, the intensity suggesting possession. His boldness surprised Kelly, but had he held her at a polite distance, she would have been keenly disappointed. Her head just reached his shoulders, so she gently laid one cheek on his chest. He dipped his head to hers. She felt his breath on her hair.

Holding Justin this close confirmed Kelly's initial speculations. His body was lean and hard. He guided her on the dance floor with fluid authority. Kelly felt herself melting to his lead. She closed her eyes and let all thoughts drain away except one. She was finally in the arms of a man who excited her.

So many months had gone by and not only hadn't she met Mr. Right, she hadn't even met Mr. Maybe—no one who could tap that deep hunger she had inside for a special person. Was Justin that someone?

What a crazy notion! Four hours ago she would have scoffed at the idea. But now, held so tenderly in his arms, she felt herself considering what a relationship with him would be like.

Unpredictable, yes. Justin could be counted on to surprise you. He generated dozens of ideas each day. At times he irritated and baffled her. Just when Kelly was sure she had him pegged, he'd do something unexpected that would force her to reassess him. Who would have guessed that he would offer to teach Sylvie to drive?

Which brought out a new, totally unexpected aspect of his personality—sweetness. He'd instructed and encouraged Sylvie with such gentle humor. Granted his famous charm affected all females, but there was nothing to gain by impressing Sylvie—unless he was really trying to impress Kelly.

In many ways we're similar, Kelly thought. *We both have this fierce desire to connect with people through television. Neither one of us backs away from a fight— or a good joke. If you examine our personalities logically, we should get along. Too bad logic doesn't always work.* With a sigh she withdrew her hand from his and slipped it around his shoulders. Now both his arms held her in a hot embrace.

Justin's increasingly firm touch made thinking difficult. His hand moved down her back, drawing her farther into him. The sheerness of her dress made every touch feel like bare skin on bare skin. She felt engulfed by Justin, lost in the exquisite sensations his body was generating in hers. How long had it been since she'd felt such aching in her breast and loins?

For someone who liked to be in control, Kelly was curiously unconcerned by her instinctive, almost helpless reaction to Justin's masculine heat. Rather, her body felt as if it were awakening from a long hibernation... and was grateful for such a delicious alarm clock. Half of her knew these reborn feelings could lead to trouble with this man. The other half was more than ready for trouble.

They drifted to the music in perfect harmony, two bodies so close as to be nearly one.

Then Justin stopped dancing. Kelly looked up and discovered that the Wild Cards had ended their one ballad for the evening. Justin relaxed his hold, but didn't release her. Kelly saw no reason to move. In fact, what she was fantasizing would have embarrassed her a few hours ago. Her face must have reflected her thoughts, for Justin bent his head down to hers. She could feel his breath, anticipate the soft contact of his lips, the taste of his mouth.

Suddenly a loud explosion reverberated through the room. The Wild Cards were at it again. Justin cursed, but the song brought Kelly back to reality. How could she be having such sexy thoughts about a man she still knew so little? The fact that he was her boss heightened the risk.

"Maybe we should get going," she said to Justin. "Just let me find Sylvie and tell her. She and Kevin will probably want to stay longer."

"I'll get the car," he told her.

On the way to her apartment, Justin wondered if Kelly would invite him in. Certainly she'd seemed to enjoy herself tonight, but a dance floor was a public place. On the other hand, inviting him in for a cup of coffee wouldn't have to lead to anything...unless they wanted it to.

The problem was that he did want it to. Dancing with Kelly had only increased his desire for her. How different she'd been tonight, with her body swaying provocatively against his, and her inky hair that fell like a waterfall over her shoulders. He wanted to run his hand through those shiny tresses and to kiss her pale ivory skin beneath the mauve silk. The dress certainly invited caresses. It outlined her full breasts, tiny waist and round bottom. Justin decided that Kelly probably looked as beautiful undressed as she did dressed, but these tantalizing thoughts spelled trouble. Come the morning he'd still be her boss, and she'd still fight his ideas.

Kelly slipped the key into her front door. All during the ride home she'd been trying to decide whether or not to invite Justin in. It would be rude, one side of her thought, not to offer him at least a cup of coffee. Another side of her snorted, *Rude my hind foot. You want him to kiss you! You've wanted it all evening!*

Kelly knew that to invite him in courted danger. Whatever happened, or didn't, he was still her boss.

He'd still have that kind of power over her professionally. Kelly liked to be in control. With Justin her feelings were so new and raw that they scared her. But
when was the last time she'd felt so alive, so aware of
herself as a woman?

And when was the last time she'd had the entire
apartment to herself? Sylvie's curfew wasn't for another hour.

"Would you like to come in for a cup of coffee?"
she asked.

He smiled. "Sure."

Kelly left Justin looking through her record collec-
tion while she went into the kitchen to prepare the coffee. She was loading a tray when she heard the deep,
rich voice of Sarah Vaughan singing a ballad. The
depth of emotion in her music never failed to stir some
answering chord in Kelly's mind.

She carried the tray to the coffee table and sat down
next to Justin. She noticed that he'd removed his suit
jacket. For a few minutes she busied herself with the
cups and pouring the coffee. Justin sipped his coffee
quietly. Sarah Vaughan sang something bittersweet by
Cole Porter.

More minutes stretched by in silence. Perhaps she'd
misjudged his interest. Kelly abandoned her coffee and
leaned back into the soft sofa. Sarah Vaughan was a
mellow antidote to her flustered thoughts.

Midway through a Gershwin tune Kelly became
aware that Justin's eyes were on her. Slowly she met his
gaze. His eyes had an intensity she'd never seen before, a directness that contained no teasing, no pre-
tense. His bewitching stare drew her in, and when his

gaze traveled to her lips, Kelly felt a small, tiny explosion in her stomach.

Their eyes met again, and for minutes no sound existed in the room except for the lush voice of Sarah Vaughan sadly detailing the risks of romance.

Justin moved closer to Kelly. She couldn't move at all, and her heart pounded so loud that she was sure he could hear it.

"The song's too pessimistic," Justin murmured.

"Is it?" Kelly said in a voice she didn't recognize as her own. "I mean, aren't there always risks in being with someone?"

"Maybe," he whispered. "But without risk we'd all be alone." He was so close that all he had to do was tilt his head down to kiss her. His lips gently grazed hers. Kelly drew back for an instant. The moment she'd secretly wanted was here, but she didn't trust it. Her cautious nature quaked at letting down her defenses with anyone, especially her boss. And how could she tell him that it had been a while since a man had been so close to her?

"Justin," she said, "I should explain. I haven't . . . I mean . . ."

"We can stop right now if you want to," he said softly.

"I just think I should tell you—"

"Don't think," he said, playing with a long, silky strand of her hair. "Do what you feel. Everything else will fall into place."

"I'm not good on impulse," Kelly whispered.

"I am." His lips claimed hers again, probing deeper one minute, lightly touching the next. Kelly felt a rush of excitement. In the back of her mind a distant bell warned that she was letting her guard down too quickly. Defiantly she banished the worry. She *wanted* this explosion of desire! She was tired, bone weary of damming these feelings.

Giving way to a sensuality long denied, her tongue met his teasing lips and, delighted, he enveloped her in a kiss that was deep and hungry. His arms wound around her torso tightly, as if he were afraid she'd be suddenly taken away from him. Her arms clasped his shoulders and neck. Kelly found herself sinking into the couch under the weight of his body. Unbidden, her own body arched against his, feeling his growing hardness.

Justin pulled away from Kelly's lips with a sigh, and began slowly kissing her eyelids, temples and cheeks. Leaving a burning trail, his lips traced her jawline and then invaded the delicate skin of her neck. While his lips were creating dizzying tingles his hand sought the curvaceous outline of her body.

Kelly moaned softly. "Justin," she whispered, "what are we doing?"

He raised his head. There was such a hot light in his eyes that Kelly's whole body tingled.

"I don't know," he said, "but I like it."

They both laughed. Justin began to nuzzle her neck.

"Ahh," Kelly murmured, "I like it, too."

"Do you like it here?" he asked, kissing the soft curve where her neck joined her collarbone.

"Yes," Kelly whispered.

"Here?" he asked, teasing her earlobe with his tongue.

"Mmm," she said, closing her eyes.

She felt his lips brush hers. It was a gentle, almost brotherly kiss.

"Here?" he asked.

"Yes," Kelly replied. Her voice sounded dreamy and far away. "But harder and longer."

Justin chuckled, and Kelly opened her eyes. "Can't resist producing, can you?" he said. He leaned back a little, loosening one hand so that he could lightly stroke her cheek.

Kelly reddened, but smiled. "I'm waiting."

Justin complied. His tongue swirled over and around hers until she joined his in an erotic duet that sent jets of molten fire through her body. The intensity of his mouth dominating hers filled Kelly with a reckless need for him. She responded with an eagerness that stunned her.

In her passion-filled haze she didn't immediately connect the click she heard with the front door opening.

"I can't believe this," Sylvie said.

Instantly Kelly and Justin scrambled to sit up. Slightly dazed, Kelly looked over to the foyer to see an embarrassed Sylvie and a smug Kevin.

"What...what are you doing here?" Kelly managed to say, furiously checking her rumpled dress.

"I live here," Sylvie explained.

"Uh, is it past your curfew?"

Sylvie held out her hand and pointed to her wristwatch. "What do you know," she exclaimed, "I'm early! We decided against getting a pizza."

Kelly was wildly embarrassed. She glanced at Justin, but he seemed merely amused. And Kevin looked like the cat that had swallowed several canaries.

"Good night, Kevin!" Kelly said bluntly.

"Good night, everyone," he said, giving Sylvie a chaste peck on the cheek.

As soon as the door closed, Sylvie looked at Kelly. Although she still seemed embarrassed, the teenager adopted a cocky stance.

"Well, Kelly, you *are* a good example to me, aren't you? And here I thought you were uptight and old-fashioned."

Kelly shot her sister a warning look. "Sylvie, there's a big difference between you and me."

Sylvie nodded. "You do it and I don't."

Kelly stood up. "We didn't do anything."

"We were just kissing," Justin maintained, although he rebuckled his belt while saying it. Kelly also noticed that his shirt had become unbuttoned.

"Yes," she said. "Let's not blow this out of proportion."

"Oh, sure." Sylvie turned to Justin, wide-eyed. "What if I'd walked in ten minutes later? What would I have seen? An X-rated movie?"

"Sylvie!" Kelly cried out.

Justin put his hand out and lightly squeezed Kelly's arm. "Easy now."

Kelly shrugged off his touch. "Justin and I are adults, Sylvie."

"Which means you can do stuff I can't."

"Basically, yes." Kelly sat down again.

Sylvie shook her head. "I don't agree. I don't think it's fair."

Kelly rubbed her temples with her fingers. "Sylvie, can't we discuss this later?"

The young girl moved nearer the couch. "What's to discuss? You're saying there are rules for you and rules for me. All my friends' parents give the same hypocritical line. It's like you don't practice what you preach." She adjusted the strap on her purse. "Well, good night, you two. Just remember I'm in the next room." With a tug on her purse she stalked off to her bedroom.

Kelly leaned her head against the back of the sofa and, in a lower voice, addressed the ceiling. "Why? Why did Sylvie have to pick tonight to come home before her curfew? It's the first time ever!"

Justin buttoned his shirt. "Don't worry about it."

Kelly glanced down with surprise. "What do you mean? What happened tonight is going to be trouble, Justin."

His drowsy eyes became uneasy. "You mean what happened between us or that Sylvie saw it?"

"I don't know," Kelly said, averting her eyes from his gaze. "Both, maybe." She glanced down the hallway at Sylvie's closed door, behind which rock music now blared. "You seemed to find this whole situation amusing."

"It's hardly a tragedy," he retorted. Justin got up from the couch. He walked over to a bookcase and seemed to examine the volumes. "I'm not ashamed of anything I did tonight. Nothing. My only regret is that we were interrupted." He turned to Kelly. "Are you sorry?"

She shook her head. Kelly couldn't lie about how she'd felt. "No, Justin, I'm not sorry. I enjoyed it as much as you, but I wish Sylvie hadn't seen us!"

He walked back to her and sat down. "I can understand wanting privacy, but what did we do wrong?"

"Nothing, but . . ."

"Well, then?"

Kelly took one of his hands and held it to her cheek. "Maybe Sylvie will think this incident is a green light to do the same thing."

Justin rubbed her cheek with his thumb softly. "Kelly, teenagers have been necking for years."

Kelly tried to laugh, but it came out an anxious gasp. "I think Kevin's pressuring her to do more than neck. Sylvie probably thinks that if she hadn't come in early, we would have made love."

Justin started to massage her neck lightly. "Would we?"

Kelly felt his warm fingers send tingles down her spine. She remembered those moments in his arms. She burned so hot for him that she wondered where it might have led.

And yet, despite all these delicious sensations, making love so impetuously to her boss would have been quite a leap for her careful nature.

She sighed. "Justin, I'm not sure how the evening would have ended, but I know I'm an adult and Sylvie isn't. And I certainly didn't do anything wrong tonight. I'm entitled to a love life."

"You sure are," he agreed, smiling.

Kelly put restraining hands on his. She had trouble concentrating when he touched her. "But Sylvie's hormones are raging, even if she's not emotionally ready to handle it. *I've* got to help her restrain those impulses until she's mature enough. I don't want her to be pressured by a fast crowd or an overeager boy-friend.''

Justin withdrew his hands. "Kelly, you're being na-ive."

Kelly stared at his perplexed face. "No, I'm not."

"Yes, you are," he replied. "It's naive to think that by being a Miss Perfect role model you'll prevent Sylvie from doing what she wants."

That was twice in one evening that Kelly had been accused of being perfect. Couldn't Sylvie and Justin see that she was actually treading water? "A good parent," she retorted, "creates an environment where the child knows what is responsible behavior." She exhaled a frustrated sigh. "Teaching sexual responsibility is tough, especially as a single parent, because my dating life impacts on Sylvie's. She takes clues from what I do or don't do. The fact that I'm an adult and she isn't doesn't change things in her eyes."

"Kelly, there aren't good girls and bad girls any-more."

"Now who's being naive?" she bristled. "There's always been a double standard. If we had made love and news of it got back to the station, just who do you think would be judged an opportunist?"

He shook his head. "You're entitled to a sex life. You can't sacrifice it for your sister, or for what other people might say. Don't go overboard."

"Overboard?" Kelly shifted a fraction away from him. "Would you mind telling me when concern is too much? I mean, two years ago I became a single parent overnight. Presto! Suddenly *I'm* in charge. Do you think I knew what I was doing? Do you think I'm absolutely sure now?" Her voice began to falter. "I know things are different now from when I was in high school, but that doesn't mean that that's good."

Justin's face softened at her distress. "Is it that bad? It seems that every generation grows up faster than the one before it."

Kelly half laughed at this understatement. "Way too fast. But my attitude can't be to permit Sylvie to do anything she wants just because 'that's what all my friends are doing.' Like it or not, I'm her example."

Justin stared at her. "Kelly, this doesn't mean you won't go out with me again, does it?"

She shook her head. "You just don't understand."

"I do, but you have a right to live your own life."

"I'm responsible for someone else besides myself!"

"So am I! I have a child." Almost instantaneously Justin's body stiffened. He glanced away from Kelly.

She sat up straight. Justin always seemed to bring up his son accidentally. "His name is Tommy, isn't it? How old is he?"

"Five," he said softly.

Kelly studied his pensive face. Now he was uncomfortable. "Why don't you ever talk about him?"

"I like to keep my private life private." He sighed. "Besides, it's painful to talk about. Tommy was very upset at my coming here. He's still unhappy. He doesn't understand why I had to take this job, why it's so important." Justin's eyes clouded over. "God, I miss him."

Kelly had never seen Justin so vulnerable. "When will you get to see him?"

"He's coming to visit real soon." He closed his eyes as if visualizing the boy's arrival. "It's just that I miss seeing him every day. When they're that young, they change so fast. I don't know. When Larry made me the offer, I thought—''

"Saving *In the Know* was too good a career move to pass up," Kelly observed.

Frowning, Justin opened his eyes. "It was, *is,* a great opportunity. I'd have been a fool not to take it."

"Who said otherwise?"

"There was a fairly judgmental ring to your comment."

"You're imagining things. Don't go overboard."

This echo of his recent advice seemed to nettle Justin further. Suddenly he wasn't the calm sage and she the hysteric. It was a situation Kelly found ironic.

"You *were* criticizing me," he insisted.

"All I meant was—"

"I know what you meant," Justin snapped, getting up. "You meant that where priorities are concerned I put my career first. *You're* the good parent, needlessly worrying over a harmless accident, like Sylvie walking in on us."

"I do not needlessly worry," Kelly sputtered.

"Yes, you do. You worry, ponder and think about everything. You're even sorry about the one spontaneous thing you did all evening. You'd sacrifice a relationship with me if you thought it might hurt Sylvie. But what have *I* sacrificed for Tommy?"

Stung and embarrassed by his words, Kelly said, "That's not what I think. That's what *you* think about yourself!"

"Nonsense."

"Yes! Why else are you so defensive? I didn't accuse you of neglecting your son. You brought up making sacrifices."

"You implied that my priority was my career," he countered. "But you're hardly indifferent to your own."

"Sylvie is more important than my career."

"Tommy is the most important person in my life! I took this job so that I can give him the kind of things I didn't have as a boy."

"Then why is he unhappy?" Kelly asked softly.

Justin paled. Regret that he had discussed this painful subject was etched on his face. He grabbed his jacket off the back of the couch and went to the front door. "I have to go." He started to open the door, then turned around. His eyes were hard. "Kelly, you are a good parent, but when do you let anything into your life but work and Sylvie?" He paused, then added, "Except tonight, of course. And, by the way, you wanted those kisses. You needed them."

"That's not fair! Your son has two parents, or at least one full time." She saw him flinch at this remark. "Sylvie has only me."

"I guess this means there won't be time for anyone outside of work."

"I've got to think it over," Kelly answered, still bruised by his comments.

Justin shook his head. "Funny," he said, opening the door, "we had our best times tonight when we didn't think, when we just followed our feelings."

Kelly gazed at the cold coffee. "Yes, and look where we are now."

She heard the door close. For a few minutes she just sat motionless. Sarah Vaughan began a song about a tender love affair, but Kelly couldn't bear it. She rose from the couch and quickly took the record off. She couldn't listen to the happy tune when all she felt was a sudden loneliness and loss.

CHAPTER FIVE

JUSTIN GAZED at Kelly across the crowded set of *In the Know*. Her delicate features were wistful, melancholy. She'd seemed distant and tense since that upsetting Friday night nearly a week ago when they'd argued. Or perhaps she was just unhappy with *In the Know*'s unusual topic that afternoon.

A couple was getting married. It had been his idea to stage a real wedding on the show. Getting married was so expensive now that young couples could barely afford more than a preacher and a ring. With *In the Know*'s help, however, one lucky couple would get a free ceremony and reception to be held live on the show. After the ceremony Gilda would interview the bride and groom, plus various members of their families. The whole event would be tasteful, warm and homey.

Kelly had protested the idea. Getting married was an important, private affair, she'd argued. To splash it in front of thousands of viewers, even for a free gown and some hors d'oeuvres, would cheapen the significance.

He'd prevailed, and now everyone in the studio and the large crowd standing on the adjoining news set were riveted to the ceremony happening before them— everyone except Justin. His mind was replaying the unhappy argument he'd had with Kelly last Friday.

How had the evening, which had started so wonderfully, turned out so cold and bittersweet? He should never have offered advice about Sylvie when his own situation with Tommy was so sensitive. Kelly seemed so ferociously competent at work that he'd assumed her private life would be as orderly. Justin chided himself. Whose private life was orderly?

Perhaps that was why he'd jumped in. Kelly's struggle to do the right thing by Sylvie achingly reminded him of a special person he might be letting down. His boy, his sweet boy, Tommy.

Kelly had spotted his overreaction for what it was—guilt. Tommy had seemed so distant and angry during his last few phone calls. Was the separation destroying their relationship? The boy's arrival tomorrow for his first visit to Boston had Justin deeply worried.

He turned his anxious eyes back to the happy wedding ceremony. Two people were becoming one. Their radiant joy in each other caused Justin to remember the other half of that confusing Friday night—the magical half when he and Kelly were discovering new things about the other. He gazed again at her lovely face. Despite their argument he still wanted her. Did Kelly still want him?

Kelly held back her tears, although it was very hard. She swallowed and glanced around the *In the Know* set to see if anyone had noticed how choked up she'd become. Hardheaded career woman though she might appear, Kelly had a romantic's reverence for marriage. Secretly she dreamed that one day she might have a reason to go searching for the perfect white dress. She even imagined walking down the aisle. It was the face of the groom that eluded her.

Kelly could see now that Justin had been right about the wedding idea. Hundreds of young couples from Massachusetts had responded to Gilda's on-air pitch. The winners were now saying their vows, and there wasn't a dry eye in the place.

Gilda, standing behind the mother of the bride, continually dabbed at her eyes. So far her performance had been perfect. Decked out in one of her more subdued outfits, she'd handled the before-ceremony interviews with warmth and just the right touch of folksy humor. The rows of audience chairs had been removed and replaced with tables around which family and friends of the couple sat. A path wide enough for a full-length gown was left in the middle for those participating in the service. The couches on the raised platform in front had been removed. In the back a buffet had been set up.

Kelly had seen to all the arrangements. If there was to be a wedding, she'd make sure it was a tasteful one. Working with the young bride and her mother had been an unexpected bonus. The young woman radiated a happiness and hope for the future that completely charmed Kelly. Her own life was so mixed up that she viewed the girl with awe and a little envy.

Since that scene on Friday night, she'd thought of little else but wondered if Justin did. His polite detachment confused her. Her nature craved the direct approach. Her motto was, *If there's a problem, talk about it.* But his maddening cool had crushed her nerve. It was almost as if he assumed she didn't want to talk about Friday night.

She shook her head and concentrated on the program. The groom was now saying his vows. "I, Robert, take thee Emily..."

Kelly closed her eyes. She was in a big, formal room. She was moving down an aisle. In front of her, Sylvie glided in a long pale yellow dress. She followed, walking slowly in her own gown, made of simple ivory satin that graced her figure but didn't overwhelm her small frame. People on either side of her smiled as she drew near. The scent of white roses wafted from her bouquet.

Ahead loomed an elderly minister, holding a Bible. To his left was another man. Dressed in a gray cutaway, this man faced the minister. But he was turning, turning to look at her. His features were hazy. Was that blond hair? Only a second longer and he'd be facing her. Her dream lover.

"Hey, it's not that bad."

Kelly opened her eyes. Justin was standing beside her. His expression conveyed that he'd just mistaken her reverie for dislike. "Bad?" she whispered. "I think it's lovely, absolutely lovely."

"Oh," Justin said, looking closer at her. "I thought... well, never mind."

The light bounced off his blond hair. For a crazy moment Kelly saw him in a gray cutaway. "You thought that because I was initially against this," she said in a low voice, "that I couldn't change my mind."

"Have you?"

She nodded. "Yes, you were right. It was a good idea."

The admission seemed to relax him. This past week he'd acted as if he always expected her to challenge him or be angry, which was odd since she expected the same from him. Now he smiled that slow, lazy smile that bewitched her so.

"Might I add," he said, "that the execution of the idea was faultless."

"Thank you," she said, turning her gaze back to the young couple. The compliment was typical of Justin lately—entirely correct but distant. Perhaps she'd blown the chance for a closer relationship on Friday night.

"Gilda seems practically one of the family," he said.

Another sore point, Kelly thought. Now he and Gilda were getting along better than ever. With that strange antenna that she had, Gilda had sensed something amiss between Kelly and Justin and had commented on the "odd chilliness" between producer and executive producer.

With barely concealed glee the star had thrown herself into the breach. Throughout the week anything Justin had asked for, Gilda couldn't wait to give. Their relationship had become closer, with Gilda spending more time in his office hatching out crazy show ideas. Now she even accepted criticism from him. In deference to a Benedict suggestion Gilda had worn her "dowdiest" outfit today to prove to him how appropriately she could dress for the wedding. Kelly supposed she should have been happy, since Gilda's performance matched the tasteful, warm ambience of the wedding.

"I wonder what the couple's future will be," she said.

"I'd say they have a fifty-fifty chance for happiness," he said.

"Just fifty-fifty?" Kelly asked, looking at him.

"Yes, about that. I think it's the national average for divorce."

"Oh, I see. That's a rather cynical attitude, isn't it?"

"Is it?" he asked, glancing at his watch. "I would have said realistic."

"You don't believe in marriage?"

His face lost some of its composure. "I do. It's just that . . ."

Kelly waited. Justin gave so few clues about how he really felt on personal matters. Friday night had been a rare crack in that facade. "Yes?" she pressed, encouraging him.

He sighed. "I have great respect for marriage. I just wonder if I could ever do it again."

"Why?"

"Because I could never bear to undo it again," he said, his voice barely audible. "As painful as you imagine divorce to be, you find yourself wishing it was only half that painful."

Kelly looked at Justin's suddenly grim face. His impervious mask had slipped for the first time since their dreadful confrontation, and some of the deep feeling she knew was there showed through. "But marriage is worth the risk, wouldn't you say?" she asked. "At least you seemed to think a good relationship was worth the risk on Friday night."

There, she had finally brought it up. He stared at her briefly and then looked away. "I said many things that night that I shouldn't have. I never meant—"

"I now pronounce you husband and wife!"

Kelly glanced at the exultant couple on the set and then turned back, but Justin had left for the control booth. The show moved to a commercial break, and she would be needed to help set up reception interviews for Gilda. She cursed the bad timing, but felt the first stirring of hope all week. Justin's armor of killing politeness had been cracked.

After the show she found him in his office, arguing with Larry Bishop, the program manager.

"Oh, excuse me," she apologized. "I'll come back."

"No, stay," Justin said, motioning her to sit down. "Larry and I were discussing the alternative cancer treatments show."

Larry pulled at his tie knot. "Kelly, maybe you can talk some sense into him. He wants to do a show on unconventional treatments to fight cancer. You know, like visualization."

Kelly sat up in her chair. "I think it's a great idea!"

Justin stared at her in surprise. Larry did, too. "I thought you were against the crackpot, far-out shows," Larry said, running his hand through his thinning brown hair.

"I'm for any show that can help people," she said. "Any show that can empower them to take control over their lives, not depend on quick fixes from psychics or con artists. I've read about these new methods to fight cancer. None of the legitimate ones are quick fixes or claim to be cures. But there are cancer patients who maintain they're in remission today because of them. The mind is a powerful tool to fight disease. And if we state very plainly throughout the program that there are no guarantees, just new thinking on the subject, I think it would be a unique show."

"What about the medical establishment!" Larry interjected. "They've stated categorically that these treatments are unproven."

Kelly shifted in her seat to face Larry. "I have a very good relationship with the medical community. They know I'm a responsible producer. Say yes to this idea and I'll get you a doctor who'll dispute the methods and one who'll at least discuss them seriously."

"But, Gilda," Larry said.

"Leave Gilda to me," Justin said.

This remark somewhat undermined Kelly's confidence in coming to Justin's office. Gilda and Justin's growing rapport tended to isolate her. A powerful mutual admiration society had sprung up between star and executive producer that Gilda sought to keep exclusive. And Justin's involvement in the show no longer made Kelly the last word on topic selection. Most of his ideas still gave her pause.

Larry threw up his hands. "All right! I can't fight you both. Just keep me informed of every guest booked." He left the office in search of an antacid.

"Ha! You did it!" she exulted.

"No, you did it!" Justin replied. "Your reputation with the medical community tipped the scales in our favor."

Kelly got up and started pacing. "I can dig into our computer to find recent articles on the subject."

"Definitely," Justin said. "There's bound to be various success stories mentioned."

"I might have to fly these people in," she warned him. "This won't be a cheap show."

"You find the people, I'll get the money," he promised.

"I think I know just the doctor to help me find the legitimate new treatments," she mused.

"If you have trouble, I have a contact in Chicago who might be useful."

"Can you call him today?" she asked.

"Consider it done."

"I'm really excited about this, Justin!"

"So am I. You know, you really ought to consider documentaries, Kelly. The format would suit you."

Kelly nodded, her mind a whirl of ideas. "Perhaps, perhaps!"

Justin laughed, his face more open and animated than it had been all week. "Who said we can't get along!"

In the euphoria of the moment Justin's small joke touched on the larger, more personal issue between them, and both knew it. Kelly's smiled faded as she sat down again. "Justin," she began, "about Friday night, I . . . I feel bad about it."

His grin vanished. In its place was a pensive half smile that looked as if some effort had gone into its making. "I feel bad about it, too."

"I'm not sure how the conversation got so heated," she said, looking down at her hands. She rubbed them together; they felt like ice cubes.

"I believe it was when I butted into your life."

Kelly glanced up. The overhead light bounced off his high cheekbones, forming shadows underneath. Suddenly he looked tired. "No, it wasn't just you."

"Yes, it was. I barged into your life and you hadn't really invited me in. I offered to give Sylvie a lesson. I suggested O'Callahan's—"

"I suggested you come to my apartment," Kelly interjected.

He smiled briefly, remembering the few electric moments between them. "Yes, but then I was a poor guest. I should never have interfered in your life. That's what started the disagreement. Sometimes my impulsiveness works against me."

"Oh, no!" Kelly protested. "Your spontaneity created what was fun about the evening."

"Until the end," he said ruefully. "I had no right to talk to you the way I did."

"Nor I."

"Then let's forget about Friday night."

Kelly was stung. She hadn't come into his office with the intention of dismissing that night. Was that what he wanted? "Oh, so you want to forget it?"

"Don't you?" Justin looked confused, and a little hopeful. "I thought after what I said—"

"I just want us to be friends," Kelly said, immediately realizing that wasn't all she wanted.

Justin's hopeful expression disappeared. "Oh... good, good." Then he added tentatively, "At least we can still work together."

"At least." She rose to leave. Disappointment gripped her heart. Perhaps they were meant to be just friends. If so, it was going to be difficult erasing that night from her mind. For one evening she hadn't been professional, and she'd reveled in the change. The unfortunate ending to it could be repaired if Justin had wanted to talk about it. Apparently he didn't want to. Now there would be just the show and Sylvie in her life, but they no longer seemed enough.

She reached for the doorknob. "By the way," Justin asked, "how is Sylvie?"

Kelly turned around. She could tell it wasn't just a polite question. "She's fine. We've gone driving twice since her first lesson, and she's getting very good. She's told me repeatedly to say hi to you."

He glanced down with a slight smile. "Tell her shifting is a snap compared to parallel parking."

"I will." She opened the door.

"Did you two patch things up after I left?"

Kelly closed the door again. He really was concerned. "Somewhat. The underlying issue of why we squabbled still remains, but Sylvie apologized for her remarks. In fact..." She paused.

"Yes?"

"In fact, Sylvie's worried that she might have ruined something between us. Now I can tell her that didn't happen."

"No, I guess not," Justin said thoughtfully. "Sweet of her to care, though."

"Yes," Kelly replied, "she's a very sweet girl. Well, I better see to tomorrow's show."

"What's Friday's show? I've forgotten."

"It's called 'Mr. Right—Where Is He?'" The irony of her answer didn't escape Kelly. "It's about how there aren't enough good men for all the single women today."

Justin whistled. "Is this a big shortage?"

"Getting bigger every day."

"Is this shortage our fault?"

"Of course," Kelly said. "We even toyed with asking you to be on the program."

"Me?" Justin sat straight up in his chair.

"Sure. A local magazine columnist named Mavis Garland picks the twenty most eligible bachelors in the Boston area every year. This morning she came out with her new list, and you're on it."

Justin positively blushed. It was such an endearing moment that Kelly didn't know how she could think of him as just a friend. "I am?"

"Yes, indeed," she answered. "Only a few short weeks in Beantown and already you're famous. Mavis says that when she saw your picture in the paper and read your station bio, she just *knew* you were list material. But don't worry. Peg has already found a couple of the top twenty willing to come on and talk about what they want in a woman and why there's this distressing shortage. You can just be our standby."

He shuddered. "Thank God. I couldn't go on live television as if I were some endangered species."

Kelly smiled. "But you are."

Justin watched her petite frame leave his office. The conversation had gone better than he'd expected. All during the week he'd thought he'd seen the same yearning in Kelly's eyes that he felt, the same bewilderment that they should be estranged. But he couldn't trust that intuition. Not after the terrible things he'd said to her on Friday night. He was grateful now that she didn't hate him. To hope for more had been foolish. Mixing business with pleasure *was* dangerous.

"KELLY, WE HAVE a problem with today's show."

Peg Lanihan nervously twisted a strand of her frizzy brown hair. They were one hour to airtime. "What is it, Peg," Kelly asked.

convenient

"Our two eligible bachelors have pooped out. One of them got engaged last night and the other got a hernia on the handball court this morning!"

Kelly sank into her office chair. The topic was correct. There *was* a man shortage. Without those two bachelors the panelists consisted of two single women, Mavis Garland, a dating service director and the author of a book on the subject. The only man was the author, and he was married. "Can't Mavis get another bachelor?" she asked Peg. "After all, we're plugging her column."

"She's tried, but it's too short notice. And it's a two-way street. We have Mavis on, and she plugs us in her column."

Kelly groaned. "We're screwed." Then a thought hit her. "Unless... Peg! I'll be in with Justin!"

Two minutes later, in a rare moment of cooperation, Kelly and Gilda had barricaded Justin in his office.

"No!" he exclaimed. "I won't do it!"

"Well, Gilda, I tried," Kelly said.

"Pleeease, Justin," Gilda begged. "We can't have a show on the shortage of good single men without a bachelor. Especially a bachelor on Mavis's list."

"I can't go on live television and talk about what I want in a woman!" he insisted.

"I won't ask you how often you make love!" Gilda said. "Although it is a fair question."

"You see?" Justin said, pointing at Gilda. "Look, I'm no expert on why there aren't enough good men. Going on the show would imply that I think I am one."

"But, Justin, Mavis Garland says that if you don't go on, she'll be very angry," Gilda said. "She says that it's some thanks for putting you on the list."

"Did I ask her to put me on the list?" Justin sputtered. His agitated state made his blue eyes sparkle. His pale olive skin glowed against his golden hair. The two no-shows couldn't hold a candle to his looks.

"Justin," Gilda said in a no-nonsense tone of voice, "Mavis Garland is a very powerful columnist. All she has to write is that she adores *Phoenix City Hospital,* and our gains these past weeks might be out the window. I do *not* want that to happen."

Between Justin's mortification and a rating point, Gilda would always choose the rating point, hands down. "Now wait a minute, Gilda," Kelly said, "Mavis Garland can't make or break this show. You can't ask Justin to bow to her blackmail."

"Yes, I can!"

Justin half smiled, as if he wasn't surprised.

"I've got an idea," Kelly said. "Have Justin on in the third segment only. It's the segment that straddles the half-hour mark, so our audience will stay with us. In the first two segments, have on the author, the dating service director and the two single women. That way the scene will be set to discuss the shortage with one of its representatives." She pointed at Justin. "Mavis Garland can be on from the third to final segment. That ought to satisfy her. Justin, you'll only be on for one segment. Surely fifteen minutes isn't too stiff a price to pay for *In the Know.*"

Justin exhaled a short, pungent expletive.

"That's a terrific solution, Kelly," Gilda said. "You saved the day!"

Justin put his head in his hands. "What time do you want me?"

KELLY PERFORMED superhuman feats getting the character generator reloaded with Justin's name, alerting the director and technical crew to the change, and informing the other guests. Mavis Garland was mollified, although slightly miffed that Justin wouldn't visit her before the show. "You know how busy executives are," Kelly said as she rushed out of the waiting room. Gilda profusely thanked her for such a "brilliant" idea, but Kelly was unnerved by Gilda's indifference to Justin's possible embarrassment.

Kelly positioned herself on the edge of the *In the Know* set, where the news set began. The show started. Gilda skillfully elicited the pertinent information from the author of *Where Are All the Good Men?* without letting him digress. The bare facts were depressing enough.

Her interviews with the two single women and the dating service director were more upbeat. She even threw in personal revelations of her own attempts to meet Mr. Right.

Gilda was at her best on shows like these, where the audience could feel she was one of them. Unfortunately, Kelly thought wryly, the star could offer no personal revelations on the death penalty or nuclear disarmament. As Gilda went to a commercial break, Justin joined Kelly. He couldn't hide his nervousness.

"Gilda's not going to ask me if I kiss on the first date, is she?" he asked, readjusting his tie clasp.

"I thought you enjoyed Gilda's unpredictability," she said, taking the clasp out of his clumsy fingers and adjusting it properly.

He tried to smile. "Does anyone at the station know I'm doing this?"

"Outside of the crew, only Larry. I had to tell him. By the time anyone else notices, the segment will be over."

"So no one will see," he said, glancing at his watch.

"Two minutes," Kelly said helpfully. "And quite a few people will see you."

"Strangers," he said.

"And joining us next," Gilda said into camera two, "is one of Boston's most eligible bachelors, who will tell us the male side of this topic. So stay around."

The stage manager gave the all-clear sign as Peg brought Mavis Garland over to join Kelly and Justin. Mavis was a grandmotherly looking woman, but her first words dispelled her appearance. "Hmm," she said, examining Justin closely, "I was right to put you on the list."

"An honor I don't deserve," he said, shaking her hand.

Mavis snorted. "Probably none of you deserves it. If you think meeting men is hard in your twenties, try finding a good man in your fifties. They all want to date women like...you," she said to Kelly.

"I'm glad there won't be any hostility," Justin muttered.

Kelly escorted the two guests to the couches and watched them get miked. Justin introduced himself to the other guests, while Gilda complimented Mavis on her dress, hair and general fabulousness. The stage manager announced they were ten seconds to air. Kelly walked back to the side of the set and crossed her fingers.

"We're back with two new guests," Gilda said. "The first is Mavis Garland, entertainment columnist for *Beantown, What's Happening!* She's just come out with her annual list of the top twenty most eligible bachelors in the Boston area. Joining her is Justin Benedict, WMAS's own executive producer and bachelor number eleven on her list. Welcome. Tell me, Mavis, was there any particular reason Justin was number eleven?"

"Money," Mavis said. "As a television executive, I figured he didn't make as much as the top ten."

Justin seemed bemused by this. "I'll ask for a raise."

"I don't think lack of money makes a man less attractive," Leslie, one of the single women, said.

"You will when you want to buy a home or a car," Mavis retorted.

"I can afford to buy my own car, Mavis," Leslie said. "What we've been talking about goes deeper than money or appearance. It's about the inability of men today to be emotionally open. They're so success-oriented. A good man can get excited about more than just his career."

For an instant Justin glanced at Kelly, who was standing in his line of sight. Tiny prickles invaded the back of her neck.

"Why can't men express their feelings to women?" Leslie asked Justin. "Getting a man to talk about his emotions is like pulling teeth. I can tell my female friends anything, but I usually edit what I confide in a lover or male friend. Why is that?"

"Men aren't interested in a woman's problems," the other single woman, Anne, interjected. "They pretend to be, but all that *sensitivity* is just to lure you into bed."

"I should be so lucky," Mavis said.

The audience laughed, but Justin didn't.

"We are interested," he said, addressing Leslie, "but we are less adept at emotional give-and-take than women."

"Cop-out," Anne declared.

"What difference does it make if he cries at sad movies as long as he can make the mortgage?" Mavis said to more laughter.

"Ah, Mavis," Justin replied, "the double standard you imply is the reason for the gap."

Mavis straightened her skirt. "What double standard? I thought I was making a point, or at least a joke."

Justin leaned forward. "What you just said is that as long as a man takes care of the externals in life—you know, the mortgage, the car payments, the career— then it doesn't matter about his private feelings. He's fulfilled his role. Women are always seen as romantics. But when you ask them to say what they look for in a husband, they always mention things like, 'Will he be a good provider?'"

"The woman's movement has changed all that," Leslie insisted. "We can contribute financially to a family now. If we can meet our share of the external world, as you call it, why can't men meet their responsibilities for the internal world of feelings and relationships?"

"Men have had nothing comparable to the women's movement to encourage them to change," Justin said. "As husbands and as...as fathers, we know we've expected women to do more than their share of nurturing. We see the problem, but our upbringing makes it more difficult for us to be as emotionally open as your upbringing has encouraged you to be."

"More cop-out," Anne proclaimed.

"No, it isn't," Justin said, an edge creeping into his voice. "Women have entered the work force, and now they know it's easy to achieve success. But it's still damn hard to learn how to love, to know when to leave the progress reports and flow charts on the coffee table to fly a kite with your kid." The expression on his face made Kelly swallow hard. "We're still learning the balance." He smiled bleakly at Leslie. "I'm sorry. You probably wanted a simple answer, and there's no simple answer. We just have to try harder."

Leslie smiled back at him, but his eyes were on Kelly.

"It *is* simple," Anne said. "A good man must be tough yet tender, vulnerable but not weak, confident but not conceited, gentle but dynamic, caring, giving, kind..."

The rest of the segment centered around Anne's personal list, but Kelly wasn't really listening. Her eyes were glued to Justin's subdued face. When the segment ended, he didn't wait for the soundman to unfasten his mike. He shook hands all around and walked over to Kelly.

His face was slightly flushed. "Did I make an ass of myself?"

Kelly smiled into his distracted face. "No, it was enlightening."

"To me, too. Look, could I see you in my office? Now."

Kelly had never left the show before Gilda's final goodbye. Today she would make an exception.

He closed the door, then seemed unsure as to where to sit. Kelly sat on his beige couch. He leaned on his desk, facing her. There were tiny beads of sweat under his hairline.

"I didn't say this morning what I wanted to say, what I've wanted to say since Friday," he began. "You were right—about me and my son. It was my guilt that made me say those unkind things to you. I regret them all. Because of my accusations it never occurred to me that you might want to talk about that evening. But you were so generous this morning, taking some of the blame, and I was so glad that we could continue to work together that I simply left it on that superficial note." He sighed, then glanced briefly at the ceiling. "Not much of a modern man, am I?"

"You're doing fine so far."

He smiled slightly. "The point is, I'm sorry for the things I said in anger."

"You were right."

Justin blinked in surprise. "I was?"

"Yes. It's hard for me to say this, but I do think too much."

"No," he protested softly.

"Yes, I do. Everything you said about what I wanted, what I needed—you were right. I overreacted when Sylvie caught us. It seems lately that I can never forget I'm a parent."

"I admire that."

"That's not the Kelly you wanted Friday night," she said, looking into his eyes. For a moment they seemed like unfathomable pools of water, but then they cleared to let the yearning she remembered so well shine through. Kelly felt a warm flush rise within her, loosening the muscles and nerves that had been constricted since she'd entered his office.

"You're a very desirable woman," he told her.

"You don't have to say it."

Justin sat down next to her. "But I want to say it. If we didn't work together..."

"Yes?"

He paused, then shifted so he could face her more fully. "Part of your charm is that you really don't know how fine you are. That Friday night you very nearly apologized for *not* sleeping around, as if experience was some sort of substitute for passion. It isn't. Technique without true feeling is my definition of loneliness."

Kelly warmed to his compliment. She'd never had the kind of confidence in her body that other women had. Those moments in Justin's arms had been a bombshell in her well-ordered life. She longed to duplicate them. No, she longed for more. He'd made the first move once before. Was it her turn?

"Maybe I'm more modern than you think I am," she said.

He leaned closer to her. She could smell his clean skin and see the tiny laugh lines around his eyes. "Labels," he said, "like modern, old-fashioned, liberated, unliberated—they don't mean anything to me. What's important is that you be true to yourself. Do what you feel is right for you."

Could she? Kelly thought she saw the answer in his eyes. She put both hands lightly on his cheeks. "Right now I feel like kissing you." And to her amazement she did.

Justin didn't react at first, so surprised was he at her move. But her probing lips activated his desire. Quickly he pressed her to him, and her arms wound around his neck. She used her tongue as a teasing weapon to inflame him, and it did. He couldn't stop his body from responding; he didn't want to. Feeling her hands massage the back of his neck, Justin knew this was Friday night all over again. Only Kelly was the seducer now.

There was no Sylvie to interrupt. His door was locked. He could change forever his relationship with Kelly, but now *he* began to think instead of feel. Impetuousness had already caused trouble between them. For all her unleashed sensuality, was Kelly ready for this change? Tomorrow he would still be the kind of father she disapproved of—that he disapproved of. A spasm of insecurity gripped him even as he felt her roving hand send warm tingles throughout his body. Despite the kiss he didn't completely believe that she approved of him.

And if Larry agreed to his new idea for Gilda's image, she might approve of him even less.

He slowly disengaged himself, savoring the last touch of her lips. She looked at him quizzically, with just a hint of humor. "Why did you stop?"

"I . . . someone might knock on the door," he stammered.

She smiled and gently rubbed her hand over his knee. "Didn't you once tell me not to worry about what other people think? 'Don't think,' you said. 'Do what you feel.'"

"Ironic, isn't it, that I should be doing the thinking and you the . . . ?"

"Fondling," she supplied.

He put his hand on hers. "Are you ready to change our relationship forever?"

Those gray eyes, so direct, so believing, stared at him. "I am right now," she said quietly.

"What about tomorrow?" he asked, cupping her pretty face.

Kelly balked at addressing the future. She wanted Justin. Reality be damned. He stirred fires deep within her that no man had ever reached. Not just the awakening of her body, but of her heart, too. But Justin had pulled away from her kiss. Was he uncertain? In the cold light of day perhaps their professional differences had made him decide a personal relationship was unwise.

His disengagement tapped another insecurity. *He doesn't really want me,* she thought. *What about tomorrow?* he'd asked. *Will I still be ready to change our relationship forever?* "Only if the man desires me," she said out loud.

Justin cast her an uncomprehending look. "Of course I want you."

But Kelly felt the cold hand of doubt. Logic dictated that you couldn't lambaste a man on Friday and make love to him a week later. Time would clarify things. "Let's wait and see, then, okay?"

"Okay."

They sat awkwardly together in silence until Kelly asked, "Isn't Tommy coming soon for a visit?"

Justin smiled. "He arrives tomorrow. I can't wait to see him."

"I'm sure he can't wait to see you."

Justin nodded, but his face lacked confidence. "I hope you're right."

CHAPTER SIX

"DO YOU WANT some orange juice?"

"No."

"How about some pancakes?"

"No."

"Cereal?"

"I'm not hungry."

Justin threw up his hands. "Tommy, you have to eat some breakfast."

The child stared at him obstinately. "I want Captain Carl's Chocolate Crunch."

Justin shook his head. "You know I don't allow you to have that cereal—too much sugar."

Those blue eyes, so like his own, looked up in defiance. "Mommy lets me."

"She does?"

"Uh-huh."

"She didn't used to."

Tommy squirmed in his chair. "I want to watch cartoons."

"First, breakfast," Justin said. "I'll make some oatmeal."

"Yuck!" Tommy stuck his finger in his mouth as if to gag.

"That's enough!" Justin snapped.

The boy fell silent. Justin sighed. Tommy could frustrate him quicker than an entire board of directors! Ever since his arrival a week ago the boy had gone out of his way, it seemed, to provoke him. Tommy never wanted to go to bed, but when Justin planned an activity, Tommy was too tired. If Justin reprimanded him for breaking long-held rules, Tommy claimed his mother let him. According to Tommy, she didn't mind what he ate, when he took naps, now much television he watched or how much noise he made.

It wouldn't do any good to call Elaine, Justin thought. His inability to get along with Tommy was *his* problem, his ex-wife would say. Justin knew that she resented his going to Boston; she'd put her career on hold to take care of Tommy.

Justin had expected a period of awkwardness with Tommy, but not this hostility. Could his son dislike him as much as it appeared? Occasionally Justin managed to break the ice, and the sweet, scrappy boy that he loved so much would peek through. Most of the time, however, Tommy remained moody and distant.

The worst moment had come last night. Bowing to Tommy's request, Justin took him out for pizza. At the restaurant the boy had made a scene, refusing to stay in his chair and throwing pizza at the waiters. When Justin had hustled him out of the restaurant, the boy had screamed that he hated him and would forever. Then he'd started to cry. Justin had held him in his arms until the sobs subsided, but Tommy wouldn't tell him what was wrong. To Justin's declaration of love, Tommy sniffled, "Okay, Daddy."

It was this refusal to talk that had Justin at his wit's end. Tommy had always confided in him. Now his son acted like a stranger, and Justin didn't know how to get him back.

In desperation Justin decided to call Kelly. Only his extreme distress could have prompted him to do this. Their heated exchange two weeks ago had made him take a hard look at his decision to come to Boston. Now the consequences of that decision were being borne out every day in Tommy's attitude toward him.

Throughout the past week Kelly had asked about the boy, but Justin had ducked the truth. He'd sensed, however, that she knew all was not well. But she'd never pried and never, neither by look nor by word, reproached him as he was reproaching himself. Her genuine concern gave him the courage to pick up the phone.

"Kelly?"

"Yes, Justin?"

"I . . . wanted to ask you something."

"If it's about the young comedians show, I really think Bobby Belcher is too off-color. When he told that joke about the donkey and the mariachi band, I thought I would—"

"No, no, that's not why I called. You can use your own judgment about him. No, it's a different matter, a personal problem."

There was a brief silence. Justin tightened his grip on the phone. He'd caught her off guard. What was she thinking?

Kelly nearly dropped the phone. Her unfinished seduction of a week ago had convinced her that Justin wanted *less* closeness. Now he was calling to confide. She felt a brief flash of elation and then remembered that he'd called with a problem.

"What's the matter?" she asked.

"It's about my son."

Now Kelly was thunderstruck. Justin had been evasive about Tommy all week. "Is Tommy sick?"

"No, no, he's fine—physically. It's just that he's . . . he's having a hard time adjusting here."

"In what way?"

"Well, I guess you could say he's having a hard time adjusting to me."

Kelly knew what a wrenching admission this was. "How is he behaving?" As Justin explained, the pain in his voice touched her heart. Still, she was no authority on five-year-olds. "Justin, I'm not sure how I can help. My dubious expertise is in teenagers."

He paused. When he finally spoke, Kelly suspended hesitation and doubt. "You're the only one I've confided in about Tommy. You're the only one I trust. We're going to the circus today. Would you like to come? I desperately need some of that honest Ferris insight."

Two hours later Kelly glanced out her apartment window in nervous anticipation. She had made a point of telling her younger sister that the big romance that Sylvie had imagined wouldn't happen. Sylvie had seemed disappointed. Kelly couldn't tell whether it was because this news dashed Sylvie's plans for more independence or because she genuinely liked Justin.

At the sight of Justin's car butterflies blossomed in Kelly's stomach. She slipped on her coat and yelled, "I'll be out all day. There's chicken in the refrigerator if I'm not home for dinner." She heard an "okay" and quickly left the apartment.

The early November weather had turned brisk and cloudy. Kelly hoped it wouldn't rain. She saw Justin get out of his car. His face looked tired and sad, but he smiled when he saw her. Those melancholy blue eyes reached out to her. She would do whatever she could to help him.

"Thank you for coming." He opened the car door for her and cleared his throat. "Tommy, I'd like you to meet a friend of Daddy's, Kelly Ferris. She's going to the circus with us."

The same hooded blue eyes stared up at Kelly in surprise and suspicion. He was so like Justin that Kelly nearly gasped. Thick flaxen hair fell over Tommy's forehead in heavy bangs. He wore overalls, a turtle-neck sweater with a tiny crocodile on it, sneakers and a coat. His lips were pursed.

"I thought we were going alone, Daddy."

Justin forced a smile. "Kelly's a friend of mine. I thought maybe she could be a friend of yours, too."

"Uh-huh."

"Hello, Tommy," Kelly said warmly. "I'm really looking forward to the circus today, aren't you?"

The boy played with his shoelaces. "Uh-huh."

"Then we're on our way," Justin said.

Without looking at Kelly, Tommy removed his seat belt and slid over in the front seat. "Okay."

Justin sighed.

As Kelly got in, she asked, "Doesn't your father have a special seat for you?"

Tommy's face scrunched up in disgust. "I'm too old for that."

"Oh," Kelly replied. She congratulated herself on getting off on the right foot.

"I don't like seat belts."

His tiny face turned obstinate, a look Kelly knew well on another person.

Justin got into the car. "Tommy, put on your seat belt."

"He doesn't like them," Kelly said, beating Tommy to the punch. Then she had an idea. "Tommy, why don't you sit on my lap? We'll put the seat belt around us, and you'll be able to see out the window."

"Is that safe?" Justin asked. "I don't know about this."

"It'll be fun," Kelly enthused. "What do you say?"

Tommy looked her straight in the eye. "I want to sit in my own seat. You can stay here."

Justin grimaced.

"Okay," Kelly said, congratulating herself on the ruse but understanding that a gauntlet had just been thrown down. She buckled Tommy into his special seat in the back. As she returned to the front, she said, "Tally-ho," eliciting an exasperated chuckle from Justin.

During the ride, Kelly pointed out unusual or funny things to Tommy, whose disposition improved slightly. She understood his reserve in front of an adult stranger, but she couldn't help Justin if she couldn't break the ice with his son.

"I hope you don't mind me coming to the circus with you," Kelly said.

Tommy shrugged. "Mommy has friends, too."

Justin and Kelly exchanged looks. "But I'd like to be *your* friend, Tommy," she said.

He looked at her. The blue eyes seemed particularly guileless. "They all say that."

This pronouncement served to make Justin more pensive—and distracted. A van pulled out in front of them.

"Justin, look out!" Kelly cried.

He swerved to avoid it, landing the car at the side of the road. "Sorry," he muttered, rubbing his eyes with his fingers. Kelly saw the worry on his face. She reached over and put her hand on his. He squeezed it, but looked away.

"Daddy! Do it again!"

Justin returned his attention to his son. "What?"

"Do it again. That was fun." Tommy bounced in his seat with the first look of interest on his face that she'd witnessed.

Justin exhaled a short laugh. He paused and then started chuckling. "So you liked that, huh?"

"Yeah," Tommy agreed. "It was like when you took me to the park, and there were those bumper cars, and we..." He fell silent.

"What?" Justin asked, turning completely to face his son. "Come on, Tommy, talk to me."

"No," Tommy said softly, "it was when you were in Chicago."

Justin reached back and massaged his son's head. "I'm here now."

Tommy shook his head.

Kelly broke the silence that followed by saying, "Well, *I* would love to hear about the bumper cars."

Tommy looked surprised. "You would?"

"Yes," Kelly answered. "Your Dad went driving with me and my sister two weeks ago. It sure was an adventure. We nearly crashed into another car "

"I wasn't the driver," Justin said, but Kelly shushed him with a glance.

"I don't know, Tommy," she said, "were the bumper cars as exciting as that?"

"Uh-huh, uh-huh," Tommy said, his whole body bouncing up and down. "It was *better*. Daddy told me he could hit all the cars—and he did!"

"He did?" Kelly prompted.

"Yeah," Tommy said, warming to the topic. "One car kept trying to miss us, but we kept chasing them. Remember, Daddy?"

"I remember, son."

"And you said, 'They're afraid of us Benedicts.'"

"They were," Justin agreed. "Every time they saw us coming, they headed in the opposite direction."

"But we caught 'em, didn't we?" Tommy said. "And, and remember you said that if we did, you'd buy me a hot dog?"

"A hot dog?" Kelly laughed.

"I love hot dogs!" Tommy stated.

He sure had the forthrightness of his father, Kelly thought. "Oh," she said. "You know there're going to be hot dogs at the circus."

"Daddy said I could eat all the hot dogs and candy I wanted."

"He did?" Kelly said, glancing at Justin.

He nodded ruefully. "The things we say to get some people to eat oatmeal."

"Okay, I bet you a hot dog, Tommy, that your dad can get us there without hitting another car."

"Hmm," Tommy said, musing over this offer. "Daddy," he said, "don't hit anybody."

"Okay, Tommy," Justin said. "But just for you. You know how much I like to hit other cars."

Tommy laughed. It was a sweet, bubbly laugh. Kelly realized it was the first time she'd seen him really smile.

Justin's relief at Tommy's change in attitude erased the worry lines that had seemed permanent fixtures on his face. He said to Kelly, "I'm so glad you came. You seem to be making a difference."

Kelly knew this was the moment for some overdue honesty. She glanced back at Tommy whose attention had been caught by a sheepdog walking by the car. Quietly she said to Justin, "I came today because of you. Because I've regretted what I said to you that Friday night, and this seemed like an opportunity to tell you that no parent is perfect, certainly not me. I do the best I can, but I blunder. There's no use pining for the days when Mommy and Daddy weren't divorced and Mommy didn't work and Daddy didn't get transferred. Those days are gone, and we can't measure ourselves against a norm that no longer exists."

He smiled gratefully and his body relaxed. Kelly sensed a door opening between them.

"You seem to have a handle on things," he said.

"No," she replied, shaking her head. "I have doubts."

His face became serious. "Speaking of doubts, I just want you to know that my pulling away from you in my office sprang from doubts within me."

This *was* a day for candor. "What doubts?"

"That you, deep down, didn't approve of me."

Kelly stared at his face, so vulnerable now in this honest confession.

"Didn't the kiss reassure you?" she asked softly.

His dimple made a brief, hopeful appearance. "I suppose it should have. I've never felt so—"

"Daddy! Come on!" Tommy whined.

Kelly had nearly forgotten about the small blond boy in the back seat, so rapt was her attention on Justin's next words. She looked at him with amusement. "Boring grown-up talk, right, Tommy?"

"Yeah," he agreed. "I want a hot dog and cotton candy and ice cream." He looked up at Kelly with a benign smile. "You can have some, too."

Justin and Kelly laughed. The boy possessed the direct charm of his father, but right now Kelly wished there were no children, no sisters, no television station, no responsibilities—just her and Justin and the words he'd been about to say. Her body felt recharged.

"I guess we better get to the circus before this boy starves to death," she said.

"To the circus!" Justin announced.

"Don't forget your promise," Tommy said.

"Don't forget what you were going to say," Kelly added.

Justin addressed his son, "Today you can eat all you want."

"Yeaaa!"

He turned to Kelly. "I'm not likely to forget what I feel for you."

Kelly settled back. Today was going to be special. She just knew it.

And it was. The circus enchanted Tommy to the point where he didn't want to go home. Kelly couldn't remember the last time she'd gone to the circus, so the experience seemed fresh and new to her. But mostly she enjoyed Tommy enjoying himself. He was such a self-possessed little boy, opinionated, sensitive. Although he'd warmed up to her a bit, Tommy still maintained a guarded distance. Kelly didn't mind. Father and son were getting along a little better. It was obvious, however, that Tommy was testing Justin to see how much he could manipulate his father.

After the second hot dog, Kelly said, "Justin, Tommy's going to have a whopper of a stomachache if he keeps eating this food."

Justin finished eating his last chocolate-covered peanut and said, "Relax, Mom, he's having a good time."

The term *Mom* slightly irritated Kelly. "I'm not trying to tell you what to do, but he might get sick."

"He's *happy,* Kelly. Why not indulge him a little?"

"He's beginning to expect it."

Justin tossed his empty box into a garbage can. "I won't ruin this day." He called over to his son, who was examining some stuffed animals. "Tommy, are you finished there?"

The boy pointed to a penguin. "Nooooo, Daddy," he pleaded, "I'm not ready yet. Buy me this."

Justin smiled. "I've bought you a million things already."

Tommy giggled. "A million? Daddy, you're silly. I want this one."

"No, Tommy, you've got stuffed animals at home."

Tommy guilelessly turned to his father. "I've got stuffed animals in Chicago, but I don't have any in Boston."

The meaning was not lost on Kelly or Justin. "Well..." Justin said, waffling.

"*Please.* I won't ask for another toy."

"Could I have that in writing?" Justin laughed. "Okay, but this is it."

The boy jumped up and down in delight. "Hey, I see ice cream!"

Justin paid for the penguin and put it under one arm. The other was laden with more treats for Tommy. "I thought the penguin was the last thing you were going to ask for."

"I said I wouldn't ask for any more toys. This is food."

"No."

"Yes."

"No, Tommy." Justin's voice was becoming starchy.

"Yes! You promised I could eat whatever I wanted."

"I've changed my mind."

The little boy clenched his fists. "Liar, liar, pants on fire!" he said to his father.

Justin stiffened. "Don't talk to me like that, Tommy." They glared at each other in mutual stubbornness.

The glow of the afternoon was fading fast. Kelly tried to retrieve it. "There'll be food at home, Tommy. Your father and I talked about making spaghetti."

He wheeled around to face her. "I didn't ask *you*," he shot back.

"Tommy!" Justin snapped. "That's no way to talk to a friend. Apologize to Kelly."

"I won't," the boy maintained. "She's not my friend. She only pretends to be my friend because of you. Just like Mommy's friends."

"Apologize."

"No!" The small voice quivered but remained defiant.

Justin closed his eyes in defeat. Kelly walked over to the shaking little boy. She knelt down to be at eye level with him. "Tommy, I care about you."

"No, you don't," he said, beginning to cry.

"Oh, baby," Kelly whispered, putting her arms around him. He didn't accept her embrace, but remained rigid, crying. Justin immediately was at their side. He set the toys on the ground and reached out for his son.

"No!" Tommy sobbed. "You don't want me. Nobody wants me."

Justin seemed crushed. "That's not true. I love you."

"No," the boy cried. "You left me, and I . . . I don't feel so good." He clutched Kelly. "I'm going to throw up."

"Oh, boy," Kelly said, picking him up and running to the nearest ladies' room.

She heard Justin yell, "Wait up," but he was encumbered by the toys, and Kelly suspected that every second counted. She was right. They barely made it into the stall before Tommy lost his two hot dogs, cotton candy, chocolate-covered raisins and milk shake. Far from feeling better afterward, he began to cry again.

"I want to go home," he said miserably.

"We are—right now," she replied, washing his face with a paper towel.

"I mean to Chicago."

Kelly put a tissue to his nose. "Blow," she said, and he did. The action gave her a minute to think. "Your daddy would be real sad if you left."

The boy inhaled a sob. "He would?"

"Yes," she said, smoothing his hair. "He couldn't wait for you to visit. He misses you a lot. A whole lot."

Disbelief struggled with hope on Tommy's face. "But he left."

Kelly couldn't explain a decision that she herself had trouble with. "He was sad to leave you. And I know he's sad now to think you're mad at him."

Tommy seemed to ponder this. He rubbed his eyes.

"Are you tired?" Kelly asked.

"Uh-huh."

"Then we'll go home," she said, taking his hand. She looked down at his forlorn face. "Tommy, I think your dad really needs to talk to you. Will you talk to him and tell him what you're feeling?"

The child glanced away from her. "I don't know."

"Please," Kelly said. "He misses you so much. He loves you."

Hearing it from another adult seemed to hearten him. "I miss him, too."

Justin's anxious face greeted them as they left the rest room. "Are you all right?" he asked Tommy.

"I threw up, Daddy. Are you mad at me?"

Justin handed all the toys to Kelly. He picked up his son and held him tightly. Then he kissed his forehead. "I'm not mad at you. How can I be mad at my best boy?"

Tommy's timid smile broke Kelly's heart. "I am?" he asked.

"The very best," Justin reassured him, "even when you upchuck."

Tommy giggled, and snuggled close to his father's chest. By the time they got to the car, he was fast asleep.

Twenty minutes later they put him to bed with the penguin by his side. When Justin closed the door, he said, "Well, at least he's talking to me. Thank you for coming today."

Kelly readjusted a comb that had become loose in her hair. "Don't thank me, Justin. I had a great time."

"Did you like Tommy?"

"Yes."

"He liked you, too. I mean, by the end of the day I think he was really coming around to you."

Kelly was unsure how to answer that remark. A real friendship with Tommy would take time. But after the trials of today, she didn't feel like clouding his optimism. "Well, I'm glad," she said, and then quickly changed the subject. "You know, Justin, a show featuring the romance of the circus might do well on *In the Know*. What do you think?"

His drowsy eyes twinkled. "I think it's a great idea. Wouldn't our viewers love to see the blindfolded knife thrower slice an apple off Gilda's head?"

I know I would, Kelly thought as they walked to the living room. She sat down on the sofa. "I'll call the circus tomorrow."

Justin put logs in the fireplace and turned on the gas jet. Flames shot up between the logs. "Instant fire," he muttered.

"It'll burn on its own in a minute," Kelly said, looking out the window. It had begun to rain. Drops pounded the leaves in the front yard. Kelly saw a world of swaying trees and icy wetness. But inside, the fire cast a cozy glow over the room. Justin knelt in front of the fire, nudging logs into position with a poker. He wore chocolate corduroy pants and a tan-and-blue flannel shirt. The firelight turned his blond hair nearly golden.

All day Kelly had waited to hear the words he'd wanted to say in the car. Now was the time.

"Justin," she began, "about today..."

"You were wonderful with Tommy," he said, getting up. "Tactful, funny, caring—I learned from you today."

Kelly didn't want her maternal virtues extolled at this moment. She'd meant her confession earlier that no parent was perfect. She struggled to do right by Sylvie, and today, for the first time, she'd seen Justin's struggle to do right by Tommy. He adored his boy, and his effort to maintain his relationship with him produced a tenderness for Justin that Kelly hadn't expected. That tenderness combined with her sensual feelings for him made his praise for her parenting skills anticlimactic. "Thank you," she said, "but I—"

"I thought my coming to Boston was, ultimately, the best thing for Tommy," he said. "I wanted him to have the things I didn't have as a boy, not realizing that what *he* wanted...was me. I also didn't take into consideration how trapped Elaine—that's my ex-wife—might be feeling with me gone."

Kelly really didn't want to hear about his ex-wife. A dislodged log turned Justin's attention away in time to miss her disappointed face.

"Kelly, help me with this fire," he said. She rose from the couch and knelt next to him. "This log isn't burning right. While I lift it slightly with the poker, use the bellows to juice up the flame under it."

"Why not use the gas flame?" she asked.

"Let's do this the more natural way."

They got the fire going again. Now, Kelly thought, was the time to do the same for *them*. Kneeling so close to him, she had a powerful urge to run her hand over the soft flannel, then edge her fingers under the material to feel his smooth, warm chest. "Justin, earlier today you wanted to say something to me."

He rubbed his hands on his thighs. "Yes," he agreed. Lit by the crackling fire, his face never seemed more handsome, more approachable. Gone was the supercool executive. Gone was her boss. He was sitting so close. The need to touch him was almost unbearable. "You've said some things to me that upset me badly, but I deserved them. I'm grateful. No, it's not just gratitude. I really respect you and your kindness."

"Please," Kelly said, holding up one hand, "you make me sound as if I deserve a merit badge."

Justin smiled slightly. In the firelight his face glowed with frank desire. He took his index finger and traced a line from her brow to her cheekbone down to her jawline, ending up on her lips. Once there, his finger gently outlined that incredibly sensitive area, sending icy tingles down Kelly's spine, even though she was sitting in front of a hot fire.

"I hadn't finished what I was going to say," Justin said softly. "Besides teaching me what a good parent should be, I also find you very attractive."

Ah, those were the words she'd been waiting for all day.

"And very sexy."

Oh, say some more.

"And I've wanted you since the first day I met you, when you spilled tea down that tight knit dress."

"I wanted you, too," Kelly confessed. "But you were my boss and, well, so many women at the station have come on to you. I've seen it."

Justin softly kissed the spot where Kelly's jawline met her ear. "I've seen how the other men at the station look at you, but you don't see it."

This news surprised Kelly. "They do?"

"Uh-huh," he murmured, pulling down her turtleneck to kiss the warm skin of her neck. "You're so completely into your work that you mistake their flirting for kidding. You don't see yourself as sexual."

He was right. Kelly knew it, but she also knew she was changing. "I do tonight," she whispered. "Tonight I'm not a producer, a mother or anyone else in a responsible position. Tonight I'm just a woman."

"And such a woman," Justin said, rubbing his face in her sweater. He took Kelly in his arms. The passion in his eyes matched her own desire.

"Show me."

Justin let out a sigh, heavy with satisfaction and anticipation. He kissed her once gently, but sensing what she really wanted, he claimed her mouth again, harder this time, his lips searing hers and his tongue invading her mouth. Kelly wound her arms tightly around his shoulders. She felt her breasts mold against the unyielding strength of his chest.

In her mouth his tongue found every sensitive crevice, defying her to resist each hot thrust. Kelly savored his urgent passion. She didn't want to compete tonight. The cool professional was disappearing. Good riddance, she thought, her body straining against his.

Justin's hands roamed across her back, finding the edge of her sweater. One hand slipped under the soft fabric and moved to the clasp of her bra. He unhooked it and gently ran his hand over the full exposure of her back. As Kelly felt the brassiere free her breasts, she became impatient with the clothes that were preventing her naked skin from touching his. His maddening talent inside her mouth escalated her need to rid herself of anything that kept the hard impact of his body from taking hers.

Kelly unwound her hands from his broad shoulders and began to unbutton his shirt. She pulled open the shirt and felt the ridges of his muscled chest. Her hands strayed over the smooth, lean expanse of it, but touch wasn't enough. She regretfully removed her lips from his and sought the area on his chest where his heart was. She gently kissed it, feeling his breath quicken and hearing his heart pounding. With her tongue she traced a line to his right nipple. In languid strokes she licked it. Justin sucked in his breath sharply. His hands massaged her hair as she manipulated him to the kind of unbridled arousal that she felt.

Suddenly they heard a cough. Kelly snapped up her head. Justin put a finger to his mouth in a shushing gesture. They both looked at Tommy's closed bedroom door and waited. When the house remained quiet, except for the crackle of the fire, Justin took Kelly's hand, got up and led her to his bedroom. When he closed the door, he said hoarsely, "No more interruptions."

Kelly nodded, her own voice coming out surprisingly husky. "No, no more." The room was warm, and the pounding rain outside created the feeling that they were the only two people on earth, that the only reality was each other. Justin eased her turtleneck over her head, and Kelly let her bra slip to the floor. Justin sighed at the sight of her exposed breasts. He ducked his head to kiss each peak as his hands unzipped her skirt and slid it and her slip over her derriere. They fell in a heap next to her bra. Kelly slipped out of her shoes and stockings and stood before him in only her panties.

"Lovely," he murmured in a strained voice. "But I want to see all of you."

Kelly slowly removed her panties, knowing that the anticipation of seeing her totally naked would excite him further. It did. His gaze thrilled her. Boldly she walked to the bed and lay down. "Make love to me, Justin. Now," she whispered.

It was amazing how quickly he shed his clothes. In the hazy light of the one lamp Justin had turned on, Kelly could see how beautiful he was. He lay down beside her and with one hand lazily ran his fingers over the curves and valleys of her petite frame.

Kelly shuddered at his touch. His urgency was apparent, but he refused to be rushed. His tongue played mad games on the rosy peaks of her breasts, but nothing prepared Kelly for when his teeth lightly nipped each crest, causing her to cry out in pleasure.

A feeling of unbearable happiness swept over her. There wasn't a part of her body that didn't thrill to his touch, that didn't strain to be touched. Without embarrassment her legs parted to allow his tormentingly sweet probing of her most private area.

She, in turn, pleased him in every way she could think of, and some, to her delight, he suggested. There was no awkwardness between them. His touch liberated her from her self-imposed shell, and she evolved into the sensual being she had always dreamed of becoming.

Kelly loved to look at his body, now faintly covered with perspiration—the slim hips rising from sturdy legs, the tapered waist, the broad shoulders. This splendid body was giving her so much pleasure that Kelly didn't think more was possible. Then he entered her.

The sensation tore moans from both of them. In an almost automatic response Kelly's legs wound themselves around his back. Justin moved slowly at first, Kelly immediately picking up the rhythm. Then he began to thrust deeply inside her.

Each murmured indistinguishable sounds—the physical release was too overwhelming for conversation.

At the exact moment Justin closed his eyes, Kelly cried out in that apex of passion that is as much emotional as physical.

CHAPTER SEVEN

"YOU DON'T HAVE to leave right now," Justin pleaded.

Kelly groped in the uncertain light for her clothes. "I do, Justin. Sylvie will worry that something's happened to me."

"Won't she be with Kevin?"

Kelly looked back at him. Lying there on the rumpled sheets, in all his naked splendor, Justin looked like a lion, a very satisfied lion. "Yes, but it's nearly time for her curfew," she said, finding her turtleneck sweater wrong side out. "She'll be coming home to an empty house."

Justin leaned on his elbow, his face cupped in the palm of his hand. "Does your curfew have to be the same as hers?"

Kelly wasn't sure how to answer that. She stepped into her panties and started to fasten her bra.

"Here, let me do that," he said.

Smiling, she walked to the bed and sat down beside him. He sat up and pretended to try to hook her brassiere. But quickly he gave up and slid his hands around her chest to her full breasts. His warm fingers on her cool skin made Kelly shiver. "Again?" he asked, kissing the nape of her neck.

Kelly was tempted, especially when his fingers started rubbing circles around her nipples, eventually settling on the sensitive peaks. Hot ripples of pleasure coursed through her veins. He closed his arms around her. Kelly felt she could remain in them forever, but . . .

"It's time for me to go," she said. "And it's not that I would be embarrassed to stay over," she quickly added. "It's just that I gave no indication that I wouldn't come home. Sylvie would worry."

"Call her," Justin suggested.

"And tell her what? That the romance I told her had ended has suddenly blossomed again and I casually decided to stay the night?"

"That's not what tonight was about," Justin said, tightening his hold.

"I hope not," Kelly murmured. Making love to Justin had seemed so right. But she knew it had also been a little reckless. Sylvie couldn't be expected to see the distinction.

Justin nuzzled her hair. "You were quite spectacular. It was like a different Kelly."

"I am different. And it's all your fault." Playfully she tickled his bare chest. He grabbed her hand and kissed the soft skin above her wrist. Slowly his lips trailed up her arm, sending waves of delicious warmth through her.

With regret she said, "Darling, I have to go."

"Darling! That's the first term of endearment you've called me." Justin laughed. "Hey, don't get me wrong. I like it," he said, hooking her bra. "Just don't forget and call me that at work."

Justin's comment brought her back to reality. "This is a dangerous game we play," she said, getting up from the bed.

"Kelly," Justin called out to her softly. When she didn't respond, he added, "Honey, darling, sweetie, dearest, angel, dumpling, snookums."

She started to chuckle. Justin could always get her to laugh, and if she could laugh, was anything that serious?

"Listen, sugarplum," he said, stretching out on the bed. "I don't intend to give you up now. Not after tonight."

His bold glance suggested that this option wasn't open for discussion. Wearing only her panties and brassiere, Kelly loved the possessive way he looked at her. At any moment she half expected him to lunge off the bed and drag her back. What passed between their eyes was elemental. She couldn't give him up, either, although she thought his dismissal of the risk a little too simple. "Justin," she said, "I want you as much as you want me. Just don't call me dumpling."

He smiled. "Why not? You're round in all the right places and you taste so good. But we must do something about your lingerie."

Kelly slipped her sweater on. "What's wrong with my lingerie."

"It's so . . . practical."

The way he said "practical" made Kelly pause. "My lingerie does what it's supposed to do. What does it matter when there's no one to see—"

"Ah," Justin interrupted. "Now there's someone to see it."

"Not at work," Kelly said, smiling.

"But if you're wearing satin lace panties, I'll know. And think about it all day." Justin rolled off the bed and put on a bathrobe that had been thrown over a

chair. Kelly noticed for the first time other garments
and objects strewn around the room. She'd been too
preoccupied when she came in.

"I'll make you a deal," she said as she finished
dressing. "I'll buy some new lingerie if you'll
straighten up this room the next time I'm here."

Justin looked around the room as if he didn't know
what she was talking about. "You think it's messy?"
When she chuckled, he said, "It's a deal. But *I'll* buy
your lingerie."

"No, I'll buy it," Kelly insisted. "Besides you don't
know my size."

"I have a fair idea of your dimensions," he said,
moving close. "Unless you would like me to measure
again." He raised his hands to massage her shoulders
lightly.

"There's nothing I'd like better than a second opinion," Kelly said, "but I'd better call a cab."

He nodded. "I'll pay for it."

"No, I can pay for it."

"*Kelly.*"

She stopped in her tracks. "You're very generous,
Justin, but I don't expect you to pay for everything.
And why is lingerie so important? Don't you like me
out of it as soon as possible?"

He laughed and ran his hand lightly over her shiny
black hair. "It's the romance of it, Kelly! Tonight you
were incredibly sensual, alive with the pleasure of your
own body. I can't match this Kelly with sensible bras
and underwear."

Kelly pondered this remark. Justin was talking about
a change in her image, albeit a private change, since
only the two of them would see it. Still, any alteration

in her identity made her hesitate. She weighed the difference—and decided to go for it. She did feel different tonight, and the feeling was intoxicating. So why should she mind if he bought her some provocative underthings? In fact, she couldn't wait to see what he would pick.

"All right," she said, "you can select the teddy of your dreams. Of course, this means that I can buy you some new underwear."

Justin picked up the phone and started to dial. "Great! I could use some new boxers."

Kelly slid her arms into the depths of his robe. She made it difficult for Justin to concentrate on giving his address to the cab company. "Some bikinis, I think," she said. "Boxers are too practical."

DURING THE DRIVE HOME and all through Sunday, Kelly replayed her night with Justin. Her body had responded to his touch in a way she had always dreamed of—with no embarrassment, no hesitation. It surprised her how very direct she became in giving pleasure and receiving it. But why not? She was a direct, candid person normally. At work she was known for her determination and frankness. In a man's arms, though, well, she'd always been less confident. Until Justin had come into her life. Now she felt totally uninhibited, and the feeling was exhilarating.

For once disregarding her bank account, she shopped for lingerie on Sunday. Justin had been right. Everything she owned was practical. But Kelly no longer wanted to be practical. Her decision to pursue a relationship with Justin was proof of that. She bought with no thought to price, only to what effect the item might have on him. That was her criterion. If the item conjured up no vision of passionate nights, if it would unsettle Justin in no way, then Kelly put it back. Those few hours in his arms had produced a sweet and long overdue release from all her responsibilities.

Perhaps diving into an affair with Justin was rash. It would certainly add wrinkles to her already hectic life, but Kelly refused to be negative. She felt footloose and free, the way she had years ago before responsibilities had submerged her needs. She gazed at herself in the dressing room mirror. A woman stared back at her. Not a producer, not a mother, but a pretty, desirable woman. She would definitely buy this hot pink nightie. The thought of what Justin would do or say before he slid it off her body made Kelly tingle.

Lying in her bed on Sunday night, Kelly debated what undergarments to wear the next day. The black lace bra and panties? With a grin she realized how unusual this dilemma was for her. But she rejoiced in the change. Kelly couldn't remember when she'd been so undone by a man. Justin was her match on every level. True, they didn't always see eye to eye on the show, but each had developed a respect for the other's abilities. And Justin knew how to have fun, a particular talent she'd misplaced recently.

She was determined to get it back. She snuggled under the covers in eager anticipation. No worries about Sylvie, parenthood or *In the Know* invaded her dreams.

MONDAY DAWNED cold and blustery. The sky was a mottled gray, just itching to burst forth with rain. Kelly heard thunder far off in the distance as she drove to work. Had she been superstitious she would have been unnerved by this ominous beginning to her day. Instead, she was just grateful that it would rain and not snow.

Life was too wonderful to let a typically late fall morning depress her. Beneath her pinstriped suit was flesh-colored lingerie so sheer that it was like wearing hardly any at all. She couldn't wait to tell Justin.

His secretary informed Kelly that he would be late. Disappointed, Kelly stopped off at the station cafeteria for breakfast. The "Top of the W," as her co-workers derisively called it, provided decent food, if a little bland. The "Gilda Simone Stroganoff" was definitely something to be avoided, however. She was chewing a limp piece of toast when she heard, "Mind if I join you?"

Without waiting for an answer Gilda sat down in the chair beside Kelly. Her appearance was a surprise since Gilda seldom arrived before eleven.

She looked particularly unusual that day in a stylish sack dress that unfortunately looked like a sack on her. Clothes, however, weren't the oddest part of her appearance. Gilda sported a shoulder bag crammed with books. And she carried a tray filled with food.

"That's quite a breakfast," Kelly commented. "You usually don't eat this much in the morning."

"I usually don't eat this much all day," Gilda said. She frowned at the plastic utensils and then poised a knife and fork over her omelet. "But Justin feels that I need more fullness in my face."

That was an understatement. Gilda's constant dieting sometimes left her looking pale and drawn. Kelly had mentioned this before, but to no avail. Gilda accepted suggestions from Justin, however, in areas where she ignored Kelly's often similar advice.

"So, Gilda, think it'll rain?" Kelly asked.

"I hope so," Gilda said, dumping two packets of sugar into her coffee. "Bad weather keeps people indoors. Viewing levels go up."

"Well, let's pray for a monsoon," Kelly replied. It had been a modest joke, but Gilda laughed appreciatively.

"Oh, Kelly, you're a stitch," she said, "although sometimes I think you're a little too sophisticated and urbane for daytime television."

"Gilda, *urbane* is an urbane word."

Gilda laughed again, a little indulgently, Kelly thought. "See what I mean? It's been an education working with you."

"Has been? Something I don't know about?"

Gilda seemed very, very mellow. "No, of course not. In fact, don't you think the atmosphere in the office has improved lately?"

She was right about that. Since Justin had come, Kelly's fights had been with him, not with Gilda. He'd become a buffer between the two women. Still, she and Gilda weren't exactly buddies. "Yes," she said, "the office is certainly different."

Gilda shook her head. "It's Justin. He's been exactly what this show's needed. Surely you can see that now."

Kelly stirred her coffee. She didn't want to discuss Justin with Gilda right now, so she changed the subject. "What are all those books for?"

Gilda's face lit up and she hastened to swallow her food. "Research," she finally said. "I'm doing research."

"On what?"

Gilda pulled a book from her bag. "Myself." She handed the book to Kelly.

Kelly read the title. "*Imaging: It's Not Who You Are That Counts, It's How You Look.* Well…I didn't know you were dissatisfied with how you looked."

"I wasn't, but Justin has made me see that I was trying for an image that wasn't *me,* that by borrowing from the clothes and makeup of models and stars, I was adopting their image instead of defining my own."

Kelly couldn't have said it better herself. She had to give Justin credit. "I think you're on to something," she said enthusiastically. "I've always thought that your style wasn't—" she searched for a tactful word "—simpatico with the general, um, atmosphere of *In the Know.*"

Gilda slapped a hunk of cream cheese onto a sliced bagel and began to spread it around. "I'm not wearing navy suits, Kelly. That's not what my research has taught me."

"But you were talking about image."

"Exactly!" Gilda stated. She took a large bite out of the bagel. Obviously the weight-gaining suggestion was a big hit. "*In the Know*'s image is changing. So I need a change, too. Besides, I never realized that creating an image was such a complicated thing. I mean, it involves demographics, ratings research. As Justin said to me last night—"

"You saw Justin last night?" Kelly asked. Immediately she regretted her quick response.

Gilda threw her a shrewd look. "Yes, we had dinner last night," she said casually. "I'm so rushed during the day that I feel I don't have adequate time to discuss the show with him."

Too busy signing autographs, Kelly thought. "So what did Justin say about your image?"

"He said I'd miscalculated, that the majority of my audience were mature women who wanted their daytime hosts to be like their best friend instead of some glamour figure. Justin showed me surveys and focus group reports to substantiate this. Since my forte is getting the personal stories from all those hausfraus we have on—" Kelly blanched at the condescension, but Gilda didn't notice "—we decided that instead of looking like a movie star, I should look like the way *they* would like to in their dreams, while still being their best friend, of course. We'll do more 'touchy-feely' shows. You know, the ones where I can talk about how my problems are the same as theirs. And I'll get involved more in preparing questions for the show to make sure they're, um, simple and easy to understand."

The bagel disappeared, as did Kelly's optimism. Gilda as everybody's best friend? She tried to figure out what upset her more—that she'd been left out of a meeting concerning the show or that the meeting involved such calculation. "Couldn't you just host the show?" she asked. "Realistically you can't be the 'best friend' to guests who are arguing over capital punishment."

Gilda eyed her coldly. "No, I can't. Every talk show host who's successful has an image, whether it's as a father figure, or motherly type, puckish boy next door or investigative firebrand. All successful hosts have an image."

"Usually the image is based on genuine aspects of their personality."

"Oh, that's naive, Kelly. *Everyone* is marketed today. It doesn't matter if the reality of their image is false. Hell, I don't want to be the best friend of most of our audience. All these books that Justin gave me last night have really helped me in seeing how I can mold my particular image. They mention everything, from which eye shadow creates a feeling of warmth down to which shades of nail polish look refined. They even mention lingerie!"

"Lingerie?" Kelly's stomach did a flip-flop.

"Yeah." Gilda laughed. "But Justin says I can wear what I want. We went over all aspects of my appearance. It was wonderful to get a male point of view on something so personal. Justin really understands the concept of image and how we can make it work for us."

"Gilda, you're not a tube of toothpaste. Your nature is grand, extravagant. You can't be trained to be... homey."

"Watch me," Gilda stated. Her huge diamond ring sparkled as she took a bite out of a jelly doughnut. After daintily wiping the powdered sugar off her upper lip, she said, "Now is my chance to really make it. I could become as famous as Phil or Oprah. You know that our rating increase has spawned syndication talk." She pointed the doughnut at Kelly. "Think big! Stop seeing *In the Know* as just a local public affairs talk show."

This advice annoyed Kelly, but not as much as having been left out of a meeting concerning the show. Justin hadn't mentioned it on Saturday.

Why should he? she argued with herself. As executive producer, he didn't have to report to her every professional meeting. Still, the secret dinner had shaken her confidence. This remolding might exclude her even further from determining the show's direction, especially since it ran contrary to her notions of honest television. She knew she had to blend her style with Justin's, but to what extent? And she knew, deep down, that the fact of the meeting bothered her less than the topic.

As illogical as it seemed, Kelly felt a stab of jealousy over Justin's involvement with Gilda's appearance. Never mind that he was trying to shape Gilda into something she wasn't; Kelly could talk to him about that. It was his intimate involvement in so personal a process that bothered her. But why should she feel threatened by his recreating Gilda? Hadn't he made suggestions about her appearance?

Ah, there was the rub. Justin's comments about her lingerie had seemed so special, his interest so individual. She wanted his opinions on such personal matters all to herself.

Gilda plunged into a juicy grapefruit. Kelly couldn't deal with any more breakfast. She excused herself. Happily Gilda pulled a book on makeup out of her bag and started to read.

On her way to his office, Kelly checked with *In the Know*'s director about the show that day on stunt-women. She went over with him again the actual stunts that would be performed. They both agreed that this would either be a great show or the set would catch fire. She continued on to Justin's office.

"Yes, Kelly, he's here now," his secretary said. Kelly walked through the door unannounced, then closed it. Justin was on the phone.

"Yes, tell the syndicator that the order was wrong, all wrong," he said. "I expected a one-hour documentary on day-care, and instead I got *The Amazing World of the Sea Otter!* I don't think otters have a day-care problem, do you?"

Upon seeing him, Kelly felt her mood lighten. Smiling, he motioned for her to sit. But Kelly had other ideas.

First, she pushed the button in on the door to lock it. Then she walked to where Justin was sitting and sat on his lap.

"Joe, um, can I call you back?" he asked. "Something's come up."

"I should hope so," Kelly said. She slowly unbuttoned her linen blouse and, for a second, revealed the nude-colored teddy underneath. "I didn't want you to wonder all day," she said, getting up.

"Ms. Ferris," his deep voice commanded, "is this accepted professional behavior?"

"Depends on what profession we're talking about," Kelly said, rebuttoning her blouse. The sight of his drowsy blue eyes made her pulse quicken. Saturday night hadn't been a dream, a fluke.

"How thoughtful you are," he said, leaning back in his chair.

"It was my way of saying hello."

He chuckled. "What a nice hello. For you, my door is always open. Or should I say closed?"

Kelly smiled. "I just wanted to show you my new lingerie. Contrary to what you might think, I can accept new ideas."

Justin got up and walked over to her. He put his arms around her. "I don't know if I can handle the new Kelly. I could barely handle the old one."

She smiled up at him. "I'm still basically the same person. I haven't radically changed my image and become everybody's best friend."

Justin looked at her sharply. "My dinner with Gilda. How did you know about it?"

"Gilda told me, of course. In breathless tones. Why didn't you tell me on Saturday?"

Justin held up one hand. "Gilda called me on Saturday morning with the invitation. Right after that Tommy dumped his oatmeal on the floor. As far as the rest of Saturday went, the show really wasn't on my mind."

In the Know hadn't really been on Kelly's mind, either.

"I tried to call you Sunday afternoon, but no one was home." He smiled. "You must have been out shopping." Drawing her closer, he whispered, "What else did you buy?"

Kelly grinned. "You ain't seen nothin' yet."

His lips touched hers. The kiss, although unbearably tender, was brief. Kelly wanted a stronger reaction. She needed to feel, even for a moment, the fire Justin had displayed Saturday night. Perhaps she needed reassurance that he still felt the same way.

Quickly she pressed her lips to his again. With a joyful greediness her tongue demanded entry into the interior of his mouth. He acquiesced, greeting her probing with the darting penetration of his own tongue. If she'd wanted a reaction, she got one. His body tensed in excitement. Boldly he explored every tormentingly sweet part of her mouth, as if searching for honey. His arms surrounded her so completely that he nearly lifted her off the floor. Her breasts rubbed against the hardness of his chest. There was no mistaking his passion. There was also no opportunity, right then, to satisfy it.

She gently pulled away.

"God," he said, his voice dreamy and ragged, "you do something to me."

Kelly ran her finger down the front of his shirt. Her voice came out a little breathless, too. "Can I be your best friend?"

His mouth curled in a small smile. "You're making fun of my idea."

"I thought we could talk about it."

The drowsy blue eyes mocked her. "You came here to talk?"

Kelly playfully patted his behind. "So tell me, will the new Gilda have a sense of humor? The old one doesn't."

He rubbed his lips with his index finger. "Why don't we sit and talk?" They sat on the couch. Justin turned toward her, his face serious. "First of all, I gave those books to Gilda to start her thinking in a new direction. We both know her appearance isn't working for her entirely."

"Yes, but—"

"Larry told me this morning that we may have a syndicator interested."

"Really? What company is interested?"

"General Video. Nothing concrete so far, just some general talk between them and Larry. I gather they like Gilda but feel her image needs more definition. I've felt this, too. So has Larry. Whether or not General Video becomes more serious about the show, now is the time to spruce up Gilda."

Kelly rubbed her hands together. "What do you mean by sprucing? Believe me, I'm not against refining her appearance, but there seems to be a more radical change brewing."

Justin's eyes dropped for a moment, as if he were pondering his next words. "I've given this a lot of thought," he said, returning his gaze to hers. "Since my arrival here, I've considered Gilda's image and whether it's working for us. You've dismissed the marketing reports and results from the focus groups who've critiqued the show, but I choose to believe them. We need to define Gilda further as a personality."

Kelly sighed. "This cult of the personality, this passion for celebrity, where will it end? I mean, I've seen news anchormen being marketed as sex symbols."

"I can't predict the future, but I do know the present. Our research has suggested that what the audience wants is a—"

"Best friend."

"Our job," he continued, "is to blend that with the structure of the show."

"What if this new personality is incompatible with the tone of the show?"

"Then we work to make all aspects of the show compatible."

Kelly felt an ominous wave of anxiety. "I have no objection to Gilda getting a new hairdo," she said, "or toning down her makeup. But I'm wary of this 'best friend' concept. I don't care how many focus groups you've hired, Gilda isn't everyone's best friend! You can change her looks, but you can't completely re-package her image. She's not a box of cornflakes or a new soft drink. She's a human being, and she can't act contrary to her nature without the audience eventually detecting it."

Justin folded his fingers together. "We're agreed that Gilda's look needs refining?"

"Yes, but—"

"Then could you give it a chance? Up till now Gilda has resisted changes in her appearance."

Justin's tactful comment didn't fool Kelly. She hadn't gotten Gilda to rethink her appearance, but he had. Since Kelly had been lobbying for this, how could she complain now? "How will this transformation take place?"

Justin leaned back on the couch. "I'm having some media specialists come in to coach her on her delivery. That will take some time. But I thought, since we're in the November rating period, and it's one of our more vital rating periods, that we could concentrate on the externals such as hair, clothes, cosmetics, culminating in a makeover show—starring Gilda."

Kelly sat up straight. "What?"

Justin sighed. "I knew you'd react like this."

"You're darn right! This is a stunt!"

Justin gave up his casual pose. He leaned closer to Kelly. His eyes seemed sympathetic, but his voice held no note of apology. "You can call it a stunt if you like.

I'd like to call it a special event. Gilda's appearance is changing for the better. We agree on that! Why not capitalize on it? Let the audience know in advance that the change is coming. Many people dream about such a fuss being made over them. Let these viewers identify with Gilda as a normal woman trying to look her best.''

"In other words, a show hosted by Gilda, starring Gilda and about Gilda. What an ego trip! She'll be impossible to deal with after that. I can barely get her to prepare properly for each show now."

Justin shook his head. "It's just one show, the beginning of a newer image. You didn't want to continue with the old one."

"I wanted less attention on it! If people tune in only to see Gilda, they'll tune out when they tire of her as a personality. I've seen dozens of talk shows go that way."

"That won't happen," Justin said confidently.

Kelly folded her arms. "Why not?"

"Because you're still producing the show, that's why. The quality you bring will hold viewers."

Kelly exhaled a short, doubtful sound. Justin's compliment may have been sincere, but his timing smacked of skillful placating. "That's nice to hear. Gilda just told me that she's going to get more involved in the production of the show. We're going to do more 'touchy-feely' shows. You know, the ones that have to do with feelings and emotions, not issues. That way she can thrust her feelings into each situation and really bond with our guests." She unfolded her arms. "Justin, I don't feel in control of this show anymore."

He gently put his hand on hers, but she didn't react. "Kelly, to you, control is total control. The host, the topics, the guests—everything has to be your call. Television is a collaborative business."

"I know that," she snapped, stung by his comment. "But before you came there hadn't been any executive producer for the longest time. I had the whole responsibility for shaping the show."

He squeezed her hand. His eyes were kind and she felt their warmth. "I know the responsibilities, both personal and professional, that you've shouldered these past few years, but I'm here now. Personally I want to be a part of your life. Professionally I have to be. That's reality. But I know we can work together to make *In the Know* a bigger success."

Kelly bit her lip. "Justin, I may find it a bit...difficult to give up control over the show, but that's because I care so much about it. The reality of the situation, to me, is that Gilda isn't national syndication material. She's too unfocused, too apt to wing it unless she's very carefully prepared."

"Then we'll prepare her. First-rate preparation— from experts—is what I've been talking about! With the proper reshaping Gilda will become a very marketable personality. Syndicators will be knocking down our doors."

For all his savvy and power, Kelly felt curiously frightened for Justin at this moment. "Depending so much on a manufactured image is risky," she told him quietly. The word she'd almost used was *irresponsible.* "You're too confident that what you hope will happen, will. Television isn't all fabricated images and exaggerated emotions. I want this show to be a success, too, but my definition of success is different from yours. Ratings and syndication dollars can't be the only measure of success."

He looked at her curiously. "I didn't expect you'd take to this image change right off, but isn't our personal definition of success the same? Don't we want the people we support to have the finer things in life?"

She gazed at his introspective face. "If by finer things you mean love and attention, emotional security and confidence, then, yes. That's what I want for Sylvie. Isn't that what you want for Tommy?"

Justin's eyes softened. "Yes."

"How are you two doing?"

He smiled. "We're doing much better, thank you. Saturday seemed to break the ice, and now at least we're talking. I made him a promise that I'd fly to Chicago next weekend."

"Oh." Kelly had had some erotic plans for then.

"But," Justin said, bending his head to kiss the nape of her neck, "Tommy's coming up the weekend after that. I think he liked you, Kelly. The three of us will have a lot of fun, and then, in the evening, the two of us will try to find something to amuse ourselves."

"Well, I'm glad you're getting along better." Although she was sincerely happy that Justin and Tommy were on better terms, she suspected her inclusion in their itinerary might not go over as well with Tommy as Justin thought. She got up from the couch. "I should go see about today's props. When exactly will Gilda's transformation be revealed?"

"I figure in about two weeks."

"And its title?"

"'All about Gilda.'"

CHAPTER EIGHT

"ISN'T THIS EXCITING?"

"Oh, Peg, not you, too!" Kelly looked in exasperation at her associate producer.

Peg emitted a throaty chuckle. "I'm sorry, Kelly, but 'All about Gilda' is sort of like a Cinderella story. I mean, look at the dress she's going to wear today for the big show. It's incredibly beautiful. Two weeks ago Gilda wouldn't have been caught dead in something so classic."

"Well, that's true," Kelly said, making sure the dress hung properly on the hanger. They were standing in the downstairs dressing room. "Gilda would have said, 'This dress belongs on a Brahman dowager with varicose veins who sits around all day clipping coupons.'"

"As if Gilda doesn't have every dime she ever earned," Peg remarked.

"No," Kelly said. "I think she's done some investing in furs."

They both laughed. Peg said, "It's kind of ironic, don't you think, that Gilda has voluntarily given up wearing her flashy furs because Justin says they won't go with her more, hmm, scaled-down image?"

"Peg, a lot of things in the past two weeks have struck me as ironic, perhaps even a little absurd."

"A lot's changed," Peg agreed, looking at the dazzling display of new, very expensive cosmetics that lay on the dressing room table.

"I wish I could say for the better," Kelly said.

Peg picked up a wrinkle-filler cream. She tried a little near the corner of her eye. "Okay, so this new image is a little fake, but it's also sort of exciting. And...I wonder if Gilda's makeup artist would give me some pointers."

"Just tell him what image you want," Kelly murmured, picking up her notes.

"A vamp," Peg said decisively, gazing into the mirror. "I definitely want to be a vamp. We *all* want to be something we're not."

The remark made Kelly glance at *her* reflection. The delicate folds of her midnight-blue dress accentuated her tiny waist, slim hips and full bosom. Two months ago she wouldn't have worn something so decidedly feminine. Two months ago she wouldn't have considered sexy lingerie as a staple of her wardrobe. Justin Benedict's entry into her life had wrought all this reassessment. He'd seen in her something she'd hoped he would, not what she *appeared* to be, but what she *wanted* to be—a sexy woman.

Today marked the unveiling of another woman's transformation—Gilda's. Kelly felt an uneasy parallel with Gilda. Each of them was changing, shedding one image for another, and largely due to Justin. The difference, Kelly thought, was that her change was real.

She left the dressing room with Peg still frowning in the mirror at her unvampish face.

Two weeks had passed since Justin had proposed "All about Gilda." Larry had given his blessing to the idea, and Gilda, well, Gilda had actually shed tears of happiness.

A huge brainstorming session was held to discuss the special show. Larry, Gilda, Justin, Kelly and Peg gathered in Justin's office to decide the parameters of Gilda's new image. Just how homey and down-to-earth did they want Gilda to become? What new look should she have and which experts should handle which changes? Lastly, how should this exciting new Gilda be shown to best advantage on the "All about Gilda" show? Justin listened to everyone's ideas, but when the session was over, Kelly noticed, Gilda's new image essentially reflected his viewpoint.

Against Gilda's wishes, Kelly was picked to oversee the cosmetic and wardrobe changes.

"You'll have me wearing suits," Gilda moaned.

Kelly smiled at this remark. "Gilda, I'm calling two very prominent Boston designers today. I'll explain what we're doing, what image we want and ask if we can see a selection of suitable possibilities. If we like what we see, I'll negotiate to get your outfits loaned to us in return for a promotional announcement at the end of the show."

"Who'll choose the outfits?" Gilda asked.

"We will."

"What if *we* disagree?"

"Then Kelly makes the final decision," Justin interjected. "But I'm sure you two will come to a consensus on your clothes as well as the cosmetic changes in your appearance."

That comment spurred a very heated discussion on the extent to which Gilda would change her appearance. A new hairdo, a new hair color, a new makeup job—these were givens. But Gilda wanted more extensive changes. She talked of having "what women dream of," in other words a massive tightening, tucking and overall reshaping of her body. She threw around such terms as *abdomenoplasty* and *liposuction* as if they were religious events rather than a tummy tuck and fat suction. With absolutely no embarrassment she waxed eloquently about the breast size she wanted and the pert nose she'd always thought she deserved.

It was a very interesting spate of self-revelation, Kelly thought. At the station's expense Gilda wanted to be reborn as her alter ego, Gilda the beautiful. She had somewhat misinterpreted Justin's description of her makeover and came to this realization with reluctance. First of all, Larry refused to authorize the thousands of dollars it would take to accomplish this overhaul. Secondly, the "All about Gilda" show was scheduled for two weeks from then and plastic surgery took time.

Some of the glow Gilda had had at the beginning of the meeting faded at this refusal. Kelly felt an odd flash of compassion for her. Obviously Gilda had been far more insecure about her looks than she'd previously let on.

"What about collagen injections?" Kelly asked.

"They don't always last," Gilda responded, but she looked at Kelly with new respect.

"What are collagen injections and how much do they cost?" Larry asked, his calculator poised in his hands.

"They're injection treatments designed to fill in facial scars and smooth wrinkles," Gilda explained, as if giving a lecture. "The procedure is done in a doctor's office, and the results can be seen right away."

"How much does it cost?" Larry repeated.

"I could get estimates," Kelly jumped in.

"I *have* estimates," Gilda replied, to some laughter.

During the rest of the meeting, other responsibilities were divvied up. Justin announced that he would oversee the reshaping of Gilda's host image, staving off any discussion of it. Larry would get the board's approval for expenses, and Justin would produce the "All about Gilda" show. Kelly hadn't wanted to produce it, but instinctively disliked relinquishing any producing responsibilities.

Walking to the set now, Kelly reflected on the craziness of the past two weeks. Producing the daily shows plus overseeing the "new look" had been exhausting and time-consuming. She and Justin stole away moments to be together. In his arms, however, her energy came back.

Not that she didn't worry about the show. She did, but her concerns were muted by other conflicting emotions—her exhilaration of having a love life and her worry over Sylvie's.

Sylvie had been delighted that Kelly's romance with Justin had blossomed. Even though Kelly had never stayed out all night, she suspected that Sylvie guessed the intensity of her relationship with Justin. Sylvie was amazingly tolerant of Kelly's many recent absences, even getting Kevin to take her to skating lessons. Despite his cheerful assent, Kelly was mistrustful of him and concerned over the increased amount of time the two teens were spending together.

Sylvie had wanted to come to the "All about Gilda" show. The promotions were all over the tube, she'd told Kelly. It would just mean cutting gym and study hall. Wouldn't Kelly give her permission? Kelly had given in, saying that after the show the two of them would go out for a late lunch and really talk.

Walking onto the set always gave Kelly a measure of peace. She walked to the cobalt-blue couch and sat down. Rows of tiered chairs spread out in front of her. Three cameras were positioned near the raised platform where she sat. Silently the metal machines waited for an image to reflect. Above, dozens of lights were suspended from the ceiling. Their combined power warmed the set. In two hours they would illuminate the new Gilda for the public.

Kelly felt uneasy. Overseeing Gilda's new physical appearance hadn't made Kelly feel as in control of it as she'd expected. Granted, the changes she'd implemented made Gilda look more tasteful, although Gilda had fought some of her decisions. And deep down, Kelly was convinced, the star still wanted to look like one.

But creating the new Gilda hadn't meant merely sprucing up or toning down the old one. Kelly had, in effect, created a new character, one that wouldn't blend in with the show but stand apart—or worse—above it.

"I think you should host the show."

She glanced toward the back of the studio. Smiling, Justin walked up the middle aisle. He sat down next to her.

He smelled so clean and piny fresh. His blue eyes twinkled with good humor and excitement. He wore a handsome pearl-gray herringbone suit with a white carnation in his lapel.

Kelly waved her hand dismissively. "I'd be a lousy host. Too opinionated."

"You?"

"Hard to believe, isn't it?"

"A tad. Mmm, I like your new dress," he said, giving her the once-over. "Is this the new Kelly?"

Kelly tried to smile. "Justin, don't joke about that."

"Okay, okay, bad choice of words."

"You joke about everything."

"You worry about everything."

"Like what if Cappy walks in here to adjust a light and sees you holding my hand."

He let go of her hand but said, "I'm nuts for you, Kelly Ferris."

She met his gaze with equal intensity. "And I'm nuts for you, Justin Benedict."

They sat there, staring at each other, not touching. But if someone had walked in, Kelly thought, they couldn't have missed the emotion passing between them. He unbalanced her so, but in a good way. She did worry too much, and Justin was adept at liberating a more spontaneous, playful side of her.

That playful side had been submerged by two years of heavy responsibilities. She'd even convinced herself that she didn't need the carefree, uninhibited aspect of her personality. Then Justin had arrived and tapped this underground spring. With him she expressed all facets of her nature. The feeling of release was wonderful.

Not that she saw him away from work as often as she'd like. Producing "All about Gilda" had fairly evaporated his free time. To make matters worse, Kelly had trouble accepting how important the show had become to Justin. After initially claiming that it was just "one show," he now saw it as the major building block in the evolution of Gilda's image.

Kelly broke the silence. "Did you want to see me about any last-minute details for 'All about Gilda'?"

Justin ran his fingers through his hair. "No, I came looking for you for another reason."

The answer surprised Kelly. Justin had been obsessed with the show lately. What else could be on his mind with less than two hours to airtime?

"It's about Tommy," he said. "He didn't go back to Chicago on Sunday."

Her expression relaxed. "Well, that's great! A longer visit. Does he like the crayons and coloring book I gave him?"

"Does he! I thought *I* spoiled him. How many crayons were in that box you gave him?"

"A zillion."

"Well, puce is a crucial color," he said. "But Tommy's artistic ability isn't what I want to talk about." He hesitated. "Tommy's having trouble at kindergarten."

Kelly's easy smile vanished. "What kind of trouble?"

"There's a bully in his class. Tommy nearly got into a fight on Friday. When I picked him up on Saturday, he was still upset about it."

"Justin! Why didn't you call and tell me? Oh, poor Tommy. I know just how he feels. Because I was so small as a child, a bully once picked on me, too.

Where's Tommy now—at his day care? I could call him and make him feel better.''

It was so like Kelly, Justin thought, to offer help immediately. ''All about Gilda'' aired in ninety minutes, but Justin knew Kelly would have offered to call five minutes before airtime. ''Actually, Tommy's in my office right now.''

''Alone?'' Usually a neighbor of Justin's, a Mrs. Bannon, baby-sat for Tommy.

''No, Sylvie came in, looking for you. She said she'd keep an eye on him until Mrs. Bannon came to pick him up. I thought it was finally time he saw my office. I also showed him the set.''

Kelly stood up. ''I'll go talk to him now.'' She started to leave.

''Kelly, wait!'' Justin called out. ''I have more to tell you.''

''Tell me after the show,'' Kelly replied, not breaking stride. She was off the set before it occurred to her that perhaps she should have stayed. Justin had looked so disappointed. But what else could he have told her that was more important than a matter involving his son?

As she passed the *In the Know* office, she heard the unmistakably smooth tones of Kevin Lucas. What was he doing here? She peeked in.

Kevin was holding court. That was the only way Kelly could describe it. The show's two female work-study students were hanging on to his every word.

''I totally agree,'' he said earnestly. ''Birth control today *should* be the man's responsibility as well as the woman's.''

"For sure," Nina, the sophomore from Boston College, agreed. "I mean, God, you are, like, the first boy I've met who really feels that way."

"Well, I do," Kevin said, flashing perfect white teeth.

"What college do you go to?" Margie, the freshman from Suffolk University, asked.

"Um, Harvard."

Liar! Kelly fumed.

"Really?" Margie asked.

"Yeah," he said, "I have a sweatshirt in my car."

"Which car?" Nina loved fast cars. She had told Kelly that many of the significant events in her life happened in cars.

Kevin walked over to the window and pointed. "There, the black BMW."

The two girls joined him. "God, like, what a righteous car!" Nina exclaimed. "I'd love to see it."

"Well, maybe I could give you a ride in it," Kevin said sweetly.

Kelly had had enough. "Why, Kevin, what a surprise to see you."

All three turned around in surprise. "Nina, Margie, why don't you check with publicity and get me a head count of who's coming from the press?"

The girls dutifully left the office. Nina shot back one wistful look at Kevin. Kelly stared at him with less affection. "Harvard?" she asked softly.

He shrugged and smiled sheepishly. "I *will* be going there."

"By then Nina will only be interested in seniors."

"Hey, I like older women."

The odd way he said it, followed by a quick wink, sent cold prickles down her head and neck. "What do you mean by that?"

He laughed. "I mean, I like women. I like talking to them. In fact, I think I'll go see my favorite woman right now."

Kelly smiled coldly. "That's where I would have expected you to be."

The two of them walked silently to Justin's office. Kelly had now witnessed Kevin lie, extend an invitation to take a girl other than Sylvie driving and make a veiled pass at herself. But would Sylvie believe such a story? Kelly suspected not. Kevin hadn't actually made a date with Nina, and pretending to be a college man probably wouldn't upset Sylvie as much as the lie upset Kelly. Finally, that he'd made a pass at herself was just one of those awful, instinctive feelings, and Sylvie simply wouldn't believe it. Telling Sylvie might produce a retaliatory anger, propelling the girl farther into Kevin's arms. How could Kelly hurt her sister without actual proof of Kevin's wrongdoing?

Sylvie was advising Tommy on crayon selection when they walked into Justin's office.

"Look who I ran into," Kelly said.

Sylvie glanced quickly between her boyfriend and her sister. "Kelly," she said, "um, isn't this great? I told Kevin that I was coming today, and his parents allowed him to come, too!"

Kelly wondered if they knew anything about it, but said nothing. Tommy was wearing blue-and-white overalls with a white turtleneck. He smiled when he saw her. "Kelly, look!" He flipped to the front of the book. "I colored this for you."

It was a picture of a swan. But not just any swan. This swan had a pink body gliding effortlessly in a blue-and-violet lake, surrounded by rainbow-colored vegetation.

"How lovely!"

"And I colored this for Daddy." He proudly showed her his progress in the book. As he talked, she sat down next to him and put her arm around him. Sylvie and Kevin slipped out of the room.

Tommy didn't shrug off her arm as he had when they first met. They were friends now. The silent, sullen little boy turned out to be quite a talker. Like his father, Kelly thought wryly.

He chattered on about his pictures. Kelly admired one and suggested that he take it to school for show-and-tell.

Tommy fell silent. "I don't like school anymore," he finally said.

She ruffled his hair. "I didn't like my kindergarten, either. Some big bully kept picking on me."

He looked up at her. "A bully?"

"Yeah," she said, "a mean boy named Bernard. He picked on me because I was the smallest person in our class. Actually, he didn't just pick on me. He was mean to the whole class."

The remark seemed to strike a chord with Tommy.

"There's a boy in my class who picks on everybody, too!"

"So I asked my dad what to do," Kelly went on, "and he said that the only way to deal with a bully was to stand up to him."

"That's what Daddy told me!" Tommy said, becoming more animated. "So I did."

"What happened?"

"He tried to hit me, but the teacher stopped him."

She smiled at his little face. "That was still a brave thing to do! I bet the other kids weren't as brave as you."

He smiled and ducked his head.

"And I bet when you go back, he won't bother you again."

He looked up with a complacent expression. "I'm not going back."

"You're going to a new kindergarten?" Kelly thought this solution was rather drastic. Once a bully met his match, he usually left the person alone.

"Uh-huh, in Boston."

"In Boston?" Kelly was confused. At that moment an elderly woman with a kindly face came into the office. "Hi, Mrs. Bannon," Tommy said. "Look what I drew."

Mrs. Bannon squinted at the drawing and chuckled. "Mighty fine, Tommy. I just saw your daddy and he says you're to go home with me now. Oh, hello, Kelly."

"Hi, Mrs. Bannon." Kelly escorted Tommy and his baby-sitter to the front door and then went searching for Justin—and some answers.

He was still on the set, talking to the director. Technical people had begun milling around. The show was less than an hour away, and last-minute details were being attended to. Several people called out questions to her. A private talk would have to wait.

She was directing the proper placement of all the flowers that decked the set when she heard, "Justin, aren't I tastefully gorgeous!"

Kelly turned to see Gilda coming out of a side entrance. The host barely acknowledged Kelly, sweeping past her to give Justin an enthusiastic hug.

He disentangled himself, then held her at arm's length to inspect her hair. "Perfect! Now the world will see how gorgeous your hair really is. And the color is so flattering!"

He motioned Kelly to join them. "Come see Gilda's hair." Kelly walked over and stood awkwardly while Gilda gazed worshipfully at Justin.

"Oh, Justin, I'm so excited," Gilda gushed. "This is the beginning of something wonderful."

"I hope so," he said. "We've sure worked hard enough for it."

"And I've got you to thank," she said. "I owe you everything."

"Now, Gilda..."

"I do. I really do."

Kelly felt unimportant, or worse, invisible.

Gilda took Justin's hands in her own. "You saw something in me that I hadn't seen. Something within me that your insight liberated."

The words hit Kelly like a sharp wind. Justin seemed embarrassed by Gilda's tribute, but pleased that she was in such a happy mood. "Gilda, all I saw was your potential."

"To be a success," she said, "to be really famous."

Fame—Gilda's ultimate dream. Being a success to Gilda meant public celebrity, impersonal adulation. These ephemeral conditions never impressed Kelly, and she thought they meant little to Justin. Still, the other aspects of success, the power and the money, he did want.

With a cold flash of pain she saw the two of them fuss over each other. Never had she felt like such an outsider.

"Kelly," Justin said, "having Gilda wear a wig last week was inspired."

"We couldn't have our viewers see Gilda's new hairdo before the big show, could we?" she said. "It's a little fuller than we originally agreed on."

Gilda touched the top of her hair lightly. "Raphael and I decided that more fullness was needed."

Kelly and Justin exchanged looks. "If you want to change the style we decided on, okay," Kelly said, "but we've paid experts quite a bit of money to create your new look. Why tamper with success?"

The last sentence got Gilda. "I can comb a little of it out. Is Bobby waiting to do my makeup?"

"He should be. It's forty minutes to airtime."

"Oooh, I better go." Gilda gave Justin's hand a goodbye squeeze and then she left for the dressing room.

When the door to the studio had closed, Kelly said, "If the new Gilda is a success, she'll stop listening to anything we say."

Justin shrugged confidently. "We helped create the look. She'll always remember that."

"Did the monster thank Dr. Frankenstein for his look?"

"I don't get the comparison."

"You will. Now let's get this show on the road."

The excited studio audience started filling their seats at ten minutes before one. Spotting Kelly with a clipboard, one young man called out, "Are you the new Gilda?" Kelly shook her head. "Aw, too bad," the guy responded. Several people laughed, including Sylvie and Kevin, who gave Kelly another one of his winks. Kelly glanced to see if her sister caught this, but Sylvie's loving smile of support was on Kelly.

Peg Lanihan tapped her shoulder. "We're ready backstage. All the guests are here, the tapes are cued up and Gilda is fully assembled."

Kelly managed a brief smile. "I should go see the finished product. She might need a small adjustment."

"Why?" Peg asked flippantly. "Justin's there."

The remark didn't improve Kelly's mood. She entered the dressing room and saw not only Justin but also Bobby Fallon, a makeup artist in his mid-twenties. Bobby dabbed Gilda's nose with a spongy material and then gave her a last-minute dusting of translucent powder.

Gilda gazed into the mirror. "Do I look classy and elegant but nonthreatening? Would the average woman trust me with her husband?"

Bobby and Justin laughed. "You're definitely a threat to any woman over forty," Bobby said.

He'd meant it as a compliment, but Kelly saw Gilda blanch slightly. The expression conveyed her true feelings. Gilda still wanted to look glamorous. The image before her was far more low-key and unalluring than she liked. Wisely Justin didn't respond to the comment.

Gilda shrugged. "Oh, well, who needs glamour? This image is going to make me rich and famous!"

"Hold that thought for the next hour!" Justin encouraged her. "Peg will come get you when we're ready. Good luck!"

Kelly turned to follow him out. "You look very nice, Gilda."

"Uh-huh," Gilda replied, nibbling on a perfectly lacquered nail. She abruptly stopped and sighed. "It's hard to chew on these damn fake nails," she moaned.

"The price of success," Kelly murmured, although she had to admit that, physically, the new Gilda was a change for the better.

From her new hair color down to her modestly heeled shoes, Gilda radiated an understated style. Gone were the platinum highlights, the miniskirts, the spiked heels. In their place was a hair color that flattered Gilda's complexion and a style that fitted the shape of her face. Due to the collagen injections and facials, Gilda's wrinkles had been minimized and smoothed out. Her makeup no longer looked as if it had been put on with a spatula. Through subtle, expert application her delicate features were accentuated, not hidden. Two weeks of steady eating had added welcome fullness to her cheeks and some roundness to her thin frame.

Gracing this frame was a full-length swirl of forest-green silk. The simplicity of the dress had made Gilda frown, but in the spirit of creating a new, successful image she had contained her distaste.

The entire effect was remarkable. Gilda really looked different. Would the studio audience be as impressed?

THEY WERE, thanks in part to Justin's shrewd pacing of the show. He didn't bring Gilda out right away. Instead, he had the station's entertainment critic come out and do a funny narration to a video called "The Gilda Simone Story." As assembled by Justin, this clever video skimmed the highlights of Gilda's life, culminating in her present position as host of *In the Know*. Photos abounded of her brief Hollywood career, with amusing pictures of Gilda as a starlet.

The intended effect was to convey a feeling of self-deprecating honesty. Gilda was depicted as a good sport, and even more important, an average person whose life had the same ups and downs as her viewers.

The video worked like a charm, putting the audience in a good mood and creating a sympathetic atmosphere for Gilda's entrance.

And what an entrance it was! After a humorous announcement that the reporter was going to "review" Gilda's new look, the show's theme music came up, and then Gilda made her entrance.

There were awed gasps from the audience, followed by thunderous applause. Smiling broadly, Gilda did a 360-degree turn for the audience before settling down on the couch. The critic gave Gilda's new look "four stars."

What followed after that, and for the rest of the hour, was a detailed description of the makeover journey. As adroitly scripted by Justin, Gilda confessed that her mature years had crept up on her. But, by golly, accepting that didn't mean she had to look like Methuselah!

So Gilda described her quest for a new look, confiding that, yes, the station had paid for all the experts. Who else had that kind of money?

Using the videos that Justin had made of her visits to the plastic surgeon and her arduous but heroic weekend stay at a fitness spa, Gilda talked about her need to look and feel her best. She brought out all the experts who discussed which makeup looked best for which age group, which fashions flattered the mature woman and why plastic surgery should no longer be considered frivolous.

"It's as much a part of good grooming as a manicure," one doctor said.

Throughout all the advice Gilda maintained a warm, intimate relationship with the women in the audience. She joined them midway in the show to get their questions for the experts. They nodded sympathetically when she confessed her fears about her looks, and smiled in agreement when she admitted that all the recent pampering was "delicious."

It was a masterful performance. At the end, when the audience gave Gilda a standing ovation, Kelly knew that Justin's creation had clicked. The overnight rating would be the real judge and jury, but if the studio response was any indication, the rating would be great.

Kelly watched as well-wishers gathered around Gilda, congratulating her. Justin joined her at the edge of the crowd. The heightened color in his pale olive skin and his wide grin proclaimed his opinion.

"Now Gilda belongs to the ages," Kelly intoned.

"It did go well, didn't it?" he said, missing her sarcasm. "I wonder how long she'll be mobbed."

"I wonder, too. We have to go over tomorrow's show."

Justin glanced briefly at Kelly and then back to the tumultuous scene. "Don't give her the research and notes until tomorrow," he ordered. "Today has been a very big day."

Kelly's mouth dropped open, but Justin didn't notice. He was still gazing at the success of his brainchild. "To quote you," she said, "'This is just one show.' Life goes on." Even as she emphasized this, however, she felt that an ominous turning point had taken place. "Tomorrow's show requires homework."

"Then I guess Gilda will have to cram," he said. "She's throwing a small dinner party tonight at Maison Française."

This was the first Kelly had heard about a party. "Are you invited to this dinner."

"We both are."

"I don't recall receiving an invitation."

He looked at her fully now, his face quiet and sympathetic. "We're *both* invited. I couldn't celebrate without you."

Justin's well-intentioned remark unfortunately confirmed Kelly's suspicion. She hadn't originally been invited. Gilda didn't want her there. The new Gilda that Justin had invented was showing her true colors. Kelly stared at the excited crowd. *I helped create her, too,* she admitted honestly. *I wanted her to look more professional. I should have known that Justin's shrewd packaging of Gilda's image would create changes that would go more than skin-deep.*

Now an entity existed called the New Gilda. This creation wasn't real, but that didn't matter. If it worked—in other words if the rating increased—then this bogus "best friend" of viewers everywhere would gain power within the show. The realization pierced Kelly like a sharp needle. *In the Know* wouldn't be a public affairs platform anymore. It would become a star vehicle.

"C'mon," he said, "let's go celebrate."

Celebrate what? Kelly asked herself. She felt Justin's hand squeeze her shoulder lightly. What did all this mean for their future? Would Kelly's clout be slowly eroded, perhaps to the point where she needed Justin not only to get dinner invitations, but to get any ideas past Gilda?

Kelly looked at his handsome face, so pleased now in the flush of success. He would go to bat for her. He believed in the quality of her producing. But how would it look for an executive producer to protect a producer—especially if it came out that they were romantically involved? Would anyone believe it was because of her professional ability?

"I don't know if I feel like celebrating," she said. "You go without me."

He smiled tentatively, "Actually, I thought we could celebrate something besides 'All about Gilda.'"

"I'm all for that."

"Tommy's going to be living with me for a while."

So that was what Tommy meant when he'd said his new kindergarten was in Boston! "Oh, Justin," Kelly said, "is the situation at Tommy's school that bad?"

"No, no. That's not the reason. I was planning on telling you earlier, but you wanted to talk to Tommy. No, this is good news! My ex-wife Elaine has been offered a once-in-a-lifetime research grant, but it involves four months of study overseas. She didn't feel it was right to take Tommy out of the country, and since she was unsure of my commitment to parenting—" Justin paused and glanced away "—she assumed she'd have to turn it down. It's something she's always wanted. She...she gave up a lot to follow me around from one station to another. Now she has her chance, but she was worried about Tommy."

He moved closer to Kelly. His face reflected a deeper happiness than the satisfied smile he'd worn after the show. "I immediately knew the solution. Tommy would come and live with me. We're practically back to our old relationship. He wasn't really mad at me, just angry that I'd left. And a change from his present kindergarten seemed like a good idea right now. I've found a wonderful school here, and Mrs. Bannon will take care of him until I get home."

Kelly stared into his jubilant face. Everything was falling into place for him now—their relationship, Gilda and now Tommy. "Justin, I'm so happy for you! Though maybe a little overwhelmed by all the changes."

"I am, too," he confessed, but then let out a quick, contented laugh. "Tommy knows his mother is coming back, and he's comfortable with the arrangement. I'd love for Elaine to relocate here, though. Lots of research opportunities in Boston. Then we could have joint custody."

"That would be wonderful," Kelly said. She couldn't think of anything else to say. This news, combined with the aftershocks from the show, had thrown her into a state of confusion. So much was happening so fast.

"I knew you'd be glad. And the three of us will have so much fun together! Tommy likes you a lot."

"I like him, too."

"Of course, Sylvie can join us if she wants to. We could give her an alternative to a night with Kevin."

"We'd lose," Kelly said. "She's in love with love." Like me, she thought to herself.

CHAPTER NINE

FILENE'S WAS PACKED with Christmas shoppers, but Tommy refused to leave until he found some saddle shoes. All the five-year-olds in his new kindergarten had them. Couldn't Daddy buy him another pair of shoes?

"He acts like he walks around barefoot," Justin said to Kelly as they maneuvered through the crowds.

She smiled, but knew their next stop would be the children's shoe department. While trekking to it, a woman with a huge shopping bag sideswiped her. As Kelly fell into a rack of polyester jumpsuits, she heard the woman yell, "Watch where you're going!"

Kelly's coat cushioned the fall, but nothing could lessen her embarrassment. She sat sprawled on the floor, a jumpsuit in one hand. She'd grasped it in a futile attempt to stay upright and not be the comic relief so desperately needed in a jam-packed department store two weeks before Christmas.

She failed. Several shoppers sniggered. "Just think," Kelly said to Justin, "that's what this woman is like *during* the season of good cheer."

He laughed, setting down his packages. Kelly felt two pairs of arms help her up—one strong, the other weaker, but no less sincere.

"Did you hurt yourself?" Tommy asked. "Are you okay? Why do these clothes smell so funny?"

His concern elicited smiles from two women who'd witnessed her fall. "What a nice son you have," one of them said.

Surprised, Kelly managed a thank-you. She looked down at Tommy for his reaction, but he was still grimacing over the jumpsuit. Justin winked at her.

His happiness over her growing relationship with Tommy pleased her. Tommy had been living with Justin for nearly a month now. Kelly understood, even liked the inclusion of Tommy in many of the things they did. Justin was making up for lost time. Father and son were getting along much better.

Was it selfish, she thought, to worry if her relationship with Justin was getting lost in the day-to-day of this newly created threesome? Not that the moments alone with Justin were any less electric. On the contrary, Kelly felt herself falling deeper for his wit, his energy and his inexhaustible passion. But those moments seemed to be stolen now from his new responsibilities—responsibilities that had become a part of *her* life. A relationship needed nurturing as much as a child.

"Justin," she asked, hanging up the jumpsuit, "what's on the agenda after saddle shoes?"

"Santa," Justin said. "We must find Santa and tell him what we want."

"Is there anything left to buy?" she asked as he loaded up with purchases.

"What do you mean buy?" he asked. "Santa brings them."

"And then they magically appear on your charge card," Kelly said. She took Tommy's hand. "What do you want, sweetie?"

The recitation of his list lasted until they got to the shoe department. While Tommy's foot was being measured, Justin asked Kelly about her Christmas list. When she told him she wanted a new blender, he refused to buy something so practical. A new silk dress or lace nightgown perhaps.

"And what do you want Santa to bring you?" she asked.

The twinkle in his eyes made her grin. "I'm not sure about December twenty-fifth," he said, "but I know what I'd like tonight."

LEAVING JUSTIN'S HOUSE on that snowy December night was not on Kelly's Christmas list. And she insisted on doing it. Justin begged her not to.

"Come on, stay the night," he said. "It's snowed three inches since dinner. I don't like the idea of you driving in this weather."

"I'm not thrilled, either, Justin," she replied, "but we've discussed this."

He sighed and wrapped a muffler around her neck. "I understand why you don't want to leave a sixteen-year-old alone overnight," he said, "but even Sylvie wouldn't want you to drive in this weather. Come on, stay. Tommy's already used to seeing you here a lot. Why not in the morning?"

Kelly jammed her cap over her hair. "First of all," she said, "I think Tommy needs more time to adjust to me than you think, and it's not just Tommy I'm thinking about. I want to be home for Sylvie."

Justin put his hands on his hips. His broad shoulders and narrow waist defined the enticing lines of his bathrobe. Kelly would have loved to shed her down coat, fleece-lined boots, scarf, hat, gloves, sweater, jeans and the lilac-scented garments underneath and snuggle into Justin's warm bed. Why she refused was becoming a mystery even to her. Sylvie already suspected the intensity of her relationship with Justin. And little Tommy did seem comfortable around her. Every day Kelly found herself drawn more and more to the boy.

She took the car keys out of her purse. Despite her growing affection for him she wasn't sure that Tommy felt totally at ease with her. He still seemed possessive of his father, and this Kelly understood, even if Justin didn't see it. Tommy didn't mind Kelly cooking for him or taking him to the movies as long as Justin came along. When left with a baby-sitter, however, Tommy pouted. So Kelly and Justin didn't leave him often.

"Kelly," Justin said, "it's been nearly a month since we first made love. Sylvie must know."

"She suspects."

Justin waved this away. "She knows." Then he smiled in a tentative way. "I'm not sure I'd care if the world knew."

Kelly gripped the doorknob. "Justin, please don't say that. You know it makes me nervous."

"It will come out inevitably, Kelly."

"I know, but not just yet. We don't need that kind of pressure yet. Or should I say *I* don't need it. The double standard always works in the man's favor."

Justin jammed his hands into his bathrobe pockets. "It'll be an adjustment for both of us."

"Less for you than for me. No matter what people said to my face, they'd gossip behind my back. They'd start to edit what they confided in me, wondering if I would repeat their secrets to you. And Gilda, wouldn't she be thrilled to find out we're lovers?"

He shook his head, as if on this point he was certain. "She wouldn't care who I slept with as long as I can get a syndication deal for her."

Kelly tugged at the fringe of her scarf. Justin was so confident lately. And why not? The past three weeks had been very satisfying for him. From the success of "All about Gilda" to Tommy's extended stay, his worries seemed to be resolving themselves like an episode of a television show that discovers a happy ending after thirty minutes. Kelly was less sure about the future. "You seriously misread her, Justin. Her ego is possessive, dictatorial. Suppose a syndication deal goes through. Will there be a place for me?"

"I'll make sure of it."

"That's it!" Kelly cried. "I don't want my career seen as a result of your protection. I want to be in control of my own career."

"You've been at the station longer than me. People trust you. That doesn't disappear overnight."

Justin rubbed his hands against the soft fabric inside his bathrobe pockets. He always felt uneasy during this kind of conversation. Nothing he could say lessened Kelly's fear of being discovered as his lover. He understood her anxiety on one level, but on another he wondered if her career might not be a safer choice than a relationship with him. Being together was a risk. And she had Sylvie's security to think of.

Justin also suspected that a close association with him would make people think she'd bought into the new Gilda idea—which she hadn't. Kelly closely protected her professional reputation. *In the Know* wasn't just her job; it was her identity. Would she worry so much about the effects of public disclosure that she would break up with him? The thought was scary. He couldn't let her leave so agitated.

"I can't talk to you if I can't see your face," he said, removing her hat and scarf. "And you'll be way too hot if you leave that on." He unzipped her coat. Kelly could see where this was leading.

"Wow," she said, removing her coat, "three times in one night."

Justin laid her coat, hat and scarf on a chair. "The evening's still young, my dear."

"Mmm," Kelly murmured as he wrapped his arms around her and she laid her cheek against his warm chest. "Why is our time together always between one and three in the morning?"

Justin chuckled. "It's when I'm at my best."

"Like Dracula."

He laughed deeply.

"Hey," Kelly complained, "laying my head on your chest when you laugh is like being next to a gong."

He gripped her and refused to let her move. Laughing even harder, he managed to say, "Whaat dooo you meaaaan?" so that his chest hummed loudly against her ear.

"Stop!" she said, although she was laughing, too. "Unhand me, you vile creature of the night!"

"Vould you like a bloody Mary?" he said, imitating Dracula's Transylvanian accent.

"Don't try to butter me up, Count," Kelly said. "I know you want my body, but you'll never have my heart!"

Justin bent down and nipped her neck. "Well, one out of two isn't bad."

They exploded in laughter. Still holding her, Justin moved the two of them to the living room couch and fell onto it. "I vant you," he declared. "Prepare to be transported to another world." He kissed her roughly while extricating his hands from under her.

Kelly adored this playful side of him. At work they were all business, although recently Justin barely tried to hide his affection for her. At home, with Tommy or Sylvie, he was genial, attentive and responsible. Seldom now did she see the teasing, wry side of him that had captivated her in the first place.

Kelly returned his kiss. Justin could get her hot faster than a camera could zoom in for a close-up. Making love would be nice, but what she really wanted was to just talk. She pulled away from his lips.

"What's the matter?" he asked.

"Nothing, I—"

"Don't you want to?"

"It's not that I don't want to. I just . . ."

She pressed her hands against his chest, and Justin let her sit up. He had a puzzled look on his face. "Did I do something wrong?"

"No," Kelly said, smoothing back her hair. "It's just that we seem to make love as a last priority—when all other matters are taken care of. What if I didn't want to always make love late at night? When would we do it?"

"Anytime you say," he insisted. "Stay the night and we'll make love in the morning."

"It would have to be at the crack of dawn," Kelly said ruefully. "You told me Tommy gets up early."

Her tone startled him. "Kelly," he said, "you seem happy to be with the two of us."

"I *am* happy."

"What began as the worst time of my life has turned into the best," Justin said, "largely due to you."

"It's not that," she said, groping for the right words.

Justin slipped an arm around her shoulders. "I realize that I've favored Tommy with my time, but you yourself suggested that he needed special attention in adjusting to living here."

"And I meant it. Special time for just the two of you."

Justin smiled and drew her close. Kelly rested her head on his shoulder. "Darling, Tommy adores you. I can tell."

Kelly had a sinking feeling. "He does like me, but he's also a little jealous of me."

Justin stared at her. "Jealous? That's crazy, Kelly. Didn't we have a great time today? Even if Santa did seem on the thin side."

Kelly smiled slightly. "Yes, we did, but the three of us were together."

"My point exactly!"

"No," Kelly said, lifting her head off his too-comfortable shoulder. "I meant you were there. That's what made Tommy happy."

She felt his hand tighten on her arm. "I feel like I almost lost him," he said quietly. "And that I have only a few months to really get him back."

"I know, darling, but a relationship between two adults needs special time, as well."

"Ah," he said, removing his arm from around her, "you're talking about us."

"I'm talking about the three of us," Kelly said. "Your present relationship with Tommy needs mending and that requires good times just between the two of you. Our relationship is still fairly new, and we need time alone, as well."

"We're alone now."

"To talk," Kelly said dryly, "to sit by the fire with a glass of spiced wine and learn more about each other. Justin, I care about you more than any man I've ever known. You've changed my life. But we still have more to learn about each other, and it's damn hard with group dates. On those I'm not a woman out with her man. I'm a mother out with her brood."

"It's wonderful to see," he said, "and I learn more about you every time."

Kelly gave up. At least for this night she was too tired to pursue the discussion. How could she explain to him, when he was so happy with her and Tommy around him, that adults needed privacy? Being a single father hadn't even sunk in yet. How could it, when she was always there to help?

His relationship with Tommy was on the mend, and he'd taken pains to develop a budding friendship with Sylvie. Kelly appreciated that. But relationships took time. Justin wanted it all, and he wanted it now. His galloping optimism swept away all doubts. Whether it was a pliant host, a contented lover or a happy child, he saw what he wanted to see. His impetuous nature balanced her cautious one, but Kelly suspected that caution was best now.

"I have to go," she said, standing up. "And I've learned quite a lot this evening myself."

Justin seemed relieved that she'd dropped the subject, but he wrinkled his nose. "Not in the mood anymore, huh?"

Kelly leaned over, put her arms around him and planted a steamy kiss on his lips. After what seemed like minutes, she pulled away and said, "Honey, I have a headache."

Justin emitted a short laugh. "I love it. You women are all alike."

Kelly put on her coat. "Yes, we are," she said. "For us, being in the mood doesn't just require opportunity. It requires the proper time, the proper atmosphere."

"And the proper guy," Justin said, rising from the couch. "I do believe he's an important part of the atmosphere."

"You're very quick," Kelly said, smiling. "Don't let anyone ever tell you different."

Justin walked her to the door. "I get the hint. Let me see what I can do about next weekend. Oh, wait, I promised Tommy I'd take him to see a Celtics game. I have PR working on the tickets—three tickets," he hastily added.

Kelly pursed her lips. "Why not just keep them at two?" she asked quietly. "You need time alone with him. And then perhaps we can be alone."

Justin nodded. "I'll work it out. I promise." When Kelly said nothing, he said, "Don't worry! You worry too much." He slipped her scarf around her neck and used it to pull her close to him. To her surprise Kelly detected worry in *his* eyes. "Tell me one thing. Are we crazy about each other?"

He'd asked the one easy question all night. "Yes," she told him.

"Then everything will be all right."

He'd given too easy an answer.

"See you at work on Monday," she said.

He draped one end of the scarf around her neck. "Tommy and I have a date tomorrow at the underwear and sock counter at Filene's."

Kelly opened the door. "But you bought so much today."

He drew up his bathrobe collar against the rush of cold air. "Yes, but what we bought today were essentials like toys. Tomorrow is the unimportant stuff."

Kelly laughed. "Just be sure and get all cotton and—" She stopped. She was falling right into a mommy mode. "You decide. You executive types are paid to make the tough decisions."

He laughed. "See you on Monday."

MONDAY STARTED out splendidly for Kelly. Sylvie announced that Kevin's family was going skiing the next weekend in Vermont and she wouldn't see him. Kelly blessed the snowy New England climate. Anything to put some distance in a romance that she discouraged but was powerless to stop. Kevin's unseemly behavior that morning before "All about Gilda" had Kelly permanently on edge, especially since she couldn't confide this episode to Sylvie.

Besides the splendid news of Kevin's vacation, Sylvie also mentioned that she would be spending the night on Friday at a girlfriend's house.

Kelly immediately saw the possibility of a sleep-over for herself. One whole night with Justin. Perhaps Tommy could be put to bed a little early that night.

When she arrived at her desk, she found roses in a lovely vase.

"Pretty high-class foliage," Peg commented. "It isn't that state senator from the capital punishment show we produced last week, is it? He sure was full of hot air."

"No," Kelly said, removing the card. "They're not from him. I'm sure his wife would object."

The card said "I vant you." Kelly smiled and slipped it into her purse.

"Is it from our illustrious leader?" Peg asked.

"What?" Kelly said, trying not to show her surprise.

"Is it from Justin? Or Larry?" Peg pressed. "Our ratings have gone up. I just wondered if they were showing their appreciation."

"Um, no," Kelly said, relieved. "These aren't a thank-you from management."

"Oh," Peg said, deflated. "I think we deserve a pat on the back. Justin has seemed so terribly pleased with us lately."

Kelly was grateful for the word *us*. "Well, perhaps he's waiting to show us in our Christmas bonuses."

"I can only hope," Peg said. The phone rang and she went to answer it, mercifully ending the conversation. Or so Kelly thought.

"Kelly, it's Justin," Peg called out, "on line four." Kelly was about to pick up when Peg whispered, "Mention that the joyous Christmas season is upon us."

Kelly laughed lightly. "Peg..."

"C'mon, do it," her associate producer pleaded. "If anyone can persuade Justin to do something, it's you. He really likes you. I can tell."

Kelly reddened despite every effort not to. "You overrate my charms, but I'll try." She picked up the phone.

Peg grinned and raised her eyebrows a couple of times in exaggerated support for Kelly's charms.

"Yes," Kelly said as blandly as she could.

"How was your Sunday?" he asked.

"Fine."

"Did you miss me?"

"Yes."

"I missed you. At the underwear counter, cooking dinner, eating—I missed you all day."

"I saw that this morning."

"Oh, you got them?"

"Yes, but you shouldn't have."

"Why not?"

"Did you know that the Christmas season is upon us?" Kelly asked, winking at Peg, who giggled.

"You can't talk?"

"That's correct. It's a warm and generous time. We here in our small office share the Christmas spirit. I was even thinking of doing a show on unusual Christmas gifts."

Peg made an okay sign and danced around their overflowing bookcase.

"Perhaps we could discuss this outpouring of festive feeling in my office," Justin said.

"I think we've done that idea too many times," Kelly said. "A different approach is needed."

Justin was silent for a moment. "How about the first-floor dressing room? No one's due there for a couple of hours at least. I'll meet you there in fifteen minutes."

"Fine, but do think about my Christmas idea. Most people really don't know what to give."

"Fifteen minutes," he said, and hung up.

Kelly replaced her receiver. "I think he got the hint," she told Peg.

"It's a warm and generous time?" Peg intoned, mimicking Kelly, "especially generous." She picked up her clipboard. "I'll go check the bumps."

"Uh, why don't I do that this morning?" Kelly offered. "It'll give you a chance to check on today's music."

"Sure," Peg said. "Checking bumps was never my favorite thing. Thanks."

She handed the clipboard to Kelly. "No problem," Kelly said. Checking the "bumps" or written material that came before the commercial breaks wasn't Kelly's favorite pastime, either, but it would be a perfectly natural reason for being downstairs near the dressing room.

As she walked down, Kelly worried again about her relationship with Justin. If it were made public, it would affect her professional reputation. Her achievements would be compromised by that most damning phrase, *you know how she got where she is.*

She pushed the stairs door open with more force than needed. It wasn't fair! Still, no one had put a gun to her head and said you must have an affair with an incredibly attractive man who makes you feel like liquid fire every time he touches you. But was that what it was—an affair? Justin talked as if she were a permanent part of his life. In her heart she felt she was. But no actual mention had been made to legalize their relationship, and Kelly would have been skittish at such a proposal.

It was all happening so fast—Justin, Tommy, Sylvie, the show. Her well-ordered world was changing faster than she had time to absorb it—or control it. She felt she wasn't connecting with Sylvie anymore. The girl was more agreeable than she used to be but less open. Their heart-to-heart talks had become little more than schedule updates. To Kelly's questions about Kevin, Sylvie merely shrugged and said things were "cool."

Kelly's hold on *In the Know* was suffering, too. She still had trouble with the "new Gilda," a growing monster that she'd helped create. That her competitive edge might have been dulled by personal affection for Justin frightened her.

"Kelly?"

She'd been so lost in thought that she didn't realize she was being addressed.

"Ms. Ferris?" Justin's voice asked again.

Kelly looked up. "Yes, Justin?" she replied in a starchy tone that made him blink.

"Could I speak with you for a minute?"

"I was just about to check the bumps in the computer room," she said.

"You're in the computer room," Justin pointed out.

"Oh," Kelly said, gazing around, "so I am."

"Randy's not back from his break yet," Justin informed her. "So unless you can work the computer, we have a few minutes."

"Fine, if you insist," Kelly said in a monotone.

They walked to the dressing room in silence. Justin turned on the lights and locked the door behind them.

"If I insist?" he asked, puzzled. He was wearing a blue pinstriped suit. The color brought out the azure in his eyes. "Did the flowers for some reason offend you?"

"Of course not," Kelly said, looking around. The first-floor dressing room was a last-minute pit stop for anchors or station talent to touch up their makeup before going in front of the cameras. Since no one used as much makeup as Gilda, the room most reflected her personality. On one wall were pictures of Gilda smiling with various stars who had been on the show. Some of them were smiling, too. Scattered all over the dressing table were the various products designed for her new image.

Gilda usually started her makeup routine about an hour before the show. That was three hours away.

"Why shouldn't I have sent them?" Justin persisted. "I didn't sign my name to the card."

Kelly returned her attention to him. At the sight of his lean frame she wondered why she'd been upset. No, she remembered why, but his presence always unsettled her.

"Discretion," she replied, putting her hands on his lapels. "My getting flowers is unusual."

He gently cupped her cheek. "Now *that* is a crime, but no one suspected they were from me, did they?"

"Peg thinks that a state senator is after me." She slipped her hands under the lapels and onto his shirt.

"Is there a state senator after you?"

"Mmm. Are we a little jealous?"

"You're not referring to that cluck on the capital punishment show, are you?"

Kelly slowly rubbed her hands up and down, feeling the ridges on his chest. "I love it when you're flustered."

"You make me flustered, but I'll do my best not to show it."

He gave her a short, soft kiss. She kissed him back in the same way. For a minute they teased each other's lips, each time threatening to go deeper, but pulling back.

"You make me kee-razy."

Justin looked up. "What did you say?"

Kelly blinked in surprise. "I didn't say anything."

"Oh, Stan, I can't wait." Suddenly the door shuddered as if a body had been thrown at it. Kelly and Justin froze.

"Easy, lover, we can't do it in the hall. What will the neighbors think?" A familiar voice came through the thin plywood door.

It was Gilda! In a shot Kelly and Justin released each other.

"Did you hear something Stanley?" Gilda asked.

"Just my heart," Stanley said in an exaggerated growl. So Gilda was with Stanley Porter, the rugged but dim sound man. "Goes in one ear and out the other" was the general comment on Stanley's professional and mental abilities. However, he was built like Sylvester Stallone.

Gilda laughed shortly. "I've had my eye on you for a long time. I just needed the right opportunity."

"That news bulletin was a lucky break," he said. "They don't need me to do audio for *Teen Talk* yet. I got fifteen minutes. That ought to be enough time."

Kelly and Justin looked at each other. What news bulletin? And how could they find out trapped in this room?

What difference did it make? Kelly thought. The jig will be up in a minute. Gilda will never believe that she and Justin came to the dressing room and locked the door for a programming conference. As if reading her mind, Justin shook his head.

The doorknob wiggled. Then the door shook. "What is it, you sexy fox?" Stanley cooed.

"The door's locked," Gilda said, trying it again.

"Open it," Stanley said. "You have a key, don't you?"

Seconds ticked by as Kelly and Justin held their breath.

"Well...well, damn!" Gilda finally sputtered. "Where is it?"

"Gilda, I'm losing the mood," Stanley said.

"Keep your pants on!" Gilda snapped. "At least for the moment. I might have forgotten to put it in this purse. I was in *such* a hurry to get here early."

Kelly looked at Justin and crossed her fingers.

"I can't find it," Gilda moaned. "I mean, I never lock the dressing room except when I'm in it. C'mon, let's go find a skeleton key."

"Anything you say. I just hope there will be enough time when we find one."

"You leave your time card to me," Gilda said. "*Nobody* messes with me anymore."

"Except me," Stanley said, and then snickered at his own wit.

At the sound of Gilda and Stanley traipsing away, Kelly let out a sigh and collapsed onto the dressing room couch.

"Don't get comfortable," Justin whispered. "She'll be back."

"Yeah, but we won't be here," Kelly said, glancing around to make sure there was nothing of hers or Justin's in the room. Justin cautiously unlocked the door and peeked out.

"The coast is clear," he said, opening the door. With as much aplomb as the two of them could muster, they exited the dressing room.

"I have to check bumps now," Kelly said.

Justin adjusted his tie. "Fine."

Overseeing the bumps gave her a few minutes to think. Justin was getting too reckless. How embarrassing it would have been if Gilda had caught them. What a tawdry way for their relationship to have been discovered. Justin didn't see the risks. He wanted it all—instant family and instant relationship, with everyone knowing.

Couldn't he see that she needed more time? The feelings they shared needed privacy to deepen and grow. Kelly wanted to be absolutely sure before the whole world knew about her and Justin.

Of course, she admitted, there were no absolutes. Life was just one risk after another. Still, moving too quickly scared her. She couldn't dismiss her worries about her future at *In the Know* as easily as Justin seemed to. Until she felt on firmer ground the station mustn't know about their affair.

How painful it would be if the relationship hit a rough patch and her co-workers knew it. She walked to Justin's office. He was alone. She closed the door. "Justin we need to talk."

"Talk?" He rose from his chair and came toward her. "You mean about the show?"

Kelly shook her head. "No, about what just happened."

He cocked his head. "Why? Shouldn't we discuss this at home?"

"We're never alone at home, and when we are I get . . . distracted."

He ran his fingers over the buttons of her blouse. "Whose fault is that?"

Kelly looked at his hand. She knew the power his hands had over her, how they made her feel. She also knew that it was time to talk about her fears, and she was afraid that if she didn't, the reckless way they were conducting their romance would take the decisions away from her.

"Justin, this has got to stop."

CHAPTER TEN

JUSTIN STRAIGHTENED UP. "What's got to stop?"

Kelly spread out her hands. "This sneaking around. We almost got caught a few minutes ago."

"I hate it, too," he said, "but it's what *you* want. I'm not proposing that we blab to everyone about how we feel, but if people should notice—and they will eventually—I'm ready."

"I'm not!" Kelly responded, so forcefully that Justin stared at her. She feared she'd just overreacted, but plunged on. "You jump in where others fear to tread. I know you think it's your strength, but acting impulsively can be hazardous, personally and professionally."

Justin's eyes widened slightly. "Hazardous?"

"Yes. It would be hazardous to disclose our relationship at this point."

Justin folded his arms. "Why?"

"Because there are still areas that need to be worked out," she explained, chilled by his unsympathetic tone. "My relationship with Tommy, for one."

Justin's pinched expression relaxed. He unfolded his arms and took Kelly's hand in his. "Is that what has you worried? Tommy loves you."

"Tommy likes me," Kelly corrected him. She squeezed his hand but let it go. "He doesn't love me yet."

Justin shrugged. "Okay, likes. But you two get along famously."

"He's jealous of my time with you."

"He's a child."

"He's a little boy who doesn't know where he belongs and is unsure of who he can trust. He knows you're a friend, but he isn't one hundred percent certain about me."

"I don't see this."

Kelly sighed. "I know you don't. That's the problem."

"Oh, so I'm the problem?"

His brevity was icy. He leaned against his desk, half sitting, half standing in a seemingly casual pose. His fingers, however, rubbed the edge of table, as if the sharp angle would keep him alert and ready. Kelly felt an awful foreboding. "I didn't say that."

"Is it wrong to see the bright side of things?" he asked. "You see pitfalls where I see possibilities. Too much caution can ruin the moment."

"It's not a 'moment' I'm speaking of. It's considerably longer that I hope these relationships will last. How's that for looking on the bright side? But relationships take time to develop, and the pressure of everyone at the station knowing about ours won't help."

Justin shook his head. "How will it hurt, Kelly? How will Peg knowing affect Tommy? Or Sylvie? You always see problems looming behind every situation."

This observation rankled Kelly. "I think I see reality."

"Oh, and I only see fantasy?"

"Right now, if you think that we're all just one big happy family, I'd say yes."

Justin's blue eyes became flinty. "Your concern for the family is just a cover up. What you're really nervous about is how the disclosure of our relationship will affect you professionally."

"Of the two of us, I'm the only one who has to worry about that." Kelly moved a few inches away. "You know what they say about women who sleep with the boss."

"This isn't some tacky affair."

"Tell that to Gilda if she'd caught us in her dressing room."

"Your paranoia about Gilda—"

"Is justified!" Kelly snapped. "The new Gilda is fast making me nostalgic for the old one. Just yesterday she point-blank refused to do a show on the state's budget crisis."

"She's entitled to make suggestions about the show. Or are you the only one who can guide *In the Know?*"

Kelly exhaled in irritation. "I think I've done my share of compromising—recently. Don't forget Gilda's new look."

"A hell of a job."

"I've come to regret it. I feel Gilda is beginning to spin out of control."

"You mean out of your control."

"Out of yours, too, Justin! You heard what she said outside the dressing room. 'Nobody messes with me anymore!' Do you think you're excluded? We've created a monster, but you don't see it. This... blindness to the dangers of all your risk-taking has me justifiably cautious about declaring our relationship. How could a few more weeks, or months of privacy—"

"Months!" he exclaimed.

"How could it hurt? We need this time to be sure of us."

Justin grew completely still. Irritation had been replaced by a more pensive expression. "I'm sure of us," he said quietly. "Are you?"

This was the moment for Kelly to declare that she was, too. Only she couldn't. Why was it so hard to believe, as he did, that everything would work out all right? Why did her wary nature keep her silent when a simple yes would end the argument? Because saying yes wasn't the truth. She simply wasn't ready for the world to know. Somewhere deep inside her a no formed. It scared her to say it, but it scared her even more not to.

Miserable over the pain she knew her answer would inflict, she said, "I'm not completely sure."

Instantly Justin's face seemed to withdraw into worried lines around his eyes and mouth. He leaned further against the desk, but this time for support. "I...see."

"When was the last time we were alone, completely alone?" Kelly asked, desperate now for him to understand her fears. "When was the last time we talked about just ourselves?" She clasped her clammy hands together. "I'm glad Tommy's here, but I feel we're linked together in your mind."

"That's not so!" Justin said hotly.

"It is. You no longer see me separate from this happy television family you've created in your mind."

He glanced around his office, with its plaques and awards. "I want *you* Kelly. I don't expect us to be a perfect couple. I just want us to *be* a couple. What do you want?"

"More time," she replied.

He looked at her. His face wasn't pleasant. "No, I don't think that's the truth."

"It is so!"

His taut six-foot frame suddenly stood very close to her. "Nope," he said, "you're a coward."

The word stunned Kelly. Of all the descriptions ever said about her, pro and con, that wasn't one of them. "I'm...I'm what?" she exclaimed. "How dare you say that to me!"

Justin waved his hand dismissively, but she could tell that his famous cool had abandoned him. "You can call me rash and impetuous, insensitive to your needs, pushing you into corners you can't get out of, and I can't call you a coward?"

"But you *are* pressuring me with your blind optimism. Pressuring me when I'm not ready. That's what I'm afraid of."

"No!" Justin said, so forcefully that Kelly started. "I'll tell you what you're afraid of. You're afraid that what's between us just might be the real thing. The only problem is that it's going to be messy. Real messy. For example, the children will have to learn to get along, not only with us, but with each other. The possibility that my ex-wife may relocate here, making Tommy a permanent day-to-day reality in my life. Then there's the uncertainty over collaborating with me, your acknowledged lover and boss. Which brings me to our co-workers, who might not be as understanding or professional about it as you'd like, making work a tense place for a while. All these things are conspiring to turn your well-ordered world upside down. And it's one show you can't produce with assurance.''

His words ripped the lid off her temper. "I'm not afraid of these things! I just don't want to have to handle them all at once."

"That's understandable, but life doesn't always deal us the hand we want. I became a single parent and started a new job, damn near at the same time."

"No, you didn't, because you had me to cushion the responsibility."

This comment surprised Justin. "Is that how you see it? I thought you liked getting to know Tommy."

"I do, but in getting to know him I've also taken him to get his booster shot because you had a last-minute meeting, I've helped pick out his new bedroom furniture, I've attended his holiday play where he was a delightful snowflake, and I've been the tooth fairy when you forgot. I've enjoyed all of it. Tommy's such a smart, wonderful little boy, but the added responsibility has me on overload. I'm having trouble dealing with all that's happened in the past few months."

"Kelly, life's events don't happen in single file. Some pile up on one another. Some, like working with you as well as being involved with you personally, are damn inconvenient and risky. But you can't put off handling problems forever."

"Now you're being rash. I mentioned weeks, or maybe a month or two. You're talking forever."

His face softened. "I can't imagine tomorrow without you, must less forever." He reached out and gently stroked her cheek.

The gesture brought tears to her eyes. She gazed into his handsome face and saw the reflection of her own misery. "I think so, too."

"If this is how we feel," he said, grasping her shoulders, "then the hell with everybody else! We'll handle their reactions together."

His face seemed so eager for her to agree. If she gave in, he would put his arms around her and kiss her. She needed those arms. Without them the world was a colder, lonelier place. But this was the wrong move. Kelly just knew it. "Justin, you're pressuring me to do something that I have serious misgivings about. And if I don't say yes, then I'm a coward, running away out of selfishness and fear."

"You can't let the outside world make your decisions for you," he said in a near whisper. "Take the risk."

Kelly felt sick, and suddenly desperately tired. "No," she said, looking down. "It's not the right time."

Justin emitted a small sigh, as if breathing had become difficult. "Will there ever be a perfect time?"

There was no mistaking the anger she heard in his voice. In trying to make him see how she felt, she'd only driven a wedge between them. Well, she was mad, too! How dare he blame all their problems on her supposed lack of nerve. Where was his patience? "I don't know. I need some breathing space."

"How much longer do we sneak around?"

His tone was a slap in the face. Kelly looked at him sharply. "We don't," she said flatly. "When I said breathing space, I meant it."

Justin went pale. "You want the ultimate cop-out," he said, "no relationship at all. I guess it's a good thing I only got two Celtics tickets."

Trembling, Kelly made her way to the door. "I guess so."

She stumbled into the ladies' room. Mercifully it was empty. She grabbed a couple of paper towels and wet them. Pressing them against her face, she tried to regain control of her heart. Thumping madly, it sounded so loud that Kelly wondered why no one was banging on the wall, asking her to keep it down. The cool towels felt wonderful, but she couldn't catch her breath.

She was stunned and dizzy from disbelief. After only a few short emotionally charged minutes, her relationship with Justin had ended. Severed, with venomously cold words. She felt wretched and ill.

As she was taking deep breaths, Peg rushed into the bathroom. "There you are!" she exclaimed. "I've been looking for you everywhere." Peg studied Kelly's pale face. "I see you've heard the news."

"What news?" Kelly asked.

"Fights have broken out in the inner city between a vigilante group and local youth gangs," Peg explained. "I think it's escalating right now into riots."

"Really?" Kelly replied. So that had been the news bulletin. It had seemed so important a few minutes ago. Now she could muster only perfunctory attention. "Has anyone been hurt?"

"Near as we can make out only gang members and a few of the vigilantes have been injured. But the neighborhoods are threatening to explode over this. The Boston Defense League maintains that they have a right to patrol streets, unarmed, as a civilian defense against crime. Local gang members are angry at the group for encroaching on their turf. The police don't want amateurs doing their job, but the neighborhood associations and the elderly claim that the League does deter crime."

"What a powder keg," Kelly said, her interest slowly returning. "What does the mayor say?"

"He wants everyone to stop fighting, first," Peg answered. "But the League refuses to stop patrolling."

"Are they planning to patrol tonight?" Kelly asked. She knew that the cloak of darkness could spell real trouble.

Peg shook her head. "No, the violence today has made them cancel their watches for tonight. But they vow to return to the streets tomorrow night."

At that moment Justin's secretary poked her head in the door. "Justin thought I might find you two in here. He's calling a meeting right now in his office."

Glancing at each other, Peg and Kelly exited the bathroom. Kelly strolled into his office, as if she hadn't just experienced, in this room, one of the worst moments of her life. She tried to compose her face into her standard professional look. She saw that Justin was trying to do the same. She sat down next to Larry Bishop.

"Is this about the Boston Defense League?" Kelly asked.

"Yes," Justin replied tersely. She noticed that he avoided looking directly at her. Was it from dislike or regret? Kelly felt a mixture of these emotions herself.

"We're waiting for Gilda," Larry said. "Luckily she came in early today to prepare for the show. She said on the phone that she'd be right up."

Gilda bounded into Justin's office, looking disheveled. Her hair seemed wilder than usual, and she smelled faintly of after-shave. "Sorry I'm late, but I stopped in the newsroom for any current developments."

"Were there any?" Kelly asked.

"What?" Gilda asked, sitting on one of the chairs.

"Late-breaking facts."

"Oh," Gilda said, "um, no."

Justin flashed Kelly a warning look. She met his glare with a tight smile.

"We're here," he said, "to discuss the situation in Boston. I'm of the opinion that this might make a terrific *In the Know*."

Gilda bounced her fist off the arm of her chair. "I couldn't agree more!" she enthused. "This situation has some wonderful elements that could result in a real breakthrough show for me."

How nice of the community to explode for your benefit, Kelly thought.

"What elements, Gilda?" Larry asked.

"Oh, Lord, they're several," she said, running her hands excitedly over her knees. "Confrontation, violence, crime, outraged victims, frustrated police, baffled politicians, and that most interesting element of all, the gangs. They're frightening, but they're also fascinating. I see the show's focus on them. Who are they? What makes them tick?''

She turned to Kelly. "I'd like to see a whole panel of different gang members, each with their own jackets, or insignias or whatever the hell they wear to proclaim who they are. We'll fill up the audience with them, too. Won't that look wild? Hmm,'' she mused, examining a beige-tinted nail, "Perhaps I shouldn't dress so dowdy for this show. Maybe I'll wear a little leather so the gangs will know I'm simpatico, that I'm—''

"Their best friend,'' Kelly finished. She straightened in her chair. "Now hold on here.''

"What?'' Gilda said, nonplussed at being interrupted. "Don't you want to do this show?''

Kelly could feel all eyes in the room on her, especially the moody stare of Justin. She picked her words carefully. "I think this *could* be a worthwhile show, Gilda, but our focus should be on the community, not the gangs. We should have all the different neighborhood groups on to discuss the situation, plus the police and the Boston Defense League. That way we'll be promoting talking, not fighting. Focus solely on the gangs and we might glamorize them. They aren't model citizens. They're volatile, angry young men. What's to prevent them from fighting on the show? It's live, you know. We can't stop tape if a fight breaks out.''

"Do you think there's a chance of that?'' Gilda asked.

Kelly pointed at her. "You see. You don't want public affairs. You want a public spectacle.''

"Stop being so noble!'' Gilda retorted. "Of course I don't want violence, but I'm not afraid of it. I'd risk a black eye or broken nose to get a memorable show.''

"What would make this show memorable is if we achieved peace in the neighborhoods," Justin said. He fixed Kelly with a cold glance. "But gang participation is a must. They're part of the situation, too."

"I never said they weren't," Kelly replied. "I just don't want them to be the stars of the show. If we create an image of gangs as exciting and glamorous, then we're setting them up as role models for any young person who might be tuning in. That would be irresponsible. I'd rather not do the show than promote that. Besides, some gang members are wanted by the police. How do we know any would come on?"

"They'll come on," Justin said with maddening assurance. "Everybody wants to be famous, even if it's just for an hour."

Kelly returned his frigid stare. "Is that what we're planning to do—make them famous?"

"No," he replied flatly, "but no one will tune in to see only community leaders argue. Gilda's right. The gangs are our key to a successful show. They're different, fascinating and very visual."

"You forgot violent," Kelly said through gritted teeth.

"Sure would be a ratings grabber," Larry said.

"I don't think it would even be that," Kelly replied. "Our viewership spans the state. Most of them aren't as interested in a section of Boston as they would be in, let's say, a makeover show."

"You're so right," Justin said smoothly. "Our broad viewership would be less interested in seeing a show about a local community problem than they would a show about the gangs and a community problem." He smiled. "I never thought I'd hear you speak in favor of a makeover show."

Larry and Gilda laughed. Peg shook her head. Kelly knew that now wasn't the time to force a decision. She quickly cast about for a way to stall. "Look, we've got shows booked this week. If this thing is settled in a day or so, then interest will peak. It will take us a day or two to book the guests, anyway. Why don't we see if the situation continues. We can start talking to the parties involved and see if any of them would consider talking to the others. By Wednesday or Thursday we should know if this is worth the risk."

When she said the word risk, she could have bitten off her tongue. Defiantly she gazed at Justin.

"Oh, by all means, let's give it some time," he agreed.

Only Justin knew what a cutting comment that was. "Yes," she said, "we wouldn't want to be rash."

"But the fighting might be over," Gilda said.

"Don't worry, honey. We'll stay on top of it," Larry promised. "Besides, I don't want to get into a fight with news over territory. Let's wait till Thursday."

KELLY STRUGGLED through the next two days. Her internal tug-of-war left her drained. On the one hand, she was absolutely positive she'd acted correctly in her argument with Justin. *He* was the one who'd gone too far, pushing her to agree with him when it was obvious she wasn't ready. Well, it had been obvious to her. Every time she thought about his insensitive impatience she became livid.

On the other hand, the loss of his intimate presence in her life hurt unendurably. The break couldn't be that irrevocable, she thought. Surely their harsh words couldn't have stopped all feeling.

If Justin had confined his reaction to their fight to cold, clipped conversations, Kelly would certainly have made an effort to bridge the glacier forming between them. But it seemed that he was using the show and his position to make his displeasure known. That Kelly couldn't forgive.

He seemed to take grim satisfaction in the worsening situation in Boston. There had been more fights, some accompanied by looting and arson. The mayor pleaded with the neighborhoods to make peace, but the neighborhoods were divided in what they perceived as the best way. Kick out the Boston Defense League? There would still be gangs. And if someone wanted to patrol unarmed, could they stop them even if they wanted to?

Each day that the tension escalated found Justin champing at the bit to put the situation on the air. Kelly pleaded that the gangs just wanted publicity. Through her community and police contacts she'd managed to reach several gangs. She'd found that there was a disagreement among them as to who would represent them on the air. At least the Boston Defense League had a president. Another problem was getting responsible community leaders to come on and debate the gangs and the League. Many thought the gangs were beneath dealing with.

To all these difficulties Justin turned a blind eye. "We can make it happen," he said. Kelly knew full well that the "we" meant her.

"The other talk shows are taking a wait-and-see attitude," she told him.

"That's why we'll be first," he said.

More and more she saw the show as a dangerous stunt, with community understanding taking a back seat to chasing the almighty rating point. Kelly was under no illusions about how the vote would go on Thursday. She could produce the show, or quit.

The notion popped into her head right before she went to sleep on Wednesday, when she knew the decision would go against her the next day. Could she afford to quit? The idea appealed to her—though not her bank account—until she realized that Justin could use her resignation as one more example of her fear of taking risks. And if the show was going to be produced, she was the best person to do it!

Yes, she would stick around. Someone had to be responsible, although if the show got out of control, it would be Justin's neck, not hers. Despite her anger at him she felt no relief from this fact. Kelly didn't want Justin to be hurt.

Lying in her bed, she wondered what she would do with all the "breathing space" she'd asked for. It seemed impossible that she would never feel Justin's arms around her again or hear his voice whisper witty, wicked things to her at night. Their fight had created a chasm between them. This show was making it deeper and wider.

ON THURSDAY MORNING Kelly filed into Justin's office with Larry and Peg. Considering that the clock read eight-thirty, it was assumed that Gilda would be absent.

Justin looked at Kelly's lovely face. Was it just two days ago that those steel-gray eyes had gazed at him with love instead of barely concealed anger? He felt an infuriating sadness. He hadn't wanted this estrangement. He'd merely wanted to take their relationship to a more open, serious, level. Wasn't that what Kelly wanted? Commit to your child, she'd said. Commit to me. Well he'd been ready to commit, and now she was backing off!

In his gut Justin knew he needed Kelly. And he wondered, deep down, if he hadn't pressured her to divulge their affair to confirm her need for him. But she wanted this "breathing space," and he was going to give it to her, even if he disliked it. He especially disliked her attitude toward the Defense League show. She was resisting it because he wanted it. So much for her much-touted professionalism.

He got right to the point. "The situation in Boston has gotten worse in the past forty-eight hours. The Defense League has been asked to disband in the interests of peace. They're having a meeting tonight to decide. If they break up, we scuttle the idea. But if they don't, we set up a show for Monday with all parties involved."

Kelly spoke up. "If they don't disband, then they'll patrol over the weekend, causing more violence."

"Kelly," Larry replied, "the gangs and the Defense League don't trust the police. Who else is going to get them to sit down together if we don't try? Nothing else has worked so far."

"It's irresponsible to have gang members strutting their stuff on television," Kelly insisted. "There are children at home."

"We'll have Gilda announce a warning that this show is for adults at the beginning of the hour," Justin said.

"Gilda," Kelly moaned softly.

Justin ignored this. "Peg, who has said they'd participate?"

Peg looked at her notepad. "Two gang members, one from the Boston Bullets, one from the Roxbury Warlords, have agreed to be on. The president of the Defense League, Paul Moran, has accepted, as has Reverend Charles Brown from the Boston Safe Community Organization. And I've got a maybe from Agnes Baker, who represents a coalition of the elderly."

Justin nodded. "Good work, Peg."

Peg smiled sheepishly. "Kelly really put this together. You should have heard her talking to the Warlords."

"Did they ask you to join?" Justin asked.

Kelly wasn't amused. "I want no credit for this show," she announced. "Just leave my name off."

She saw Justin frown slightly. He didn't like that. Good. He wasn't going to like the next thing she was going to say. "I also want to bring up another point," she continued. "I think we ought to consider having another host besides Gilda for this show."

"What?" Larry asked.

Kelly held up one hand. "Hear me out, Larry. This will be a delicate show to handle. A lot of preparation will be involved. You know that Gilda likes to shoot from the hip. She rarely reads all the research we give her, and for this show that's a must. More importantly, Gilda likes to inject controversy into even the most innocuous topics. This show will hardly need that. But you heard her on Monday. She *wants* fighting to break out. Her ultimate goal isn't peace in our inner city but a hefty rating and personal immortality. Such an attitude can backfire on the reputation of the show. We're trying to achieve peace with this show, aren't we, Larry? We're not hoping for a brawl, right?''

''Of course not,'' Larry said, straightening his tie, ''but now Gilda *is* the show. We've spent a lot of money for that identification.''

''Who did you have in mind for a substitute?'' Justin asked. So far he'd been strangely calm over her idea.

''Andy Hopkins,'' Kelly replied. ''He's been the reporter covering the story from the beginning. He's also very knowledgeable about the problems in the inner city. I've sounded him out on the possibility of hosting the show, and he's eager for the opportunity.''

''That was rather unwise,'' Justin said, a hard tone to his voice. ''Who gave you the authority to do that?''

Kelly met his cold stare. ''I gave me the authority as producer of this show. I talked with him in confidence, and I made no promises.''

Justin shifted forward in his chair. ''A move like that should have been discussed with me first.''

''And me,'' Larry said. ''What will Gilda say?''

''That's not the point,'' Kelly said, although she knew Gilda's reaction would be volcanic.

''No, it isn't,'' Justin put in. ''The point is that to replace Gilda with another host, even for one day, is a major decision. I should have been consulted.''

Kelly saw Peg and Larry glance at Justin with uneasiness. The tone of his voice, the tapping pencil, the turbulent blue eyes all testified to an inner fury. Kelly realized she'd committed a breach in protocol but felt justified for the good of the show. "Andy could cohost the show," she offered.

Justin dropped the pencil into its holder so hard that it bounced. "*I'll* decide who hosts this show," he snapped, "just like I decided that this show will take place on Monday if the Defense League refuses to disband, as I expect. So talk to me tomorrow with a firm guest list, and assemble the research. Larry, could you stay for a moment?"

She was being dismissed. With as much dignity as she could muster Kelly left his office, followed by Peg. When they were in the *In the Know* office area, Peg said, "Boy, Kelly, replacing Gilda! I sure give you credit for nerve."

Kelly dropped her Defense League file onto her desk. "Do you think I'm wrong, Peg?"

Her associated producer shook her head. "No, but couldn't you have talked with Justin first? He might have been more agreeable to a cohost idea."

"I doubt it," Kelly replied, although she knew Peg was right. Had she gone looking for a fight? Now that she and Justin had merely a professional relationship, had she wanted to test his reactions, probe for hidden feelings?

Peg picked up her stopwatch. "Well, I don't want to be the one to tell Gilda."

Kelly started sorting through her notes. "If Justin decides against it, she'll never know we even considered it."

"Unless Larry spills the beans," Peg said, walking to the door. "He has such a big mouth."

Two hours later Gilda stormed into the *In the Know* office area. She hadn't put on her makeup yet, and curiously, she looked far prettier than when she had it on. Kelly didn't have a chance to tell her that, because Gilda screeched, "How dare you suggest that I be replaced!"

Count to ten before replying, Kelly cautioned herself. "Did Larry discuss the show with you?" she asked blandly.

Gilda dumped her huge purse onto a chair so violently that it flew open. An under-eye concealer and a can of deodorant popped out.

"Yes," Gilda hissed, "he did. Oh, he started off in that oblique way of his. 'Gilda,' he said, 'how comfortable do you feel about the Defense League show?' I said I felt fine, that it would be a cinch. When he continued that line of questioning, I knew something was up. After some subtle threats, he admitted there had been a discussion on who the right host should be, meaning there must have been doubt about me! Now, I asked myself, who would think I wasn't qualified? Certainly not Larry. He swore up and down that the discussion was academic, and he was behind me one thousand percent."

Gilda took off her coat. Underneath she wore a tasteful powder blue knit dress, with low-heeled navy pumps and pearl necklace. Kelly marveled at the new Gilda and how the gracious, bland exterior contradicted the real woman. Right now, however, the true Gilda was coming out.

"So," Gilda continued, "I narrowed it down to you and Justin. Actually, it was no contest. I knew it was you. Admit it! This was your idea."

"I won't lie to you, Gilda," Kelly said. "Although I think you're excellent for some shows, I don't think your talents are specifically suited for this one."

Gilda fanned the air with her hand. "'Specifically suited,'" she mimicked. "Fancy words for saying unqualified. Well, let me tell you, Ms. Ferris. I am the *perfect* person to host this particular show, and do you want to know why?"

"Frankly, no."

"Because I'm not tainted with journalistic pretensions."

Kelly rose from her chair. "Tainted?"

"Yes, tainted. Oh, you can pretend all you want that this show might help the community solve its problem, but deep down our viewers won't tune in to see that."

"You underestimate them."

"I understand them. How many hours does the average home watch television per day? I know it's several. And what with news shows, documentaries, talk shows, special reports, made-for-TV movies with serious themes, viewers are bombarded with *problems*. Oil spills, toxic waste, the ozone layer, child abuse, battered wives, drug addiction, divorce, day-care, poverty, the homeless." She took a breath. "Viewers are *numbed* by the tonnage of depressing facts hurled at them. So, to me, the future direction of *In the Know* is clear. Stop making the viewers think. Divert them with the offbeat and sensational, like the gang show. Make *me* the draw instead of dry topics like taxes. I'll make America love me."

Kelly gagged at the thought. "Gilda, the American public isn't as shallow as you portray them. And talk shows can be more than sensationalistic pabulum. The gang, uh, the Boston Defense League show especially needs a calm hand. Do you know the history of Boston's neighborhoods? Are you aware of the problems down there? If you cater to the gangs, are you prepared for the possible consequences? I mean, will you know how to handle a gang member if he gets out of hand? Think, Gilda!''

For a moment neither spoke, and Kelly had a wild hope that Gilda actually understood.

It was Gilda who broke the silence. "I know what you're doing," she said slowly, "and why you're trying to undermine me. I know what this is really about."

"What?" Kelly asked, disappointed.

"This is about power," Gilda stated, "or should I say the balance of power around here." She took two confident steps forward. "It's shifting away from you, and you can't stand it. Before Justin came here, you pretty much called the shots. But then he and I turned this show around and now *we* have the most say. Being a third wheel must hurt like hell. I figure that's what provoked this unsuccessful little trick of yours."

Shrewdly Gilda had zeroed in on Kelly's deepest fear. Nevertheless, Kelly met the star's smug smile with one of her own. "As hard as this might be for you to believe," she said, "I was thinking about the show, not about myself. And my 'trick,' as you called it, may not have been unsuccessful."

Gilda's smile remained. "I assure you it was."

Kelly shoved her hands into the pockets of her skirt to keep Gilda from seeing them shake. "You talked to Justin?"

"Of course," Gilda said. "He and I are on the same wavelength about the show—about everything, really. This syndication deal may take the two of us to the top. It's you who aren't part of the team anymore."

Kelly struggled to control her face. *Don't let Gilda see that you're stung by this,* she ordered herself. Justin couldn't have decided the host issue without speaking to her. But she remembered that she'd explored the possibility of using an alternate host without consulting him, and perhaps this was the payback. "Oh, I intend to remain part of the team all right," Kelly said as forcefully as she could.

Gilda folded her arms. "That remains to be seen."

Kelly felt a small prickle at the back of her neck. "What's that supposed to mean?" she asked, as if the answer were of small importance.

"It means there may be some changes around here," Gilda said, fingering her pearls. "And I don't mean the replacing of *me.*"

Kelly's mouth went dry. "Oh, there's been some talk about replacing me?" She was grateful to find that her voice remained steady even if her nerves didn't.

"Uh-huh," Gilda said, examining a small snag in her dress.

"Or have you been doing all the talking?" Kelly added.

Gilda looked up. "You'll be interested to know that a suggestion came up recently for you to leave this show from a source that surprised me."

"Who?" Kelly asked, dreading the answer.

"Justin," Gilda replied.

When Kelly didn't speak, Gilda said, "It's just in the talking stage right now, kind of like your idea about replacing me."

"I don't believe you," Kelly said.

Gilda walked to the door. "Ask him," she said, "but if I were you, I'd start taking home personal items from your desk." With her bag and coat in tow, she sashayed out of the room.

Kelly stood rigidly for a minute in case Gilda wandered back to shove in another dagger. When it looked as if she wouldn't, Kelly crumpled into her chair. Her head throbbed so badly that she had to rest it on her desk, cradled in her arms. In the darkness she tried to collect her thoughts, but all she felt was an overwhelming devastation. This couldn't be true. Justin wouldn't! Kelly waited for the tears to fall, but her eyes remained dry. As she recovered from the shock of Gilda's cheerful announcement, she felt anger growing.

How dare he so cavalierly discuss her future—with Gilda no less! He must have known how humiliated she would be to have it divulged like this.

Kelly raised her head. She would make Justin explain. Whether he wanted to or not, whether they never made love again. He would explain what he was trying to do to her.

She stood up and went to the mirror that Gilda had put on the wall for office touch-ups. Looking into it, Kelly composed her face and smoothed back some strands of hair that had strayed from her French twist.

All her life she had waited for someone like him. Her very being resisted the notion that he could be this vindictive. Something inside of her just didn't believe.

She walked down the hall, oblivious to the hellos from various co-workers. A remark she'd made to him earlier in the week kept echoing in her brain: *Tommy... doesn't know where he belongs and is unsure of who to trust.* Kelly felt a sad kinship with Justin's son. Where did she belong? Who could she trust? Was Justin lost to her now? The pain twisted like a slowly tightening knot deep within her heart.

Justin would explain. To her face he would tell her what he was trying to do to her.

CHAPTER ELEVEN

JUSTIN'S SECRETARY was away from her desk, but in any case Kelly had no intention of announcing herself. He might pretend he was busy. She boldly opened the door. Justin looked up from a folder lying on his desk. He was alone.

"What are you trying to do to me?" she demanded, slamming the door.

His head jerked back slightly in surprise. "What?" he exclaimed.

Her barely controlled anger made it impossible for her to sit down. Besides, she felt better standing. "Justin, what are you trying to do to me?" she repeated.

"Do to you?" he asked. "Don't you have that backward?"

Kelly nodded, as if she had expected those very words. "Okay, I realize that perhaps I should have consulted you before talking to Andy Hopkins, but—"

"Perhaps?" Justin's eyes flashed with anger. "Perhaps!" he repeated. "You were way out of line, Kelly. We hadn't even agreed to do the show when you talked to him."

"Oh, we were going to do it," she scoffed. "I could tell your mind was made up on Monday."

"So why not try a little sabotage? Whip Gilda into a frenzy so that we'd skip the show to avoid the aggravation?"

Kelly rocked back on her heels. Surely he knew she wasn't that underhanded, but then she wasn't sure she knew him anymore. "How dare you accuse me of that," she said in a voice roughened by pain. "My talking to Andy might have been premature, but it wasn't sabotage. I was honestly thinking of the show."

Justin's eyes didn't meet hers for a moment. When he replied, his voice was softer. "All right," he said, "perhaps I misjudged your motives. But your idea was presumptuous and you failed to consider the repercussions."

Kelly let out an angry sigh. Now they were getting to it. "I didn't mean for Gilda to know before the issue was decided. *I* certainly didn't tell her."

Justin stared at her. "I didn't tell her, either."

"I know. Larry jumped the gun."

"By the time she came to me, smoke was coming out of her ears. I had to calm her down."

Kelly leaned forward. "So you did talk to her."

Justin looked puzzled. "Of course I talked to her. I talk to her all the time."

Kelly asked the next question quietly. "About me?" she said.

His eyes narrowed. "Rarely."

"But sometimes."

He returned her stare evenly. "I have once or twice. But then I've spoken to you about her more than once."

"True," she admitted, "but you never said anything to me that in all conscience you couldn't have said to her face."

"The same goes for when I spoke to her about you," he stated. "I've never said anything to her that I couldn't say to your face."

Kelly gasped. Her look of misery so shocked Justin that he stood up. "Liar," she whispered as tears welled up. Justin blinked as if he hadn't heard correctly. "Liar," she repeated, louder this time, reaching for the door.

Instantly he was around his desk to grasp her arms. "What are you talking about?" he demanded.

Kelly gazed into his handsome face, with its sharp lines and magnetic eyes now etched with worry and confusion. How she loved him. She would never love anyone like him. She would never be able to trust a man again. "I know," she said, suddenly wondering where all the oxygen in the room had gone, "that you talked to her about replacing me."

It was fortunate that Justin gripped her tighter. She felt faint. "What!" he exclaimed. "I did what?"

"You... you talked to her about having me replaced as producer for *In the Know.* She told me." Kelly's arms began to ache under the pressure of his hands. "Do you deny it?"

Justin released her. He glanced away. Kelly knew him too well not to know there must be some truth to her accusation. She couldn't stop the tears from falling down her cheeks. The tears seemed to anger him.

"I never spoke to her about replacing you," he said roughly. "Never. Recently I mentioned to Larry that I thought you would be perfect to produce the upcoming Boston Harbor documentary, but I never meant for you to leave the show permanently. It would have been a temporary assignment."

"Oh, so you talked to Larry."

"He's my boss," Justin snapped. "I'm supposed to discuss new ideas with him, just like you're supposed to discuss ideas with me! I regret that Larry mentioned the suggestion to Gilda, but producing a documentary is hardly an insult."

"Gilda used the information like a weapon," Kelly said quietly. "It was humiliating."

"I never meant for her to know," he maintained.

"Besides," she continued, "who asked you to suggest anything on my behalf at all? Why did you meddle in my professional life without consulting me?"

Justin's breathing came quicker now. The heightened color in his cheeks and the stormy blue of his eyes only increased his attractiveness. Kelly wondered how she could find him so appealing when he was breaking her heart.

"Kelly, I mentioned documentaries to you once. Remember? You seemed excited by the possibility."

"Sometime in the future."

"The future is today," he said firmly. "When opportunity comes, you've got to grab it. I know what the programming department is planning for the next year, and this might be your only chance. I didn't mention it to you because the project hasn't been fully approved. I didn't want to get your hopes up."

"Get my hopes up!" Kelly exploded. "I'm supposed to look forward to being replaced? That's how it would look."

"To whom?"

"To everyone at this station who knows of the tenuous relationship between Gilda and me," Kelly said. "To everyone who's felt her ego run roughshod over them because she's got star clout. I'd get 'congratulations on your documentary' to my face and 'Gilda's acing her out' behind my back. Because after I produce this one earthshaking documentary, do you think Gilda would let me come back—no matter what you promised? Or was this to get me gracefully out of the way when the syndication deal went through?"

Justin's eyes became slits. "The syndication deal is in the talking stage right now. I suggested this documentary because I believe in your talent, period. Truthfully I think you're too good to just produce shows on psychics."

Kelly refused to be mollified by this blatant attempt at flattery. "Saying someone is 'too good' for a job is really just a way to finesse them out of it."

"I'm telling the truth!"

"The truth is whatever serves your purpose! You charm and manipulate, all for a rating point."

"You aren't without schemes yourself! You breached professional standards by trying to replace Gilda for this show."

"My idea was for the good of *In the Know*. Gilda plus gangs equals disaster!"

"Must we all share your vision or be labeled lowbrows? I'm looking out for the future of this show, too," he insisted.

Kelly sighed deeply. "I can see the future. One morning I'll wake up in your arms—unemployed."

Justin inhaled sharply. If Kelly had wanted to hurt him as much as he had hurt her, she'd succeeded. Despite her own misery she paled at his wretched face. She raised her hands to touch him, then realized she no longer had that right.

"I can't believe you'd think I'd ever try to hurt you like this," he said softly.

Kelly wiped the tears off her cheeks with her fingers. "You did hurt me."

His blue eyes were wells of sorrow. "I only tried to love you. I thought you loved me. I guess we were both mistaken." He opened his door and exited, leaving Kelly alone with her desolation.

How she made it through the rest of the day, she didn't remember. Her body simply functioned, permitting her mind to retreat into numbness. Later that evening she turned on the television. As Justin predicted, the Boston Defense League refused to stop patrolling. More violence was expected. The show was on.

Curiously Kelly didn't care as much anymore. One show could hardly compete with shattered love. The pain vacillated between unbearable and excruciating. Fortunately Sylvie seemed wrapped up in her own thoughts that evening, and thus didn't recognize her sister's anguish. Kelly couldn't believe that she and Justin had come to this point. So how could she explain it to Sylvie?

The routine of living moved her forward. She made dinner, cleaned up, took a bath, set her alarm. But her mind remained locked on those few crucial minutes that morning. In such a short time harsh words had hardened into implacable, unreachable sides. He should have told her about the documentary! Producing it did appeal to her. Why had Justin held back the news?

Accusing her of sabotage cut deeply, too, but the unkindest cut of all was his last words. *I tried to love you. I thought you loved me. I guess we were both mistaken.* She hadn't wanted to part. All she had asked for was some breathing space. That simple request, made with the expectation that he would understand, had snowballed to this impasse because he hadn't.

With her most private dreams in ruins, Kelly turned off her reading lamp and tried to sleep. She wished for unconsciousness to stop the awful pain.

Seven hours later she was still wishing. Kelly thought she'd dozed off at around three in the morning, but she didn't feel as if she'd gotten any rest. She took a long shower and brewed a particularly strong pot of tea. Her cat Cecil rubbed against her bathrobe, begging for attention. She stroked his white-and-tan fur, wishing that love could be dispensed so easily.

Sylvie came into the kitchen. She smiled a good-morning at Kelly and then did a double take. "Do you feel all right?" she asked, moving closer for a better look.

"I didn't get much sleep last night," Kelly said. "The Defense League won't quit patrolling, so we're doing a show on their fights with the gangs on Monday."

"Real live gang members and Gilda?"

Kelly nodded.

"Oh, Kelly, I'm sorry. Maybe you can be sick that day. You look like you have the flu."

Kelly tried to laugh. "No, I don't think so. This is one show I can't afford to miss. It sure will be a long weekend, though." She looked up from her mug. "Hey, how about catching a movie tonight?"

Sylvie looked surprised and, Kelly noticed, a little rattled. "Don't you remember? I'm spending the night at Andrea's tonight. I told you last weekend."

Kelly closed her eyes. The break with Justin had temporarily blown Sylvie's schedule from her mind. "That's right. You did tell me. I forgot."

"Aren't you seeing Justin tonight?"

"Uh, no, I'm not seeing him."

"Oh?" Kelly saw Sylvie eyeing her with worry. "You two having some problems?" the teenager asked.

Kelly couldn't bring herself to say the romance was over. Something in her resisted this accurate if terrible statement. "All relationships have their ups and downs" she replied, trying to sound philosophical. "Why aren't you seeing Kevin tonight?"

Sylvie started to scramble some eggs furiously. "Kevin's skiing with his family, remember? Seeing girlfriends is important, too, you know."

Kelly smiled, remembering now this piece of good news. "I couldn't agree more. I've always believed that."

Sylvie glanced around with a grin. "I know."

Kelly finished her coffee and contemplated the eggs that Sylvie had thoughtfully made for her. She tried some. They tasted like paste. Maybe she was getting the flu. Somehow the thought cheered her up, and she went to get dressed.

Driving to work gave her a chance to tick off the various confirmations she would need that day from the panelists. Thanks to her diligence, the show was practically booked and the research nearly done. If this show succeeded, the irony would be that it would probably be one of her last.

She couldn't stay. As painful as the decision was, she knew she had to leave *In the Know*. Working with Gilda would be impossible now that the star felt she could run to Justin to countermand anything Kelly wanted. And working with Justin would be—Kelly could hardly contemplate it.

As the day progressed, she became convinced that she was right. Not surprisingly it was decided that Gilda should host Monday's show. Gilda pretended to be vitally interested in the research, but her comments centered less on the issues than on which gangs would be in the audience, whether or not the press had been alerted and would extra security really be needed. The security issue went all the way to Justin, who sided with Kelly.

Kelly was in a tumult as to how Justin would react to her. She hadn't seen him since yesterday's fight. She expected anger or biting sarcasm. Instead, he was quiet, almost formal. His confidence in the show remained high, but his manner was subdued. The hollows under his cheekbones seemed more pronounced, the lines under his eyes deeper. She wasn't the only one who had experienced a rocky night. His eyes unsettled her the most. They radiated a bleak incomprehension, as if he, too, couldn't believe that they had come to this.

Sensing his lonely confusion, Kelly felt an overpowering desire to reach out to him, to hold him, and confess that she was wretched, too. In her reverie she pictured that he would embrace her tightly and admit that he regretted withholding his plans for her. He only wanted her to grow, he would say, and not be forever under the tyranny of an outrageous host. She would thank him and say that she believed in his honesty. Then she would proclaim her love for him. Let the world know, she would say. And they would live happily ever after.

Somehow the opportunity never came. Despite moments when his gaze nearly brought tears to her eyes, Kelly encountered nothing in Justin's words to warrant this gesture. A wall of words had been erected and no dream would tumble it down. Kelly wondered if she wasn't putting too much into his tortured stares. Perhaps it was anger, not sadness in his eyes, and he wouldn't want to hold her, even if she offered.

To her surprise, management was divided on the show. Justin and Larry were for it, of course, but the vice president and general manager, Lew Brady, had misgivings similar to her own. Justin had taken a bigger risk than she'd realized. If the show failed, Justin, not Larry, would take the fall. In a spate of more irony, Kelly wondered if, after Monday, both of them would be jobless.

The day finally ended. Never had Kelly felt so exhausted. A nice, hot bath and a soft pillow would be her reward. She was thankful that Sylvie was at Andrea's.

Kelly arrived home at six o'clock. She puttered around the kitchen, throwing together a mixture of odds and ends that she was sure would be delicious once they were stir-fried together. The result didn't meet her expectation, but she didn't care.

Taking her plate into the living room, Kelly turned on the television. When the news popped on, she immediately switched to a station that was showing a rerun of a classic sitcom. There had been enough reality for one day. Unfortunately the show ended with Lucy and Desi proclaiming their love for each other, despite a stupendous misunderstanding. Groaning, Kelly turned it off.

Weariness consumed her. She figured she had enough energy to take a bath, but not enough to do the dishes. Dumping her plate into the sink, she contemplated her bath. To bubble or not to bubble? Should she smell like a raspberry or a summer's day? She could handle decisions like these.

As the bubbles began to rise, Kelly remembered she had forgotten to tell Sylvie that she wouldn't be able to attend Sylvie's skating class tomorrow morning. She had some last-minute show details at the station. Kelly turned off the ultrahot water. She walked into her bedroom and dialed Andrea's phone number. Her mother, Susan, answered.

"Susan! Hello, this is Kelly Ferris."

"Well, hello, Kelly, how are you?"

"Fine, just fine. Can I speak to Sylvie?"

"Sylvie's not here."

"Oh. Did she and Andrea go to a movie? Perhaps you could give her a message for me?"

"Andrea's up in her room, listening to her stereo," Susan explained, her voice a shade less cheerful. "Was Sylvie planning on stopping by?"

Kelly was surprised. She knew she'd been distracted this morning, but she distinctly remembered Sylvie saying she intended to spend the night with Andrea. She told this to Susan.

"Well, this is strange," Susan conceded. "Let me call Andrea to the phone. Andrea! Andrea, turn down that music! Thank you. Pick up the phone in my room. Kelly Ferris is on the line."

"Hello?"

Kelly recognized a tentative hello when she heard it. Why should Andrea be nervous? "Hi, Andrea, this is Kelly. Listen, maybe we got our signals crossed, but I distinctly remember Sylvie telling me she was going to spend the night with you tonight."

"Um, no."

"No?" Kelly was startled. "Did you two decide to meet at the mall maybe? I mean, she told me twice she was going to your house tonight. Once, last weekend, and she reminded me again this morning. It seemed very definite."

"Andrea," Susan prompted, "did you invite Sylvie to spend the night?"

"Well, I..."

"Andrea," Susan said in a deadlier tone, "did you invite Sylvie to spend the night like she told her sister?"

Kelly heard a barely audible "Yes."

"Then why isn't she here?"

"Um, she changed her mind."

"Changed her mind?" Kelly was now very worried. "She said she was going to be at your house, Andrea! Did she, by any chance, decide to spend the night with another girlfriend?"

"What? Uh...yeah. She went to someone else's house. I can't remember who, but don't worry. I know she'll be fine."

Unfortunately for Andrea, neither her mother nor Kelly accepted this assurance. "Andrea, I have to know where she is," Kelly pleaded. "Think. Who did she say she'd be with?"

"I can't remember." Andrea's voice was now plaintive.

Her mother didn't buy her memory lapse. "Andrea, I have a sneaking suspicion that you do remember. And I'll give you five seconds to recover from amnesia."

Kelly heard a nervous groan. Where could Sylvie be all night that would warrant this deception? The answer was obvious, but Kelly didn't want to believe it.

"Andrea, is Sylvie with Kevin?"

The silence that followed confirmed Kelly's worst suspicions.

"Andrea," Susan said, her voice like a stiff, winter wind, "this is serious. You will tell us everything—right now."

Kelly heard a sigh, but she knew Andrea was going to confess. "Okay," the teenager said, "but it wasn't my idea. Kevin's family is away for the weekend, and he and Sylvie thought it might be a great idea—"

"Damn it!" Kelly exploded.

"It wasn't my idea," Andrea whined.

"No," her mother said, "but you were a party to the deception. You're responsible, too. Do you think they're at Kevin's house right now?"

"Yes."

"Then I suggest we hang up and let Kelly handle the situation. Then you and I are going to have a talk about honesty. Kelly, call me back if you need anything."

"Thank you, Susan." She heard two clicks. As she put the receiver down, she noticed that her hand had perspired so badly that the phone was slippery.

Sylvie had lied to her, bold-faced. Kelly could have cried. Then she got angry.

She thought her closeness to Sylvie would have outweighed Kevin's pressure. Sure, she'd been more involved with her work lately and hadn't had as much time to talk to Sylvie. And, yes, Justin had also been eating into Kelly's spare time. *Had*—the word stung. But she'd tried to remain Sylvie's confidante and emotional compass. More than the actual reason for the deception, Sylvie's lying to her hurt the most.

Well, Sylvie wasn't going to get away with it. Kelly knew where Kevin lived. She would go over there and...for a moment she recoiled from the scene her visit would cause. She wondered if she should call first. No, she decided. Kevin might lie and say Sylvie wasn't there.

A wave of anxiety and heartache engulfed her. Kelly squeezed her eyes shut to stop the tears, but she failed. Those she loved best were moving away from her. With deep sobs she wondered how to get them back.

The phone rang. Instantly Kelly picked it up.

"Hello, Sylvie?"

"No, Kelly, this is Justin."

Kelly sat up on the bed. Although it surprised her, the sound of his voice made her irrationally happy. "Uh, hi, Justin. Is something the matter?"

"Have you watched the news tonight?"

"No."

"Well, the Defense League just clashed again with a gang. This one was called the Skull and Bones."

Crying had made Kelly a trifle hoarse. "Someone will eventually get killed over this."

"I know," he agreed. "I wanted to talk to you about beefing up security."

"Now?" Kelly asked. Frankly the show wasn't a priority with her at that particular moment.

"Is this a bad time?" He paused. "Are you going out?" he asked hesitantly.

"Yes," Kelly sniffled. She searched her night table for a tissue.

After a brief silence, Justin said, "You sound funny. Are you okay?"

She blew her nose. "I can handle it."

"You've been crying."

"So what?"

"So... what's the matter, honey?"

The way he said "honey" dissolved her. It was so sweet, so kind.

"I...I...Sylvie lied to me," she sputtered. "She said she'd be over at Andrea's...but she's not. She's at Kevin's. And she's planning to stay all night. So I have to go over there now... and I—"

"Whoa," Justin said softly. "Let me see if I follow this. You say Sylvie said she'd be at Andrea's. Andrea is a friend."

"Yes." Kelly quickly explained what she'd learned from Andrea. The explanation helped calm her. Having someone to confide in made the crisis seem less overwhelming. "So you know I have to go over there," she stated.

"Alone?" he asked. "Is that a good idea? Wait! I have a better one. I'll come with you."

The suggestion filled Kelly with gratitude, but this was her fight. "Thank you, Justin, but I couldn't impose. It might be unpleasant."

"All the more reason for me to be there. I eased things once before. What if Kevin's been drinking?"

"Well . . ."

"And you sound very upset. You really shouldn't drive."

"Justin, I don't want to embarrass Sylvie any more than I have to."

"You take care of Sylvie," he replied. "I'll take care of Kevin. Pick you up in ten minutes."

Kelly heard the phone click. Energy surged through her tired body. She wouldn't have to go through this alone.

Eight minutes later she saw Justin's car pull up in front of her building. She ran down her apartment stairs.

Justin got out of his car and came briskly forward to greet her. In his eyes she saw compassion. In his chin-up smile she saw comfort.

Awkwardly she reached out her hand to shake his. "Thank you, Justin." He shook his head and enveloped her in a hug. It wasn't a hug of passion, but a lovely hug of support.

Justin held her a second longer than the nice, friendly hug he'd intended. "Oh, Kelly," he whispered. She was in his arms again. He regretted the problem with Sylvie. Kelly looked enormously upset. But he was so glad to be with her.

During the drive to Kevin's house, Justin stole glances at her pensive face. A feeling of unbearable tenderness swept over him. Could they turn back the clock? Reluctantly he realized that time couldn't be manipulated. Bridges had been burned, mistakes made.

As Kelly directed Justin, they passed large Colonials, mellowed Cape Cods and a few imitation Taras. Everything seemed gracious and expensive.

"Turn left here," Kelly ordered. "Kevin's house is number 3413." Justin pulled into the circular driveway of a brick Colonial. Kelly noticed that a light shone from a curtained upstairs window. The porch lights were in the shape of kerosene lamps. They blazed a curious welcome.

"How cute," she commented as she got out of the car. "I wonder if they own a spinning wheel."

"Easy," Justin said. "How, exactly, do you plan to announce yourself?"

"The normal way," she replied. "Walk to the front door, ring the doorbell, say hi. I wish I'd thought to bring a coffee cake."

Justin laughed shortly. "You could make a wisecrack in the middle of a tornado."

Kelly was far from merry. The joke had been a way to lessen the butterflies in her stomach. She rang the doorbell, which resembled a pretentious gong.

"Are you sure they're here?" Justin asked when Kelly rang for the second time.

"Someone's home," Kelly answered, pointing to the lit second-floor window.

"Um, perhaps they're occupied," Justin said as tactfully as he could.

"Oh, great!" Kelly groaned. Then she brightened. "Maybe they're listening to his stereo and can't hear the doorbell."

Justin cleared his throat. "You enjoy a little background music, too."

Kelly glared at him. "I'm not leaving."

He touched her shoulder. "I'm not suggesting that," he said gently, "but we could go to a gas station and call. It could save some embarrassment."

"Then it could be too late." Kelly felt his hand press lightly.

"It may already be too late."

She sighed. "I know, but I'm taking her home. Then we'll have plenty of time to talk."

Justin nodded. "Okay, but let's go around to the back door. Teenagers are forgetful. It could be unlocked."

Kelly followed him around the stately home. She glanced up at the sky and made a wish on the brightest star.

Justin tried the back door. To their surprise it opened. Before they entered the house Justin turned to Kelly and said, "Some people might applaud us for what we're doing. Then again some people might call it trespassing."

Kelly shivered. "I know. I'm very grateful you're here."

He smiled and held the door open for her. They found themselves in the kitchen. It was immaculate except for a greasy cardboard box on a counter containing one stiff piece of pizza. In the distance rock music blared.

"Someone's home all right," Justin whispered.

Kelly's mouth went dry. Her resolve never faltered, but the reality of what she was about to do made her throat tighten. Justin took her hand. Squeezing it slightly, he said, "Let's go."

Following the sound of the music, they made their way to the main staircase at the front of the house. It wasn't difficult. A few lights were on.

Kevin's mother had exquisite taste, but the furnishing didn't distract Kelly, especially when she heard the unmistakable giggle of her younger sister.

They silently climbed the carpeted stairs. Luckily the door to the room from which the giggle and music came was closed. "Get ready," Kelly said. "I'll knock on the door, announce myself and then go in."

"Why did we decide to do this without the Marines?" Justin asked.

"Because we're doing the right thing," Kelly said, although at that moment she would have preferred a root canal to barging in on her sister. "I'll go in alone in case...well, Sylvie may not be dressed. If I yell, come in after me." She squared her shoulders and rapped briskly on the door. The giggling stopped. "Sylvie! This is Kelly. Please come out."

Gasps filtered through the closed door. "Go away," came the growled response from Kevin. Sylvie did not reply, which worried Kelly. With manufactured confidence she strode into the room.

The scene she walked in on made Kelly angrier. Kevin's room smelled like a brewery. Beer bottles lay everywhere. Strewn on the floor were Kevin's shoes, socks, sweater and shirt. On the rumpled bed, sitting up dazed and shocked, was Kevin, clad only in faded jeans, and Sylvie, clutching a sweater to her naked chest. Thankfully she had jeans on, too.

The two of them stared at Kelly as if she were a Martian. Sylvie was the first to speak. "Iss my sister!" she slurred, turning beet-red.

Kelly walked over to her. "You're not at Andrea's, Sylvie. Now we're going home."

Sylvie looked stunned. "Wait! I didden mean to lie. I just wanted to be with Kevin."

Kelly glared at Kevin. "If you needed a six-pack to do it, then there must have been a little pressure involved."

"That's a lie," Kevin said, scrambling off the bed. "How dare you sneak into my house."

Sylvie bent her head. She mumbled something about "being nervous." Then she looked up defiantly. "You had no right barging in on us," she said, slipping the sweater on. "No right!"

"Yes, I do have a right," Kelly said, picking up Sylvie's shoes and shocks. "From where I sit I had an obligation."

"To humiliate me?" Sylvie refused the socks. She took great pains to pronounce her words correctly, but a slurred consonant here and there couldn't hide her intoxication.

"Believe me," Kelly said gently, taking her arm, "I don't want to hurt you. In fact, I can think of many things I'd rather be doing tonight."

"Like sleeping with Justin," Sylvie replied. Kelly reddened but held her sister tightly. "All that talk about saving myself for the right boy when you were fooling around yourself," Sylvie continued. "Coming home after midnight. I wadden born yesterday!"

"You could have fooled me," Kelly snapped, trying to pull her recalcitrant sister up from the bed.

"Let her go," Kevin warned.

"Hypocrite," Sylvie taunted.

The word struck Kelly as forcefully as a blow. She released Sylvie so quickly that the girl fell back onto the bed. Taking a deep breath, Kelly stepped back and gazed at her sister. "You throw words around like *hypocrite* and *rights,* but you're not the only person with rights! It's my right as an adult to assess a relationship and decide if I'm ready for intimacy. This right didn't come to me magically at sixteen or eighteen, but through experience and maturity. Since you don't have either yet, it's my responsibility to counsel you to wait, when I can decide for myself not to. It's not hypocrisy. I was ready. I felt—and still do feel—that you're not."

"I am ready," Sylvie insisted, but burst into tears.

"Oh, sweetie," Kelly said, walking back to her and putting her hand on Sylvie's wild, curly hair. "Let's go home."

"Take your hands off her," Kevin ordered. He'd obviously been drinking, too, but not to the degree of Sylvie. Perhaps that had been the plan, Kelly thought, as she saw him walk around the bed to face her. Still, his face was flushed and he projected a volatile hostility.

"Stay out of this, Kevin," she said.

"I will not. This is my house. You can't take her against her will. I won't let you."

Kelly took in his strapping frame, his clenched fists and eighty-proof breath. "Justin," she called.

Sylvie gasped, and Kevin whirled around as Justin came in.

"Justin, he—"

"I heard," Justin replied. "I kept the door open a crack. Listen, kid," he said to Kevin, "Sylvie's a minor."

"Hey, she wanted it," Kevin boasted. "I hardly had to make her—"

"I'd shut up if I were you," Justin said. He walked to the foot of the bed.

"Yeah, make me man," Kevin snarled.

"You little jerk," Kelly rasped as she got a weeping Sylvie to her feet.

"He's not a jerk!" Sylvie said through tears. She tried to free herself, but Kelly kept one hand firmly attached to her sister while using the other to hold Sylvie's clothes.

"Calling him a jerk was generous," Justin said. "Real men don't pressure women, and they don't get them drunk."

"Hey!" Kevin shouted. "I don't have to force girls to sleep with me. There are plenty who'd dump a date just to be where Sylvie is now."

"I'm sure your parents will find all this very interesting," Kelly said. She started to pull Sylvie from the room.

"Tell them!" Kevin shouted with alcoholic bravado. "You broke into our house. That's a crime around here." But he said this to Justin, as if Sylvie was no longer the issue, but besting Justin was. He pointed to Kelly, making slow progress with a near-hysterical Sylvie. "She's not going anywhere." He lunged at the couple, jerking Sylvie nearly out of Kelly's grip.

"Kevin, you hurt me!" Sylvie cried, managing to pull her arm away.

Justin maneuvered himself between the women and Kevin.

"Get out of my way," Kevin demanded.

This wasn't the smartest request. Justin may have been an inch or two shorter than Kevin, but he had sobriety on his side.

"Whoa, boy," Justin said, blocking Kevin's attempt to reach Sylvie.

"Who're you calling a boy?" Kevin snarled.

Justin stared him down.

"Either move out of the way or I'll make you move," Kevin threatened, putting up his fists.

Justin sighed. He glanced at Kelly. "Where are the Marines when you need them?"

CHAPTER TWELVE

"YOU'RE GONNA BE SORRY," Kevin said, advancing toward Justin.

"I'm already sorry," Justin replied, positioning his body for an assault.

Kevin swung. Justin dodged it. Kevin swung again and missed.

"Kevin, stop," Sylvie pleaded, but she might as well have been talking to a brick wall. He straightened up for a moment, as if assessing Justin differently, and then lunged at him.

He caught Justin in his midsection. The charge sent both crashing against a dresser. Justin gasped in pain as his head hit polished mahogany. To Kelly's horror she saw blood trickle down his face and his eyes glaze over. Sylvie started to cry.

Immediately Kevin took advantage of Justin's dazed condition, pounding him in the stomach. Justin deflected the blows as best he could, but at that point he was the weaker of the two. He slowly slid to the floor under the beating.

Kelly couldn't stand by and let this happen. She dropped Sylvie's arm and moved to help Justin.

She needn't have bothered. On the floor Justin wrapped his feet around Kevin's legs, and in a hard thrust unbalanced the young man. Kevin fell backward, enabling Justin to get up. He waved Kelly out of the way. Kevin scrambled to his feet and made an unwise second lunge at Justin. This time the boy's jaw connected with Justin's right hook, sending the surprised teen toppling onto his bed.

Sylvie rushed to his side. Her tear-stained face seemed barely able to comprehend what was happening. "Are you all right?"

Kevin lay there motionless for a moment. Then he raised his head. Already a bruise was forming on his right cheek. "Get out," he said hoarsely.

Sylvie recoiled from this response. "But, Kevin..."

"Did I break your jaw, kid?" Justin asked, accepting a tissue from Kelly.

"Get out," Kevin repeated distinctly.

"I guess not," Justin said, dabbing his wound. The tissue quickly turned red. "I need to go home," he said to Kelly.

"You need to go to a hospital," she replied.

He shook his head, then winced. "No, I think the bleeding's stopped. Let's go home."

"I'll drive," Kelly said, linking her arm with his. "Sylvie," she called out softly, "is Kevin all right?"

Her sister was still leaning over Kevin. "Are you okay?" she kept repeating. "Do you need a doctor?"

"Get out!" he yelled, turning away from her and curling up on his bed.

Sylvie fled the room. Kelly found her in the Lucases' ornate bathroom crying and shaking. Gently she helped Sylvie to Justin's car. The ride back was silent, punctuated by occasional sobs and sniffles. Sylvie finally stopped crying, but she announced to Kelly that she would never speak to her again as long as she lived.

Kelly wasn't nearly as worried about this vow as she was about the purple bump forming on Justin's head. The bleeding had nearly stopped, but the cut needed immediate attention.

Justin's neighbor, Mrs. Bannon, gasped when she saw him. A mere bump, Justin assured her. But he asked if she could stay a little longer so that he could take Kelly and Sylvie home.

"We'll take a cab," Kelly said. "You've done more than enough for us this evening."

"Nonsense," Justin replied in a voice that brooked no refusal. Mrs. Bannon tactfully retired to the den, and Kelly hurried to get an ice pack, bandages and disinfectant. Sylvie repaired to the bathroom to wash her face, so Kelly tended Justin in the kitchen.

"Ow!" he protested when she patted medicine on his head.

"I thought you said it was a flesh wound," Kelly commented.

"Yeah, but it's my flesh," he pointed out.

They laughed. It was the first time Kelly had done so all evening. Sylvie joined them in the kitchen, where Kelly had served Justin some strong coffee laced with brandy. Sylvie's face was red and puffy, but she seemed sober—and angry.

"You humiliated me tonight," she accused Kelly.

"I didn't mean to," Kelly said, dropping bloody swabs into a garbage can.

"Couldn't you have called?" Sylvie shot back.

"Would Kevin have admitted that you were there?"

"He . . . uh, I don't know," Sylvie said.

"Well, I do," Kelly said, sitting down. "He would have lied to me, and I would still have had to come.

Only you two, once alerted, might have left to finish your...business elsewhere. And then I would have worried about you all night.''

Sylvie colored but still gazed furiously at her sister. ''Now it'll be all over school on Monday.''

Justin put the ice pack on his head. ''No, it won't.''

''Why not?'' Sylvie asked.

''Because then he'd have to explain that he got the bruise on his cheek from a man nearly twenty years older than him in a losing fight over a seduction that he didn't bring off.''

Sylvie blushed. ''Yes, I'm the same 'nice girl' that I was this morning,'' she said sarcastically. ''I'm just about the only girl I know who is.''

''That's not true, honey,'' Kelly said.

''Kevin says—''

''Ah, Kevin again,'' Justin interposed. ''That authority on everything. I bet he said that if you loved him, you'd prove it.''

Sylvie looked down. ''I do love him.''

''I respect that, but are you ready to express it in this way?''

The teenager twisted a tissue in her hands. ''I'm...I'm not sure.''

''Don't you have the right to wait until you are sure?'' Justin asked.

Sylvie looked up, stricken. ''But then...''

Kelly waited on tenterhooks for her answer. When Sylvie fell silent and tears trickled down her cheeks, Kelly lightly squeezed her arm. ''Then what?'' she asked softly.

Her sister inhaled a sob. ''Then I might lose Kevin,'' she said, and started to cry again.

"Oh, no, don't cry," Kelly said, scooting her chair over to Sylvie's. Her sister's misery swept all anger from her. She put her arms around her, even as she feared that the young girl might reject this peace offering.

To Kelly's great relief, Sylvie eagerly accepted the embrace. She returned the hug, little drops of tears falling onto Kelly's shoulders. "I know the decision of when to make love is one of the hardest," Kelly murmured. "I just don't want you to do it because of pressure."

"I was so nervous," Sylvie sniffled.

"Nervousness is normal, so is awkwardness," Kelly said, "but needing a six-pack is pressure."

Sylvie pulled away from the embrace. "He did get a little crazy, didn't he? I . . . I thought he was defending me, but I wonder now what he would have done if I had decided not to and you weren't around."

"I wonder, too," Kelly said grimly.

"But we were," Justin said. "And now it's all over."

Although her face was still red and wet, Sylvie smiled. "Thank you Justin. And, Kelly...I'm sorry for lying."

Tears came to Kelly's eyes. What a wonderful ending to a rotten day. She smiled at Justin in gratitude.

"Kelly, why are you crying?"

Kelly looked around and then down. Standing in the doorway was Tommy.

"Hi, honey," she said, opening her arms.

He ran to her, and she lifted him onto her lap. "Why are you crying?" he asked again.

"I'm crying because I'm happy."

"Oh," he replied, stumped by this peculiar answer. Turning to his father, he pointed at the ice pack. "Daddy, what a funny hat."

The room exploded in laughter. Tommy laughed, too, but asked, "What's so funny?" Encouraged by his father, he went over to try on the "hat." "It's cold," he squealed.

"Come on, big guy, I'll tuck you back in," Kelly said.

Tommy frowned. "I'm not tired."

"I'll read you a story."

His face lit up. "Okay."

Kelly walked with him to his room. Tommy bounded onto his bed, slipped under the covers and grabbed his penguin. He settled into his standard listening position.

Kelly picked up a book and sat on the edge of his bed. "Mmm, okay, *The Ghost of Haunted Hollow,* chapter one—"

"Kelly?"

"Yes?"

"Why haven't you come to see me?"

The question threw her. She knew Tommy was perceptive, but he was also just a child.

"I've been real busy, sweetie."

The big blue eyes looked questioningly at her. "I missed you. I asked Daddy where you were, and he said you were busy, too. But he got real sad."

Kelly closed the book. Breaking up with Justin meant that she would probably see very little of this wonderful boy. She'd been so stunned at the rapid disintegration of her relationship with Justin that she hadn't dealt with what it would mean to Tommy.

"I'm . . . sorry, Tommy."

"Will you come ice-skating with us tomorrow?"

"Um, I don't know."

"You promised to help me bake Christmas cookies, remember? You said boys should know how to cook, too."

Kelly smiled at this, but her heart was heavy. "I'm not sure, honey," she managed.

He sat up, worry on his little face. "You aren't going away, are you?"

She saw that this was his biggest anxiety. Who could blame him, considering the events in his life this past year. The breakup of his parent's marriage, followed by the separation from his father, must have left him craving for stability. Now, due to circumstances he couldn't understand, she was leaving him.

I don't want to, Tommy! she almost cried out. *I can't believe it's come to this.* The thought of not seeing him, playing with him, hearing his funny, perceptive comments filled her with a terrible sadness. She reached over and hugged him, so that he wouldn't see the tears. She held him until she had her face under control, wiping her eyes on his pillow. "I better read you this book, young man, before it's morning."

He leaned back on his pillow and saw her spotted face. "Were you crying because you were happy?"

The question tore her to pieces. "Sort of."

She began the story. After five pages his eyelids drooped. On the sixth he was sleeping. Kelly turned off the light and tiptoed from the room.

She rejoined Sylvie and Justin. "I think we should go home. Sylvie and I have some talking to do."

Sylvie smiled.

"Fine, I'll drive you," Justin said, holding up one hand when she started to protest. "My head is fine. It'll take more than a bureau to make any real dent in it. I'll go tell Mrs. Bannon."

The drive back to the apartment was subdued. Sylvie fell asleep, exhausted by the emotional roller coaster she'd ridden. She woke up as Justin pulled into an illegal parking space. "I'll see you both to the door."

Kelly let Sylvie enter first and watched the teen make a beeline for her bedroom. She intended to thank Justin again, but now that the moment had arrived, she felt awkward.

"Justin," she began, "I want to say again how much I appreciate what you did tonight."

He shook his head. "Please don't."

"No," she insisted, "I want to. I owe you for...so many things."

His blue eyes looked into hers. There was sorrow in them and another emotion that she couldn't quite figure out.

"You don't owe me a thing," he said. "I just want you to know that you can depend on me, that my word—" he paused "—is still good."

The self-contempt in his voice was as cold as the winter night. Kelly couldn't let him leave in this frame of mind. Not after the heroic way he'd stood up for her and Sylvie tonight. "I...you're being unfair. I depended on you tonight, and you were wonderful. You're much too hard on yourself."

He emitted a short laugh, but it was ironic. "Being too stringently honest with myself has never been one of my failings."

"Being too blunt is one of mine," Kelly whispered, remembering her harsh accusations of just two days ago. She had questioned his word about the documentary. She'd outright insulted his integrity. And all because of a television show.

"No," he said softly, "at least I get the truth from you."

The truth? Kelly didn't know what the truth was anymore. All she knew was that Justin had helped her tonight, generously and unselfishly. Feelings that had never really disappeared guided her hand gently to his cheek. "Do you want the truth, Justin?" she asked. "You were remarkable tonight. You treated Sylvie with such kindness and compassion. I thank you from the bottom of my heart." Before she could analyze what she was doing, she reached up and kissed his lips.

She felt him stiffen slightly, from surprise or discomfort, she couldn't tell. Then his lips did seek hers. There was a moment of urgency, of longing, but the kiss became guarded, as if he didn't really believe in its power to heal anymore. As his lips left hers, Kelly recognized a bittersweet aftertaste.

"Thank you," he said almost formally. "I'm glad I could help. Tell Sylvie I'll be thinking of her on Monday." The mention of the day of the much-debated show seemed to bring all its acrimonious baggage back in front of them. Awkwardly Kelly dropped her hand.

"I'll see you on Monday," he said. Glancing down, he turned on his heel and strode quickly down the hall of her building. She heard his departing footsteps. Each step seemed to hammer home one thought: *I've lost him.*

That night Kelly was unable to sleep. In fact, rest proved elusive during the entire weekend. Recent events, playing over and over again, filled her mind with worry and regret. Despite the fact that she had hurt him, Justin had still come through for her. Their parting at her doorstep had been heavy with unspoken feeling. She'd been wrong to run away from him, to run away from love. And she did love him. Knowing that, what did it matter what other people thought? She felt Justin still loved her, but their horrible fight, aggravated by the show on Monday, had driven what seemed like a permanent wedge between them.

The stakes from this show were high. If Kelly was right and things went awry, management would turn against Justin. His career would be damaged. She could see him standing there, amid the chaos, waiting for her to say, "I told you so."

But she wouldn't say it. Suddenly Kelly knew she would do whatever she could to help Justin with this show. He'd been there for her when she needed him. She would do the same for him.

Monday morning dawned cold and gray. Both Kelly and Sylvie viewed the day with extreme trepidation. Sylvie couldn't eat breakfast; she was so nervous about what Kevin would say about Friday night. Kelly dropped her sister off at school, giving Sylvie a hug for support. When she entered the *In the Know* office area, she was immediately bombarded with problems.

"Kelly, the Warlords and Bullets won't sit in the same waiting room with the Defense League. What do we do?"

"Kelly, Agnes Baker of the Coalition for the Elderly is angry that we can't make half the audience seats available for her group. What do I say to her?"

"Kelly, the Boston Defense League president Paul Moran wants to have editorial approval over our open. Do we let guests do that?"

"Kelly, they all want to know if there's going to be a makeup man, uh, person. Did we arrange for that?"

To Peg, Kelly answered, "I want four waiting rooms when our guests arrive—one for each gang, one for the Defense League and its members and one for Reverend Brown of the Boston Safe Community Organization and Agnes Baker. Use conference rooms. And we never give editorial approval to any guest over our open. They'll have plenty of time on the air to explain exactly what they stand for."

To Phil, the stage manager, she said, "Tell Agnes Baker that the audience seats were rationed equally between the various interest groups coming today. I did arrange for ramps to be installed so that wheelchairs can be accommodated. That will have to satisfy her. And," she sighed, "this isn't a network. Everyone will have to do their own makeup."

She threw down her coat and decided on some mellow herbal tea. She heard the door close and someone ostentatiously clear her throat.

She turned around. There, in the doorway, stood Gilda in a beautiful but wildly inappropriate black leather suit. The outfit sported shoulder pads, a tight, short skirt and a funky design that clashed entirely with Gilda's new image—and age.

Kelly felt her hopes sinking. "Why, Gilda?" was all she could manage.

Gilda twirled around, a happy smile on her face. "I spent a great deal of time pondering which outfit would be right. I think this will show the gangs that I'm not stuffy but, as a suit, still satisfy Reverend Baker."

"It's Reverend Brown, Gilda," Kelly said. "Agnes Baker is with the Coalition for the Elderly."

Gilda shrugged off this correction. "I have my handy-dandy crib sheet," she said, pulling a small index card from her pocket.

"Did you read the material?" Kelly asked.

"Sure," Gilda said. She admired her black leather suit in the office mirror. "But the research you gave me didn't have nearly enough background information on the gangs. Remember, they're the key to the show."

Alarms went off in Kelly's brain. "Gilda, we're here today to deal with a specific issue. Does the Defense League have the right to patrol the neighborhoods? Are they, as they claim, just a neighborhood watch group, or are they vigilantes aggravating an already tense situation? Focusing on the gangs will give undue attention to them. Law-abiding citizens like Reverend Brown deserve equal time."

Gilda pursed her ruby lips. "I don't intend to have this show sound like a city council meeting."

"We'll be lucky if it does."

"No," Gilda said, moving to the door, "I know just what this show needs."

She left the office, stopping just outside to accept a compliment from a surprised Peg. Kelly sipped her tea, hoping that the leaves really did soothe the nerves.

"Gilda looks...unique," Peg said as she entered. "I wonder what happened to the burgundy pleated dress she was supposed to wear."

"Too stuffy," Kelly said.

Peg ran one hand nervously through her frizzy hair. "The show could come off, you know, if she just sticks to the material, doesn't try to glamorize the gangs or the Defense League, gets everyone's name right and doesn't interject her own opinions."

Kelly laughed. "You're absolutely right! Why am I worried?"

Peg grinned. "I got the waiting rooms, and I called Moran."

"Great. Now will you check the bumps, music and graphics? I want to write the open."

"Sure," Peg said, passing Justin on her way out.

His presence always had a physical impact on Kelly. His fluid gait and lean, tough build continually unsettled her in a very primitive way. She'd seen this body without the gray suit. She'd felt its power.

Now he stood before her, radiating power of another kind. Today's show, both in tone and content, was basically his call. His risk. Would he believe that she now wanted to share that risk?

"Sit down," she said softly. "How's your head?"

"Fine," he said, lightly touching his bandage. "I told people that I slipped on some ice and hit my head. Everyone believes me because, as I've discovered, everyone's done the same thing."

As he sat, Kelly noticed the circles under his eyes and the pensive expression on his face. "I came to tell you that security's been beefed up. And every audience member will be searched with a metal detecting device to find any guns or knives."

"The old people, too?" Kelly asked. "Is that necessary?"

"I'm doing my best to keep this show nonviolent," he said defensively. "Isn't that the big worry?"

"I thought the big worry was boredom," Kelly quipped, but Justin didn't laugh at her attempt to lessen the tension.

She knew that now was the time to reassure him. He could believe her or not, but she wanted to set the record straight. "Justin," she said, "if you think the metal detector will do the trick, then I'm all for it."

His tired eyes flickered with surprise.

"Perhaps," she continued, "I haven't shown my support as . . . professionally as I should have, but that doesn't mean I wish for trouble today. The possibilities in this show are clearer to me now. Lots of things are clearer to me now. So if you need help today, just ask."

Justin's head jerked back slightly in disbelief. His eyes searched her face for any trace of lingering disapproval. When he didn't find it, his body relaxed and color seemed to return to his pale complexion. "Thank you. That means a lot to me."

"Friday night meant a lot to me," Kelly said.

The declaration produced a near smile. One of his dimples made an achingly sweet, all too brief appearance. "Did it?" he asked softly. "I spent the weekend wondering."

Her pulse quickened at this admission. "I spent the weekend thinking about you, too. And Tommy."

His haggard face became alert. Kelly saw in his expression a hopefulness and the faintest glimpse—it couldn't be her imagination—of a stronger need. A need for her. "Any conclusions?" he asked.

Only that I love you, and I believe you never meant to hurt me, Kelly wanted to say, but at that moment Larry Bishop walked in.

"The Warlords are here," he announced, rubbing his hands anxiously. "A couple of them went into the newsroom and demanded to see Sally Forsythe because, and I quote, they thought the anchorwoman was a 'foxy chick.' What have we gotten ourselves into?"

Kelly and Justin exchanged glances. Was this really a preview of more trouble to come? Kelly began to worry. Unfortunately Justin perceived her apprehensive face as critical rather than concerned.

"Let's not blow this out of proportion," he said to her, although it was Larry who had made the comment. "I'll go and handle it."

"I'll help," Kelly said, anxious to dispel his misperception.

"No." He said the word a shade too sharply, then caught himself. "Um, thank you, but why don't you see to the other guests?"

Kelly watched him go, upset over the misunderstanding. But there was no time now to explain. The rest of the morning flew by in a crush of last-minute details. All the guests arrived and were escorted to their separate rooms. At first the gangs refused to be searched. But after Kelly threatened to cancel the show if they weren't, ego won out and they consented. Unfortunately not just knives were found. Mace and brass knuckles were confiscated, the Mace from two elderly ladies. All this contraband made upper management very nervous.

"I can't believe they brought knives to the station," Larry said, mopping his brow with a handkerchief.

"These aren't your average teenagers," Kelly said. She had an easier time with the Defense League, who couldn't wait to prove that they carried no weapons. Reverend Brown and Mrs. Baker needed no frisking. They were just concerned that the show not get out of hand. It was an assurance Kelly couldn't promise.

She'd gone over the format of the show again with all participants. Profanity, she warned the Warlords and Bullets, was prohibited. Finger gestures of any kind were forbidden. Decked out in his Warlords leather jacket, Jerome White shrugged at every comment. Luther Jackson, president of the Bullets, wore his silver Bullets shirt. He just wanted a chance at the Defense League, he told Kelly, so he would "try" to watch his language.

Gilda had wanted to speak with the gangs before the show started, but Kelly, backed by Justin, refused. He was annoyed that Gilda's burgundy pleated dress had "disappeared" and that, despite Kelly's research, Gilda seemed unprepared. Kelly went over the open with her, and Peg tried to review the important points.

"I know what's important and what isn't," Gilda yelled at the two of them in her dressing room.

Kelly walked to Gilda's dressing table and stared into the mirror, watching Gilda reapply her red lipstick. The ruby color was dramatic but unflattering.

"Gilda, we're just trying to help," Kelly said.

"I know what I plan to do," Gilda replied coolly, her eyes never straying from her reflection.

Peg closed her file and lightly squeezed Kelly's shoulder before she left. Kelly kept staring at the mirror. It was pointless to try to coach Gilda now. The star was definitely beyond Kelly's control or anyone else's.

The upcoming show promised to be a hair-raiser. And yet Kelly's thoughts weren't on the show. Her mind kept returning to those few hopeful moments earlier with Justin when his face revealed for an instant that she still mattered to him. She now had the courage to tell him how she really felt. She couldn't wait for this show to be over. "I'll leave you alone now," she said. "We'll be bringing in the audience in about ten minutes."

Kelly found Justin and Larry in the control room. The director was giving last-minute instructions to the camera people. The technical director, whose function was to push the camera-two button when the director yelled, "Take two," was checking his board. The sound man waited for the guests to be escorted to the set so that he could mike them. It was a crowded hub.

"I'm bringing in the audience now," Kelly said.

Larry chewed on his lower lip. "Is everything secure?"

"As secure as anything can be on live television," Kelly replied.

He smiled sourly. "I wish I hadn't eaten the Stroganoff for lunch."

Justin glanced at his watch. "Let's do it."

With a resolute sigh Kelly went out to welcome everyone to a very special edition of *In the Know*.

CHAPTER THIRTEEN

"I WANT TO WELCOME you all to *In the Know*," Kelly began. "Today we have a special show on a most important topic—the increasing violence in Boston between the Boston Defense League and gangs of local youths. The first two segments will be strictly conversations with our panel. But in the four after that we'll throw the show open to questions from our audience. So I encourage you to be thinking of questions that you might like to ask."

"Whaddaya doin' tonight?" a voice shouted.

It came from a Bullet. They all wore the same identical silver shirts. Some of his buddies laughed, but other gang members chided him.

"Hey, shut up, man," a Warlord said.

The other audience members looked warily at one another and at the security guards posted at the far ends of the set, out of camera range.

Kelly ignored the invitation. She saw Peg come onto the set with the panelists.

"Here come our panelists now," she announced, waving Peg forward. Applause mixed with a few boos greeted the five guests. Jerome, the Warlords' president, raised his fist to his fellow members. They returned the gesture, causing a small, ominous murmur in the audience. Agnes Baker was helped onto the set by Reverend Brown, who carried a Bible. Three small couches were arranged in a semicircle around a slate coffee table. Kelly sat the two gang leaders, Luther and Jerome, at opposite ends of the semicircle. Separating them seemed like a prudent idea. Paul Moran, the Defense League's president, turned out to be a sandy-haired man in his late thirties.

"In a moment Gilda Simone will join us," Kelly continued. "Please be quiet during the open. And please respect whoever is speaking. There's plenty of time for everyone to be heard."

Peg joined Kelly. "Is Gilda ready?"

"As ready as she'll ever be," Peg replied. They walked off the set just as Gilda made her entrance from the other side.

"Hello! Hello everybody," she sang out. "Welcome to *In the Know.*" She stopped to shake hands with several audience members, even attempting a hip handshake with a few Bullets and Warlords. One of them whistled appreciatively at her studded leather jacket. Reverend Brown, Kelly noticed, seemed less impressed. He shot her a disbelieving look, as if she had lied in her promise that this show would be handled seriously. Embarrassed, Kelly felt a small but definite erosion in her credibility with community leaders.

Gilda announced, "I hope we're all here to work today. Yes, I said work. Work for a better Boston." Her voice dropped an octave. "And I mean that sincerely."

"Gilda, thirty seconds!"

She nodded to Phil, the stage manager, and sat down. Luther took a long look at her legs. Kelly closed her eyes and made a brief but fervent prayer.

"Amen," Peg murmured.

The open went smoothly. In a refreshing change of pace Gilda read it as written. And her first question was to Reverend Brown, who in concise words peppered with a few Biblical allusions, explained the position of the average citizen caught between the gangs and the Defense League. Her second question to Agnes Baker resulted in a feisty, delightful speech on why senior citizens welcomed the League if they could coexist with the police. The elderly wanted more protection, she said, not factions fighting one another.

Kelly began to breathe normally. Gilda was behaving impeccably.

"Now after a commercial break," Gilda said, gazing seriously into camera three, "we'll talk to the actual combatants in this explosive situation, the Boston Defense League and—" she paused for dramatic effect "—the presidents of two gangs. Stay with us!"

When Phil gave the all-clear sign, Kelly walked over to where Gilda was having a discussion with Luther.

"Terrific, Gilda," Kelly said. "Keep it up for fifty more minutes and we'll have an Emmy on our hands."

The host smiled happily. "The best is yet to come. I was talking to Luther here, and he says the Bullets have a very interesting sexual code of conduct."

Kelly's smile vanished. "We're here to discuss a serious situation, not do an exposé on gangs."

Gilda shook her head in a bemused way.

"Fifteen seconds!"

"Gilda, listen to me. Continue the way you are."

The host examined a chipped nail. "Their insignia is very interesting, too."

"Gilda—"

"Ten seconds!"

Kelly had to return to the side of the set. She saw Gilda huddle with Luther again. Reverend Brown looked distinctly unhappy.

"Get Justin," Kelly whispered to Peg. Peg scampered off.

He appeared just as Gilda was welcoming the viewers back.

"What is it?" he asked.

"Fasten your seat belts," Kelly warned, "Gilda's about to rap with the gang leaders about their sex lives."

Justin stared at her. "Are you exaggerating?"

"I only wish I was."

"We've spoken so far with Reverend Brown and Agnes Baker," Gilda said. "Now I'd like to talk to the gang members themselves to see how they feel, to get a sense of their world. And it's a pretty unusual world at that, with strange rituals and codes of honor. You might even say that gangs are like mini-armies in the urban jungle."

Kelly winced.

"Tell me, Luther, what is the insignia of the Boston Bullets?"

"Well," Luther preened, "it's a bullet with blood on it. Like this." He turned around so that the viewing audience could see that on the back of his silver shirt was the very same insignia. "We like to think the bullet's goin' up," Luther explained, turning back to face

Gilda, "always straight and always *hard*. It sort of expresses how we are as men, if you know what I mean."

A few audience members tittered. Gilda seemed very impressed.

"Remind me to speak with Luther when we do a show on teen pregnancy," Justin murmured to Kelly.

"What does the blood mean?" Gilda asked.

Luther stared at Jerome. "It means no one better mess with us or they'll be sorry."

Several Bullets hooted their support. Jerome merely bared his teeth in what Kelly hoped was a smile.

"Now, Jerome," Gilda continued, "what is the insignia of the Warlords?"

"A skull with a knife through it."

"How interesting! Does the knife express how you feel as men?"

He stared at her. "You lookin' for a demonstration?"

Gilda laughed as if the retort was worthy of Noël Coward. Justin shook his head.

"Remember, this is daytime television, Jerome," Gilda said. "Now I've heard that gangs have unusual initiation rituals. Could you tell me what one has to go through to be a Warlord?"

"Lady, I don't want to be talkin' about that," Jerome said. "I want to talk about the League comin' into our neighborhoods and actin' like they're cops, only they ain't."

"We never said we were cops," Paul Moran interjected. "We want to help the police."

"Man, you carry sticks."

"Only for self-defense!"

"And you strut around like you own the place! If you can carry weapons, *we* can too."

"Neither of you should carry weapons!" Agnes said.

"If it weren't for gangs and the trouble they cause," Moran said, "we wouldn't be in your neighborhoods at all!"

"That's a lie!" Jerome snapped. "All we do is defend ourselves!"

"Your violent posturing, with the insignias, the slogans, the guns and knives, it aggravates an already tense situation," Moran countered.

"Yes, but Mr. Moran," Gilda said, her face barely concealing her delight in stirring things up, "doesn't the Defense League have an insignia, a slogan and weapons?"

Moran colored at this remark. He straightened up on the couch. "Walking sticks are *not* weapons!"

"They are if you get hit with one," Jerome snapped.

"And I deeply resent you making comparisons between us and the gangs," Moran shouted. "We're a responsible group whose only goal is to protect the citizens of our neighborhood!"

The quiet voice of Reverend Brown interjected, "But you don't live in the neighborhoods you patrol, do you, Mr. Moran?"

"We live in Boston!"

"Ah, but you don't live in Mattapan, Dorchester or Roxbury. These are the places you patrol."

"Yeah!" Luther said.

"They're the places that need it!" Moran said.

"Who asked you?" Jerome snorted.

"Yeah, who asked you?" an audience member shouted. Immediately the audience erupted in shouts and catcalls. Gilda's expression turned smug as she took in the heightened tension.

"She's enjoying herself," Justin muttered. "She's having such a good time stirring things up that she won't know when she's gone too far until after it happens."

Kelly felt helpless sympathy for him, the show and the whole damn world.

"Please, please," Gilda called out. "Everyone will get his turn." When the audience quieted, she turned back to Moran and asked in her most pleasant voice, "So, what you're saying is you're not a gang, but you do bear some resemblances."

Moran's eyes nearly popped out of his face. Hisses wafted down from the bleachers. Kelly saw a Bullet shove a Defense Leaguer. He was restrained from shoving back by another Leaguer, their blue berets moving back and forth as they argued with each other.

Justin's eyes were slits of angry blue steel. "How many minutes left in this segment?"

"It's the longest one," Kelly groaned. "We have at least eight more minutes."

"We are not a gang!" Moran roared. "We don't terrorize schoolyards. We don't push drugs!"

"Hey, man!" Jerome said, standing up. "Don't be puttin' that rap on the Warlords. We don't push that sh . . . stuff. Maybe the Bullets do, but we don't."

Luther, who had been thoroughly enjoying himself, choked in surprise. He stood up, too. "Don't you say that, Jerome. Don't you say that about the Bullets. Just 'cause we kicked your butt last weekend!"

"Keep talkin', Luther," Jerome said, "and maybe you just might believe that."

"Boys, boys," Gilda interjected, as if the two youths were merely being high-spirited. "Let's talk about drugs for a moment. Gangs *have* been accused of being pushers."

Jerome gave her a look that wiped Gilda's complacent smirk off her face. "Prove it," he said, "and don't *ever* call me 'boy,' old lady."

Gilda gasped. Justin quickly walked to the head security guard, and Kelly saw them engage in a serious conference.

"You see," Moran said, standing in anger, "you gangs are the reason the Defense League is needed."

"Get out of my turf!" Jerome shouted, putting a fist in Moran's face.

"Don't threaten me, sonny," Moran said.

"Gentlemen, sit down and let's talk," Reverend Brown suggested. "As the Bible says—" But his voice was drowned out by the rising ferment in the audience. Warlords were arguing with Bullets, and both were arguing with Defense Leaguers. The police representative, Kelly noticed, checked his gun. The elderly seemed frightened, as—for the first time—did Gilda.

"Please, everyone, sit down!" Gilda pleaded.

"Hey, lady, you started it," Luther sneered. He turned to his comrades and yelled, "Bul-lets! Bul-lets! Bul-lets!"

They stood, fists in the air, and chanted their name. The Warlords, not to be outdone, rose and repeated their name over and over again.

"Get out, get out, get out!" Luther yelled, obviously loving his role as cheerleader. In response the

Defense Leaguers got to their feet and shouted, "Hell, no, we won't go!'

"Can't you do something?" Kelly heard Agnes ask Gilda.

The answer was clear. Gilda couldn't do anything. The fracas she had encouraged now scared her. At the far end of the news set Kelly saw Larry Bishop and Lew Brady, the vice president and general manager, scurrying over.

Justin returned from his emergency conference. "I'm stopping this," he said, walking over to Phil, the stage manager.

But at that moment a Bullet lunged at a Leaguer. The Defense Leaguer more than returned the blow. An elderly woman screamed as the Bullet fell on her after receiving a particularly nasty punch. His fellow gang members took up the gauntlet, and suddenly fists were flying everywhere. It happened so fast that the security guards couldn't stop the fighting from escalating into chaos—on live television.

In a flash Justin jumped into the fray. Kelly screamed for him to stop, but her words were wasted as Justin separated gang member from Defense Leaguer, and gang member from gang member. People were screaming as they jammed the ramps to get out. Unfortunately the stampede blocked the ramps, preventing the security guards from getting at the fighters. Bloodstained knuckles and faces greeted the shocked viewer who tuned in late. The cameramen, trained to shoot any action, did just that. Still miked, the panelists pleaded with the fighters to stop. Home audiences heard Gilda Simone's teary, ineffectual plea.

A voice began to be heard, however, over the shouts and screams. Unsuccessfully at first, but with growing force, Justin called on the fighters to desist. His cool head and shrewd mouth began to make a difference.

Suddenly a shot rang out. Fists froze as everyone strained to see who'd fired it. The police representative stood next to Justin with his gun pointed at the ceiling. He looked to Justin for approval, but Justin shook his head.

"We won't have any more violence," Justin said to the hushed crowd. "This is what we gathered here today to stop."

"We didn't start it!" a Warlord yelled.

"Neither did we!" a Defense Leaguer answered.

"You're all to blame!" Justin cried. "Anyone who threw a punch is to blame! Violence will not be tolerated on this show!"

As he calmed the crowd, another gathered around Kelly. The news department wanted to interview the fighters. Andy Hopkins again offered his services as moderator. Larry Bishop shooed away dozens of curious gawkers while Lew Brady ordered a production assistant to get an old sitcom rerun on standby.

Kelly fought through the tugging hands to confront Brady. "You can't end the show like this!"

Brady shook his head vehemently. "What show? It's degenerated into a brawl."

"What if they sue the station?" Larry moaned.

"You can't end this with the viewing audience thinking this situation can never be resolved," Kelly insisted.

"It can't," Brady replied. "This is a matter for the police."

"The police have failed so far!"

"So have we," Brady said, looking at his watch. "We might still be short with the comedy, so I want you to throw up public service messages to fill the gap."

"No."

Brady looked up. "No?"

"No," Kelly stated quietly. "We have a real opportunity here. Justin's calmed the crowd down—"

"They could still go at any minute!"

"Not if they see there's hope!" Kelly said. "Let Andy take over. He knows the problems. He knows the players. Let the people see a host who cares. These people came here today to try to solve something."

"Not all of them did," Brady said, pointing at the set. Kelly looked out and saw Justin talking down a still-belligerent Bullet. The security guards were escorting the injured people off on the other side. Thankfully there seemed to be only a handful, and the injuries seemed minor.

"Yes, perhaps some of them did come for the publicity," she said.

"Like you predicted they would," Brady said. He pulled a linen handkerchief out of his expensive suit and mopped his brow.

Kelly hated to have her words thrown back at her. "But I was wrong. Most came to help their neighborhoods. We have a chance here, on live television, to help a community heal itself."

Larry grabbed her arm. "Even Justin would say to end it now."

"Then the risk is mine," she stated.

"Kelly, this isn't worth it," Brady said.

"Yes, it is, Lew. *In the Know* has always stood for something. If you end the show right now, then we'll be seen as sensation seekers who irresponsibly riled up gangs for a rating point."

"That was Gilda! She—"

"Don't end the show, Lew. Let people know we really care. This show can be turned around!"

"Lew, don't do it," Larry pleaded, his portly face flushed with anxiety. "Think of our insurance."

"Think of the people," Kelly replied.

Brady stared at Kelly for a long moment. Finally the general manager sighed and waved his hand. "Okay, we'll stay on. But go to a commercial," he commanded the stage manager to tell the director over headphones, "and we'll bring Andy out."

The viewer was suddenly stunned to see a floor wax commercial. Kelly walked onto the set with Hopkins. "Justin, we're staying on the air."

"I don't know," he replied, looking drained. "I've restored order, but I'm not sure how long it'll last." His bandage had loosened on his head. He absently tried to fix it. "What a mess."

"The show can be saved," Kelly insisted. "Lew agrees. But we're going to have Andy take over."

Justin shook his head, unconvinced.

"Reverend Brown! Good to see you," Andy said. He called, by name, several community activists, Defense Leaguers and gang members. Reverend Brown joined him to shake his hand and talk to the audience. Seeing that her show had been taken away from her, Gilda burst into tears and ran off the set. Agnes breathed a sigh of relief. So did Paul Moran.

"When we come back from the commercial break," Andy said, "we're going to talk about some solutions to this problem. A little scuffle isn't going to stop us."

"Those of you who want to stay and help, please do," Justin said, "but those of you who intend to disrupt this show again, I can guarantee you that it won't be tolerated. If one punch is thrown, we pull the plug."

A few Bullets and Warlords left the set, but most remained. Everyone else resettled themselves. Kelly and Justin joined Lew and Larry on the side.

"Welcome back to *In the Know,*" Andy said, fastening Gilda's mike to his tie. "I'm Andy Hopkins, filling in for Gilda Simone, who was terribly upset over the incident that just happened here. We hope she'll feel better soon, but for the duration of the show I'll be your host. And, ladies and gentlemen, this show will continue. Too much has been left unspoken and unresolved for us to stop just because the going got a little rough. We intend to remain here, even if the show is longer than an hour, until we come together as a community."

The audience burst into applause.

"What?" Larry asked. "We've got *Bowling for Bucks* on after this."

"Not today," Lew said. "Today I think we're going to lose a few. But," he added, clamping Kelly and Justin on the shoulders with his hands, "I'll be proud if we do."

Justin tried to smile, but Kelly saw that he couldn't. He looked dejectedly out onto the set.

"Mr. Moran," Hopkins began, "you say the people want you to patrol. Would you be willing to put that to a test?"

"Of course," Moran said.

"There's some talk about a special vote in the city council to address that very question. If the vote indicates the people want you to leave, will you?"

Moran squirmed in his seat. "Well, uh, you've put me on the spot here."

"Would you abide by the people, sir?"

"I would have to confer with the entire League," he waffled, "but I'm confident that the people want us. So I would abide by the vote."

"Jerome, the city council has called an emergency meeting for this Wednesday. Would you agree to a cease-fire until then?"

Jerome sat forward in his chair. "Will they still patrol?"

"The cease-fire should include all parties, Andy," Reverend Brown interjected.

"But the people, the elderly, still need protection," Moran insisted, looking to Agnes Baker for support.

"I think we elderly fear the increased violence caused by your fights with the gangs more than the protection you want to give. I agree with Reverend Brown."

Moran sighed but acquiesced. The audience burst into applause again. For the rest of the hour and a half that the show lasted, Hopkins skillfully tackled the many issues that brought the League into existence. If the problems between the gangs and the Defense League couldn't be solved completely—the Bullets and Warlords couldn't speak for other gangs—they were at least diffused, and promises for a cease-fire were given on all sides.

It was television at its best, Kelly thought. The prolonged applause at the end was completely justified, as was the flock of newspaper reporters and newspeople from the competition.

Justin handled the questions and compliments with diffidence, Kelly noticed, giving praise to others. Bombarded with questions herself, she didn't have a chance to speak with him.

As the crowd thinned out, she saw him slip away. Excusing herself, she followed him.

He walked briskly, barely acknowledging the praise from co-workers at the station. Kelly was waylaid more than once by admirers so that when she got to his office, she found his door closed. She tapped lightly but got no response. She went to his secretary's desk and buzzed him through the intercom.

"Lou, I'm taking no calls," he said.

"This isn't Lou, Justin. It's Kelly."

She waited a long moment before she heard, "Okay, come in."

She opened the door, expecting him to be, if not happy, at least relieved. But he looked depressed. His mouth was pinched in a grim line. His eyes contained no triumph. He sat behind his desk as cold and impenetrable as a statue. The black mood surprised her and made her tentative.

"You sure don't look like a man who's just produced a shoo-in at the Emmys," she said, sitting down.

He stared at her face, as if searching for something. "Go ahead."

"Go ahead and do what?" Kelly asked, uncomfortable with his abruptness.

"Go ahead and say I told you so," he replied, throwing the show file into a desk drawer. He slammed the drawer shut so forcefully that his desk shook.

His bitterness unsettled her. "What for? The show was a success."

He gazed at her quizzically. "By the sheerest, most unbelievable chance, this show succeeded, but that was after a riot broke out and five people needed medical attention."

"Superficial cuts and bruises," Kelly said.

"Oh, so that makes it okay? I should feel grateful that *only* five people got hurt and not wretched that anyone got hurt at all!"

"Of course not," Kelly said, "but the show turned into a miraculous achievement. These communities started to heal themselves. By achieving a cease-fire this show *prevented* violence."

"I deserve a medal."

"Management thinks so."

He laughed unpleasantly. "Then I should be very happy."

"Justin, I—"

"You'll get offers from this. Oh, I know your name wasn't on the credits today, but people in this town know you produce the show. I wouldn't blame you for leaving."

"I have no intention of leaving."

He acted as if he hadn't heard her. "You were right. Focusing on the gangs invited trouble. But I wanted this show to succeed so much that I turned a blind eye to the risks."

"Justin, the show was a success."

He looked at her cynically. "What part of it did you like the best? The part where Gilda asked about the blood, or when she called a Warlord president 'boy'?"

"Well, Gilda wasn't—"

"Prepared? Tactful?" Justin laughed, a frighteningly bitter laugh full of self-mockery. "She was *terrible,* as you predicted she'd be."

Kelly stared at his tormented face, wondering how she could find the words to express how she felt. Mistakenly she had thought this would be easy. A few hours ago a look on his face had made her believe that a declaration of love might be welcomed. But now, seeing how far he was distancing himself from her, she wondered if she could convince him that she liked him, much less that she loved him. What if her declaration had come too late?

"Justin," she said, "you think I came here to gloat. Nothing could be farther from the truth. I came to apologize."

At first she thought he hadn't understood her, so grim did his face remain. "Apologize?" he murmured.

"Yes, I came to apologize for not having the guts to see that this show, even with Gilda, was a risk worth taking. Sometimes you have to take a leap, often a scary one, to achieve a greater good. I only saw the negatives. *You* saw the possibilities."

"Yeah, of a nine rating and a thirty share," he said dryly.

She shook her head, her courage building. "No, I don't believe that was your only reason. You agreed to wait to see if the situation resolved itself. I should have seen that when it didn't our show might have been a legitimate hope. No other talk show but ours tried to deal with the situation.''

''*Sunday Roundtable* did.''

''They had on one Defense Leaguer and one community activist. They didn't even have on a gang!'' She could see that the remark had surprised him. ''I know how I felt about the gangs, initially,'' she emphasized, ''but their presence was a must. You saw that.''

He smiled, a truer smile this time but one still filled with self-reproach. ''Kelly, what I really saw in the gangs was the possibility of a show so exciting that syndicators would beat down our doors for it.''

''That wasn't your total motivation.''

''Maybe, but it was the overriding one. Oh, I could give you all kinds of reasons for my need to succeed—money for Tommy being the biggest—but those reasons shouldn't have clouded my judgment. Your judgment wasn't clouded.''

If only he would stop complimenting her! ''My judgment was clouded,'' she protested. ''Deep down I feared this show would bring syndicators beating down your door, wanting you, wanting Gilda, but not wanting me. I was afraid I'd lose *In the Know*. My dire warnings about the gangs didn't totally spring from lofty principles. I'm not so very noble.''

''You just happened to be right.''

''That's only because we stopped working together! I refused to admit that this show could make a difference, and you refused to see that my way of producing it was the more prudent. Don't you see, Justin, that a combination of our talents is what will make *In the Know* great! Your fundamental sense of where the conflict is, mixed with my ability to produce it! This show got out of kilter because we stopped listening to each other.''

For a moment she thought she'd reached him. He swallowed painfully. ''That's kind of you to say, but I'll be glad to give you a reference.''

She had hoped for a different reaction. *Some* thaw in his determined effort to remove himself from her life. ''I don't want to leave, Justin,'' she insisted. ''I want to stay and learn more from you.''

His eyes searched her face for any trace of irony or contempt behind that remark. Because there was none, his features softened, but he spoke sorrowfully. ''What's there to learn? How to be reckless? How to take the facts of life and mix them up until they agree with how I want them to be? I've acted like a buccaneer all my life, wheeling and dealing, unmindful of the costs. Today I nearly had to pay the price, but I got lucky. The show, miraculously, succeeded. But I deserve no credit. In fact, I'm ashamed.'' He got up and came around to her. She stood and took his hands. They were like ice. She rubbed them a little, but he withdrew them.

''I've always tried to manipulate reality to fit my needs,'' he whispered. ''I can't anymore. I see clearly who was right in this situation. Perhaps I can learn from you, but I haven't the faintest idea what you can learn from me.''

With a look of profound sadness and regret he said, ''You don't need me.'' Before she could reply he walked out the door.

CHAPTER FOURTEEN

KELLY DIDN'T SEE Justin for the rest of the day, nor could she get him on the phone that night. Mrs. Bannon, baby-sitting Tommy, merely said he was out. Sylvie had also wanted to speak with him, to tell him that Kevin hadn't said a word about Friday night. She wanted to thank Justin for helping her, and for being so right! Kelly agreed. His calm and supportive advice that night in his kitchen had hit just the right note with Sylvie. Kelly wanted to tell him that. She wanted to tell him so many things.

The next day he was absent on "personal business," his secretary told her. He would be back tomorrow.

Frustrated and worried, Kelly tried to busy herself with the show, but her thoughts kept coming back to his words: *You don't need me.*

She did need Justin—in countless ways. During the past two years, she'd become too rigid. Producing *In the Know,* raising Sylvie—these heavy and sometimes scary responsibilities had forced her to adopt a strictly serious attitude, for fear that letting down her guard would show how unprepared she was to be a mother or how unsure she occasionally was as a producer. Compromise meant admitting that she couldn't handle it all. Through Justin she now saw the need for compromise. Bending to accommodate someone else's thoughts and talents didn't signify weakness but strength. No longer did she want to control the show, or Sylvie, or Justin. She wanted to let life unfold in all its unpredictability.

Was this a new Kelly? The question made her smile. In a way, she was much different than before Justin had blown into her life like a tornado. He'd renewed confidence in her identity as a woman and increased her appreciation of people who viewed the world with a laugh. Yes, she'd definitely changed.

Deep down, however, Kelly suspected her new self wasn't so much a change as a reacquaintance with her former self, the one that existed before responsibilities had altered her personality. The new Kelly was bits and pieces of the old one, plus added confidence inspired by a loving man. This image felt comfortable, natural. It was a true reflection of her real self.

Justin had been the catalyst for this transformation. Kelly remembered the meeting she'd had with him at the Channels Bar the first week he'd been in Boston. He'd asked her what women dreamed of. Her own inner fantasy had whispered, "True love." Well, Justin was that love, but this knowledge had come too late.

The show was no longer the refuge that it had always been, even with a more docile Gilda. Since her ouster from Monday's show, Gilda had been nervous and pliant. She did everything Kelly asked for Tuesday's show, and Kelly called all the shots. But *In the Know* wasn't fun without Justin. Tuesday's show on the hole in the ozone layer was flat and boring. Her experts talked in dry, scientific terms. Justin would have somehow found a way to make this topic pertinent and personal to the viewer. Combine the mind and the heart. One without the other was lonely, as Kelly now understood.

On Wednesday she drove to work early to try to catch him before the others came in.

At first she couldn't find him. His briefcase was on his desk, but he wasn't in his office. Finally she found him in the downstairs dressing room, rooting through the closet.

"What are you looking for?"

Justin nearly lost his balance. So Kelly hadn't left! The sight of her surprised him. After Monday's show he'd assumed...but then why analyze it? She was back! Mixed with his elation, however, was the melancholy certainty that if their professional relationship continued, their personal one would not. He was to blame, and the knowledge haunted him.

He'd pushed so hard to get what he wanted. Usually his charm or his clout moved people to agree with his ideas, and his manner was so engaging that they invariably did it with a smile. He'd chased success recklessly, kidding himself that there were no sacrifices in the pursuit. Only Kelly had challenged his smug assumptions. Only Kelly had made him see what his single-minded race for success had done to his son, and his own standards of responsible television. Kelly had cared enough to penetrate his smooth image. From her he'd received more than acquiescence, more than admiration. He'd been given honesty and love. Unfortunately he'd discovered this too late.

He loved Kelly and he needed her badly. Much had happened in the past twenty-four hours, much that he wanted to talk to her about. She might even be proud of what he'd done.

Ah, he chided himself. Why should she be proud of him? Monday's show was a mere two days ago. Who could forget it so soon?

And yet here she was, standing in the flowered silk dress he'd given her as a present. And her beautiful black hair, which he loved to touch, tumbled freely down her back.

Why was she here so early? He wanted to ask her this and a hundred other questions. He wanted to explain how he felt, but all he could manage was "Damn! You surprised me!"

He pulled away from the closet with a start, knocking off several items on a rack at the top. They fell half on him and half onto the floor.

Kelly walked over to him and parted the tie and panty hose that had fallen on his head. "Oh, I'm full of surprises today," she said with a laugh. Inwardly her heart did a back flip in nervous anticipation.

He smiled in a constrained way and pulled off the items. "I guess the first is that you're still here."

She put her hands softly on his cheek. "It will take more than one measly show to get me out of your hair."

His eyes widened at her touch. He put his hands over hers and gently pulled them away, but didn't let go. "I don't want you out of my hair," he said softly. "I just assumed—"

Quickly Kelly disengaged one hand and put if over his mouth. "Don't assume," she said. "Let me tell you how I feel."

She led him to the couch, feeling the slight tremble in his hand. Or was it in her hand? They sat down, so close to each other that Kelly had an overwhelming desire to kiss him. Later, she promised herself. First, she had to convince those vulnerable eyes that she loved him.

She tried to clear her throat, but her mouth was so dry that she could barely swallow. Her voice came out shaky but impassioned. "Justin, you said on Monday that I didn't need you, that I couldn't learn anything from you. Well, you're wrong on both counts. I need the very qualities that you disparaged in yourself the other day—your risk-taking and your wonderful sense of adventure. I don't mean just on the show, either. From you I learned when a situation or person is worth taking a chance on, even if your mind warns you not to. And I've learned that sometimes caution is really selfishness."

He began to look at her strangely, as if her words weren't at all what he'd expected. The subtle change in the atmosphere spurred Kelly on.

"I've come to see the drawbacks in a too-ordered life. It's a way of hiding, and I'm not going to hide any longer."

She saw his body uncoil. His face remained closed, however, resisting her words of praise. Only a barely perceptible change in his eyes told Kelly she was beginning to get through.

"Who are you hiding from?" he asked.

"You might think I was hiding from you," she said, "but really I was hiding from myself. I saw my world as one of responsibilities, and the only way I could handle them was to be in absolute control. I shut out the emotional side of myself to achieve this. When I met you, you unlocked that side of my nature. But the change scared me because I was no longer in control. I was so frightened of letting go and taking on the new responsibilities in our relationship that I didn't see what I would get in return.''

She tucked her sweating hands into her skirt. ''I accused you once of failing to really commit to your son.''

''You were right.''

''No, I...'' She faltered. This was the hardest confession of all. ''I have no right to criticize anyone when I'm just as guilty. You offered me your love. You made me feel like no other man has ever made me feel. I took your love, and all you asked in return was that I commit to you. Which I'm sure you thought wouldn't be all that hard since I had been lecturing you on the very subject.''

''I asked more of you than that,'' Justin said, his face finally losing its remoteness. ''This past week I've begun to realize just what I had asked of you, in terms of Tommy, that is. I talked about family this and family that, pushing you to take over as equal partner, even though you aren't really Tommy's parent. I pushed too hard. I expected too much too soon.''

''You had a right to expect someone you loved to love you back,'' Kelly said. ''My backing out was unforgivable.'' She glanced down, feeling the tears on the edge of her eyelashes. ''At least I can't forgive myself.''

''I can.''

Tears blurred Kelly's vision, or else she would have seen the change on Justin's face that she'd been praying for. So she didn't believe her ears. "I know this might be too late," she cried, putting her face in her hands, "but I had to tell you. I need you. I...I need your crazy sense of humor, your fearless plunging into new things and the fun you find everywhere! *In the Know* was never as important as you. It's just a show, not my life. You're my life, you and Tommy and Sylvie."

She felt strong arms envelop her. "Shh, shh," Justin murmured as he held her close. Kelly felt the soft wool of his jacket and smelled his clean skin and knew she was home.

"Oh, Justin," she said, pressing her face against his jacket, "I love you so much! I never stopped. But do you still care? Is it too late?" She pulled her face away to get the answer to her worst fear.

He didn't have to utter a word. His face told her everything she wanted to know. Joy mixed with incredulity, happiness shaded by enormous relief. His eyes, which could freeze with a glance, sent out warmth and elation. He began to kiss her, not one big, lingering kiss, but dozens and dozens of kisses all over her face, neck and collarbone. Kelly closed her eyes and felt life returning to her body. She thought she felt his tears mingle with her own.

He paused and asked, "Does this answer your question?"

Kelly opened her eyes. Justin's smile canceled every doubt. The world seemed like a magical place. Here she was, being kissed by the man of her dreams, when minutes before she'd wondered if he still cared for her. It was a day for miracles. "Say you accept my apology."

He raised her trembling hands to his lips and kissed each palm. "I'll accept yours if you'll accept mine," he replied.

"I accept unconditionally," Kelly said, grazing his lips with hers, "but what am I accepting?"

"A promise, actually," he said, looking deep into her eyes, "that I'll always love you, that you and Tommy and Sylvie and—" he paused "—any children we might have will always come first before business. And I will be a full partner in their upbringing. Lastly I promise that there will never be another show like the one on Monday."

She noticed a smudge of mascara on his oxford cloth shirt, and found it strangely endearing. "Are you asking me to marry you?" she inquired, running her hands inside his jacket.

"Yes," he replied. "I want you to marry me. I love you. I love your honesty, your spunk, your integrity, your wicked sense of humor and—" he smiled, slowly glancing down "—your great body. Of course, I don't love you just because your figure is so wonderful."

"Really?" Kelly asked dreamily. "Your body is the main reason I love you."

They laughed, but Justin's face turned serious. "Kelly, before you give me your answer I have to tell you about a development that came up yesterday. Elaine has decided to relocate to Boston. We talked and agreed to share joint custody of Tommy. It's time I became a full-time father."

So that had been the personal business that had kept him away from the office!

"Justin, that's wonderful!"

His eyes searched hers. "Do you mean that? Being a stepmother isn't easy."

She kissed him gently on the lips. "I know it won't be easy, but I'll get Tommy's friendship in return. And being a stepbrother-in-law is no snap, either. When you helped me with Sylvie, I learned that two heads are better than one. I actually realized that I enjoyed you taking some of the responsibility in my life. Not having to control everything is liberating."

"So is finally learning what my real priorities are," he said. "I want to share everything with you. Together we'll shape a new *In the Know* and a new family."

She put her arms around his neck. "Just as long as the show doesn't become too stuffy."

He shook his head in amusement. "By the way, did Kevin—"

"Nope, not a word."

His face broke into a huge smile. "Then say you'll marry me, Kelly. Stand beside me, sleep with me, bear our children so that we can be a Nielsen family." They broke out into giggles. "You haven't answered my question," Justin said.

She gazed into his happy face. "I'll marry you. I would be an awful fool not to."

He kissed her, only this time it wasn't a cascade of them but one deep, thrilling kiss that seared his promise to hers. She clung to him, returning his passion with her own fierce desire. Tears streamed down her face again, but these were tears of joy. No reality existed during those minutes except her body pressed to his. Their passion wasn't entirely sexual, but rather the overwhelming ecstasy of two people who had teetered on a disastrous precipice but hadn't fallen off. They had saved each other.

Neither heard the door open.

"Justin! Kelly! What are you doing?"

Both looked up to see Gilda standing in the doorway with Stanley Porter. Stanley had a big pink smear on his lips.

"Making out, Gilda," Justin replied. "Isn't that why you're here?" Justin and Kelly looked at each other and then burst into peals of laughter. They laughed so long that Gilda became even more furious than she was when she entered.

"Are you laughing at me?" she asked. When neither of them could catch their breath to reply, she said, "Look, I want to know. Are you two messing around?"

Kelly wiped off the remainder of her mascara. "We're engaged."

Gilda's mouth dropped open. She glanced from Kelly to Justin, who smiled and nodded. The host's face turned a violent red as she assimilated this bombshell. Kelly almost felt sorry for her.

"I . . . I can't believe it," Gilda said.

"Believe it," Justin said. "Kelly and I have decided to make love not war."

"And all this has been going on *behind my back!*" Gilda exclaimed. "A cheap, tawdry affair!" She glanced at Stanley, and then ungraciously shoved him out the door.

"Oh, not cheap," Kelly said. "This affair has had a very high cost."

"But you disagree on almost everything about *In the Know!*"

Justin put his hand on the back of Kelly's head and lightly ran it over the silky locks of her hair. "We're beginning to work together."

Gilda chewed her lip. "Sleeping with the boss is the height of unprofessionalism, Kelly," she taunted.

"Sticks and stones, Gilda," Kelly said with a smile.

Justin got up from the couch and went to the closet. "Speaking of unprofessionalism," he said, reaching in deeply, "it's unprofessional to hide your wardrobe, Gilda." He pulled out her burgundy dress and handed it to her. Kelly laughed in surprise.

"I have a contract," Gilda said in a deadly tone. "You two can't do anything to me. I'm going to see Larry!" She slammed the door hard.

"She had better not give Larry an ultimatum today," Justin said, taking Kelly into his arms again. "I think her clout has evaporated. You know, she's going to tell everyone."

"Oh, good," Kelly said, snuggling against his strong chest. "It'll save me the expense of putting an ad in the paper."

He raised her chin with his hand. "You're suddenly very cavalier about the station knowing about our engagement."

She shrugged. "I suppose it might be awkward at first, but producing *In the Know* is just a job. It's a great one, and I love it, but basically it's just a job. It's not my total identity anymore."

He rubbed his face lightly in her hair. "There are two people who I'd like to tell real soon."

"Sylvie and Tommy?"

"You read my mind. See how well we work together?"

HARLEQUIN
Romance

**This June, travel to Turkey
with Harlequin Romance's**

**THE JEWELS OF HELEN
by Jane Donnelly**

She was a spoiled brat who liked her own way.

Eight years ago Max Torba thought Anni was self-centered—
and that she didn't care if her demands made life impossible
for those who loved her.

Now, meeting again at Max's home in Turkey, it was clear he
still held the same opinion, no matter how hard she tried to
make a good impression. ''You haven't changed much, have
you?'' he said. ''You still don't give a damn for the trouble you
cause.''

But did Max's opinion really matter? After all, Anni had no
intention of adding herself to his admiring band of female
followers....

**THIS JULY, HARLEQUIN OFFERS YOU
THE PERFECT SUMMER READ!**

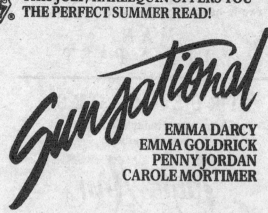

**EMMA DARCY
EMMA GOLDRICK
PENNY JORDAN
CAROLE MORTIMER**

From top authors of Harlequin Presents comes
HARLEQUIN SUNSATIONAL, a four-stories-in-one
book with 768 pages of romantic reading.

Written by such prolific Harlequin authors as Emma Darcy,
Emma Goldrick, Penny Jordan and Carole Mortimer,
HARLEQUIN SUNSATIONAL is the perfect summer
companion to take along to the beach, cottage, on your
dream destination or just for reading at home in the warm
sunshine!

Don't miss this unique reading opportunity.

Available wherever Harlequin books are sold.

THE LADY AND THE DRAGON

Dragons were the stuff of legends and Prince Charming only existed in fairy tales. Despite her romantic inclinations, Professor Katherine Glenn knew better than to wish for make-believe. But when she came to visit her "middle-aged and scholarly" friend Michael Reese in his Welsh castle, reality blurred with fantasy. Michael was twenty-eight, gorgeous and *never* quoted poetry. His lovemaking thrilled her but she realized they both were hiding secrets. And somewhere in the castle of Aawn something lurked . . . breathing fire. . . .

Enter a world of magic and mystery created by Regan Forest, author of MOONSPELL, in this very special Editor's Choice selection available in July 1991 (title #355).

Available wherever Harlequin books are sold.

HARLEQUIN *Temptation*

LADY

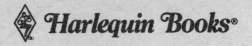
Harlequin Books®

Dear Reader,

Over the past few months, a new schedule for on-sale dates of Harlequin series has been advertised in our books. These dates, however, only apply to the United States. We regret any inconvenience or confusion that may have been caused by this error.

On-sale dates have not changed in Canada, so all your favorite Harlequin series will be available at your local bookstore on their usual dates.

Yours sincerely,

Harlequin Books

HREADER